Black Toad

(Kronegyn hager du)

Tom Herrington

Ugly Little Toad Publishing

Copyright © 2025 by Tom Herrington

The moral right of the author has been asserted.

All characters and events in this publication, other than those clearly in the public domain, are fictious and any resemblance to real persons, living or dead, is purely coincidental.

All rights reserved.

No portion of this book may be reproduced in any form without written permission from the publisher or author, except as permitted by U.S. copyright law.

If you allow AI to scrape my manuscript, I may come and do the same to your car. If you copy any parts without correctly referencing, you are an ass.

ISBN: 9798309672875 Paperback 1

ISBN: 9798319094247 Hardback 1

Ugly Little Toad Publishing:

Tollgates House

Battle, East Sussex. TN33 0JA

*For my dear daughter Jet (Peg), for her dedication to everything.
Love, Dad.*

Nature's silence is its one remark, and every flake of world is a chip off that old mute and immutable block.
– Annie Dillard

Introduction

I wouldn't dare dream of doing the place a disservice, nor would I allow it to be guilty by association to either the protagonist, or any of the godawful antagonists of this gruesome tale. Therefore, in good faith, I have set aside the introduction for a little local geographical and historical background of the humble Cornish village of Trebrowagh (*Tree-Brow-ugh*), where our story begins. This will be followed by the main course, a thoroughly modern Cornish gothic thriller, with a healthy wedge of nineties nostalgia and a side serving of simple countryside stereotypes.

Situated inland, 150m above sea level, at a confluence of the A30, A39 and A392 to Newquay, Trebrowagh is a stopover village where once carriages and stagecoaches would have rested their horses and passengers at the inn. A curious place, it is accidentally attached, through decades of development to the far prettier St Kres and almost adjoins the newer St Columb Road at the northern end of the village. Trebrowagh was established in 1820 to provide homes and a community for those working in the then burgeoning kaolin mining industry. As such the village has traditionally always had a proud, honest and hardworking spirit. People looked after each other there, the colourful Victorian terraces in Trebrowagh centred around the chapel and public house.

You should understand it is not as attractive as those chocolate-box coastal fishing villages you see on the television, or as dreamy as the bucolic rural hamlets hidden down impossibly narrow country lanes. Trebrowagh is a pit village. Local legend maintains that Pocahontas once lodged at the inn on her way from Falmouth to London, and that she'd been so adored by the miners that she'd left behind an oil painting of herself as a memento. The landlord was so touched he had renamed the pub after her – The Indian Queen. Her painting hung in the pub until the 1960s, when it was knocked down. Who knows where the portrait went, but there is a Pocahontas Close now, where they built the prefab bungalows.

You might imagine the inn was probably once a reliable place for a brawl and to indulge in a little light smuggling. Undoubtedly, the Indian Queen would have been good for a jug of warm nut-brown ale and a game of shove ha'penny in its heyday.

There's not a great deal else to say about the village, apart from that the outskirts quickly become very rural, beset with farms and endless acres of arable land, with breath taking and far-reaching views of the moors, taking in the manmade Toothpaste Mountains', or Cornish Alps as they're known locally. Oh, and there's a secluded Methodist preaching pit, formed in an old tin mine. And they have a McDonald's.

Now, a little housekeeping. Based on a true story, the characters in the novel have been molested as little as possible, with perhaps only their names being changed to protect their identities. Any resemblances to people you know, either living or deceased, are purely coincidental.

As for our story, the horror becomes apparent as two intertwined timelines are woven together, finally closing thirty three years of secrets, deception, denial, revenge and redemption.

You are now invited to relax, dream away to a warm and sunny rural idyll, pour a tea, set out your scones, slather them with jam, then a dollop of cream *on top* and join us out on Bodmin Moor, where our fable begins...

Act I: Ugly Little Toad

Chapter 1

Amuse bouche

'S'gustin', Jed! There were tiny little bits of her everywhere. Literally everywhere mate. Lumps of arm and fingers on the bar, one of her cheeks were on the door at the back, and the blood, it's all over the walls, all over the ceiling, ain't nowhere it ain't...An' the flies, Jed. The dirty flies. Bluebottles and wotnot.' Trish stooped to wipe her hands clean on the front lawn between the pub and the old A30.

'Yeah, you said about the flies, Trish. But, tell me again, deep breaths, slowly, how did you come to discover them?' Sergeant Bosanko tugged at his cheeks, dragging his face down to his chin in despair. Thirty three years on the force, and, mainly due to the geography of his patch, he'd never had a morning like this. Neither had he ever been sick on the job, until five minutes ago, which was surprising considering his generally weak constitution. Sure, there'd been some pretty grotty road traffic accidents and a handful of agricultural mishaps over the years. But this morning had been a total bloody shocker. *It's like something off that blooming Netflix.*

Firstly, there'd been that suicide down the clay pit over in Trebrowagh. That was a total mess, and now these two. *Madness.*

Trish continued her attempts to clean her palms, this time rubbing them on the back of her navy shorts. When she'd finished she put her hands on her hips and continued her story. 'So…it's proper sunny this mornin', right. The sortin' office ain't got too much goin' through, just junk mail and a few TV licence reminders, so we're all like, we can get everything done before eleven if we get out quick. You know, get down the beach for the day. Marli says she's gonna barbeque some mackerel an' that.' 'Trish the Post', as she was known locally, was now reclining, she was resting on the front of her shiny pillar-box-red van and alternating between placing and lifting her palms on and off the hot bonnet to affirm how warm the morning was. Not even nine a.m. and the mercury was cruising towards the late teens. Considering her grim discovery, she was holding herself together very well.

'Okay, Trish, so you got here early? Am I right?'

She rolled her eyes. 'Correct, Jed. I just told you that. So…I has this package for the old bastard, signed-for post. So I'm like, oh bollocks, got to get out and knock for the dirty pig. I swing the van in right? *Hang on Trish,* I says to myself, *tis proper quiet up here…Eerie like.* Here's the thing Jed, get this, I knew the moment I turned into the drive something weren't right. You know how you just get a feelin'…?'

Jed was struggling to concentrate. He had an horrific homicide-suicide on his hands. A messy one. And he'd known both the deceased almost all his adult life, he'd go as far as to call them friends. But all he could think about in this moment, was Trish's mouth. He was mesmerised. He couldn't for the life of him understand why anyone would want to make their lips so big.

'Does it hurt when you get that done? You know, with the...mouth...you know, your lips?'

'JED! What in the hell? Are you unwell? What is wrong with you mate? There's an old lady been blown into a million pieces being eaten by flies in the bloody pub!.' She pointed towards the heavy open door of the bar. She shook her head at the sergeant in astonishment and nodded towards the block of garages. 'An' her husband's dangling from the fuckin' rafters over there in the garage. And you're asking about my bloody aesthetics?! Mind boggles, Jed.' She raised her thick black eyebrows and huffed at the embarrassed policeman. He slapped his face in an attempt to snap out of his daze.

'Yeah, sorry, you're right, Trish. I dunno what came over me. Sorry, it's all proper disturbing. Right, I need to get forensics over from Truro. Trish, you must be shaken up. Can I get you a taxi home or something?'

'Nah, you're alright, Jed. I'll finish me round if you don't mind. Letters ain't gonna post 'emselves, ya know. Need to wash my hands too, got old lady all over them.' She flicked her fingers to the ground, in an effort to shake off a small and fresh morsel of flesh she'd noticed on the back of her hand.

'Sure. Okay, go on if you feel okay. I'll pop by later to get a statement if you don't mind.'

'Tomorrow, Jed. I'm meeting Marli later. I just told you that.'

'Loud and clear, Trish. See you tomorrow.' Jed tipped his hat and waved as she got back into her van and pulled out onto the old A30 towards St Kres.

He took from his trouser pocket a pristine white handkerchief and wiped the sweat from his neck and brow, before putting his hat back on. He was the first officer here, so this was his crime scene. He'd get it taped off and wait for the white coats to arrive. Jed couldn't face going back into the pub again, it blew his mind just how much blood and body parts could possibly come from one human. He'd leave the myriad pieces of old Annie as they were. But he was compelled to return to the garage block. He pushed the door gently, letting the sharp morning light pick out the floating dust particles as it flooded across the front of the dusty old Rover panda car. He covered his mouth with his hand, he couldn't help himself from gagging as he looked up at the monstrous size-eleven feet of his old boss gently swaying three feet above him. Those handsome black Oxford shoes had always been so perfectly polished, and this morning was no different, but interestingly, until this moment he couldn't recall ever having seen the soles – *exceedingly well looked after*, he thought. *The state of it here. My guess is the fool had a bit of a barny with old Annie, blew her from here to Boscastle, then done himself in. I'd never have thought this'd be the end of them two though...I'm proper gutted, I just don't understand.*

Still convulsing, the sergeant squeezed his nose to try to fight back the impeding vomit. *I mean, seriously, Jed. What manner of shithousery has occurred here?* He couldn't process any of it. Finding it difficult to breathe, he had to return to the car park to await the reinforcements. He squatted down on the lawn, buried his face in his palms and screamed.

Absolute carnage.

Chapter 2

Wenna Hawkey

May 2024 – Ten days earlier

I'm starting to recognise the route by now. Take the second turning for Trebrowagh, not the first. The hawthorn and hazel hedgerows rise as the lane narrows and I'm mindful to mentally record any possible wider parts of the road I may need to reverse into at any given time. According to the locals, it's the 'bloody Amazon vans' that have usurped tractors as the number one traffic nuisance these days. To be fair, I'm not sure Amazon are the only culprits here.

It's warm this morning and a real treat to have all the windows down and it cheers me to hear seed pods popping in the sun as the car trundles towards the farm. I'm also surprised to smell the sweetness of honeysuckle on the air so early in the summer. It's wonderfully rural this side of the village. In my experience, I've always found countryside as pastoral as this a blessed tonic for the nerves when I have grizzly and angst-inducing jobs to undertake. I raise my eyebrows at myself in the rear-view mirror and accept that I may be wasting my time with these people. I certainly wouldn't have picked this job unless I had to. Anyhow, this is the lot I got, and what a lot I got! I manage to just about force out a self-appreciative smile for that sentence.

Stopping the car to open the gate at the Hawkeys' farm, I'm conscious that this is the last chance I have to grab a few lungful's of clean air and absorb in the breath taking views across the plains before entering the stuffy bungalow nestled into the gravel drive below me. I park next to the decaying silver Vauxhall Vectra, straighten my tie, ruffle my hair, and draw an unnecessarily long breath, holding it for thirty seconds before exhaling. And I repeat. Twice more.

Wenna is waiting for me on the doorstep. She smiles, it's a welcome and honest smile. She pitches a little wave at me from waist height. I already feel that she is more relaxed today than last weekend. We greet each other warmly as she holds the back of my hand softly whilst I formally shake hers. She holds the front door open and ushers me into the lounge.

The room is a reasonable size, maybe three sofas long and two sofas wide. The large window at the end of the room stretches from wall to wall. It has two outward opening panes at each end, and a large sash in the middle. It looks out beyond a large wooden tiled barn over endless gold and green fields, sporadic clumps of flourishing deciduous trees and onwards, over the granite horizon to the bleak and alluring Bodmin Moor sleeping under flaxen skies. The curtains are a pink, blue and cream chintz print. They are thin and unlined. Behind them, cheap white net curtains protect from prying eyes. The carpet is an orange, brown and maroon hellfire piece of art, like you'd expect to find at a working men's club or unloved seaside boozer. There is a flattened path worn into the shagpile from decades of Wenna's shuffling from the kitchen to the La-Z-Boy chair and back.

The armchair I'm invited to sit in is too soft for my liking and is dressed superfluously in loose arm covers, horse brasses and a lace headrest. It takes a bit of fidgeting to get comfortable. But it's not just the chair to be honest, it's this whole missing persons case. It's getting me down, chronically, to the extent I feel utterly miserable about all of it. Everything I've read so far in the patchy police files and my experience to date with these peculiar people has led to me feeling hideously unsettled. I catch myself furiously waggling my right foot.

Picking up from my last visit, I feel I may as well get straight back into the investigation. I really want to get into her head this week, I believe she's beginning to trust me.

'Wenna, start again for me. I want us both to be absolutely clear about this. From the beginning. When did you first meet, or at least become aware of him?'

She itches the side of her nose with a talon-like finger which is somehow both bony and chubby, she slowly leans in towards me. I hear her draw a deep breath into her chest as she starts to speak, the sound whines like a wintry draught creeping under the front door of an old house. She's certainly one for looking you in the eye.

'First memory of the boy was him coming to the fenister for a nub of butter on one of thems Ryvita's.' Her voice is a peculiar and jarring blend of calm and disturbingly husky. 'He always came to the window, most every day. Always hungry. He were proper dirty too. All soot and peg – should 'ave given 'im a proper wash. Would've too if I could have caught 'im, flitty, squiggly little toad.'

She tugs at her sheer Nora-Batty tights, stretching them up from her cedar-like trunk of a leg so I can make out her very round and corned-beef-coloured knee. She looks to the ceiling and sucks her top lip into her mouth; it squeaks as she releases it.

'I'll tell you what, Doctor, you wouldn't believe the sight of him. Such a grubby little urchin he was. I'll draw you a picture of the little maw if you wants...'

'Maw means boy? Right?'

She looks at me as if I'm a half-wit. 'Course it is, Doctor.'

She seems encouraged to draw me a picture and reaches for a pencil and a pad of Basildon Bond paper from the top of a once beautiful console table. I say 'once beautiful' as it appears somebody has sawn the table in half, clean down the middle, and tacked on a length of wood in a vain attempt to create a new leg. I've thought about this table on previous visits. It is, or once was, an exquisite piece of furniture. My guess is it's rosewood. I'm compelled to ask about it.

"'Tis m'ogany.' Wenna smiles and winks. 'Edern says it be worth least a thousand. Was worth two before they split it.' She's very pleased with this outcome. 'Edern and his brother got left it from old Nell, you know, when Nell moved on. Neither of 'em could agree on where to keep it. So, when the auction man says it's worth two thousand, Edern says to Pascoe, his brother, that they gonna have half each. Pascoe saws it in two, puts on a new leg for both sides, and now they both gots a table worth a thousand. Well, that was five years back, worth more now, I s'pose. Can't say it looks better, mind...'

Her rambling storytelling makes me chuckle. I kind of like Wenna, she's a very simple, straight-talking lady, innocent or perhaps ignorant of modern ways. The words pour out whilst she thinks, there is no filter, she just chatters away. Her West Country twang is as warm as it is incomprehensible. It sounds unfair, but I'll put it out there, she's not the quickest of wits, none of the Hawkeys are.

She must be in her early seventies. Today she's wearing a floaty and floral mauve dress, the fabric looks more synthetic than natural. I couldn't say where it was from, but I can only imagine she shops in Bodmin or Wadebridge, as they're the nearest towns. I doubt she gets out too much. To be honest, I can't really picture her out of the armchair, let alone out of the house and away from the ramshackle farm bungalow here on the outskirts of Trebrowagh. You may have already noticed that Wenna speaks with a Cornish accent as thick as clotted cream. All the Hawkeys do. They have adopted their own dialect, which has taken me the last couple of weeks to begin to understand. I swear they make words up on the spot half the time, there's always a new word or phrase I've never heard before.

After a minute, Wenna shows me the picture she's drawn of the boy, and quite frankly it's a ridiculous drawing and only just resembles any kind of human at all. Pointless. She is pleased with it though. The Hawkeys are a most curious breed.

To date she hasn't been comfortable with my questioning, but I persevere.

'Why do you think he came here? The boy, the maw?' I ask.

'You're the shrink, you tell me.' She shrugs, looking at me for answers.

'Well, I might argue that he was hungry? Or lonely? Maybe he came to see *you*, Wenna? How about that? Maybe you were of comfort to him. Perhaps your home was a safe place?'

She stares at me, looking puzzled as she screws up her face and gently teases the peachy fur on her cheek.

◈

I'd been sent to interview the Hawkeys by the Devon and Cornwall Police's Historic Crime Department. The beaks in Truro had decided to revisit an unsolved missing-persons file. This particular mystery was the case of a boy from a hippy / New Age traveller commune in Trebrowagh who went missing in 1991 without a trace. It was already accepted that he would have been the boy at Wenna's window. It had been common knowledge locally that he often made visits to the Hawkeys' farm. To be frank, it strikes me that nobody had ever really taken the time to concern themselves about him back then. It was a fact that there was a local urchin (or '*maw stret*', to use the Hawkey dialect) in the village. By all accounts he was grubby, always seen with a dirty, unwashed face and tatty clothes. The poor thing was scrawny too, but the most intriguing part of all is that he was mute. The case records describe him as a selective mute.

The police had never found any reason to suspect or evidence to suggest that the Hawkeys had been in any way involved with the boy's disappearance. Reports agreed that they had always been compliant, often going out of their way to make tea and put out sandwiches or cakes. True, they were understood to be an odd bunch, I mean very weird. Complete misfits. I'm pretty certain that every village in the land has a similar oddball cast of residents. They liked to keep it in the family, if you know what I mean. The mere mention of the Hawkey name down at the Blue Rose Inn would invariably trigger endless quips about six toes, curly hair and dads being uncles...Wenna, Edern and Wenna's son, Jago, are a very local family, but I don't believe we could call them a criminal one.

However, as I told Wenna two weeks ago, a new top bod at Truro Police had got a bee in her bonnet about the case and her gut instinct told her that the Hawkeys knew more than they would let on.

As a psychologist and psychotherapist, the Historic Crime Department believed I could develop a deeper, somehow more personal relationship with them, which might shed new light on the missing lad. They wanted me to get to know the Hawkeys, to get in their heads and under their skin. So, in an unorthodox move I went to their home. The Hawkeys seemed happy enough to invite me in. And thus, our investigation began. This is now my third visit to the farm. I'd visited the last two weekends on the trot, but once they warmed to me, I figured I'd stay locally for a few days, to get to know them better.

The difficulty with this case has always been a serious lack of any useful evidence. That, and dubious information from the missing boy's own community. What we do know is that an eleven-year-old boy had been recovering from a violent altercation with another local child when, without any warning, and apparently against his character, he simply disappeared, never to be seen again – these are always the most peculiar - all is not what it seems, kind of cases.

I'm firmly of the belief that the police couldn't be bothered with the case at the time. The original records don't reveal much of an investigation. A handful of people were questioned, a man was charged but 'conveniently' died in custody, and that was it. No search for the boy or a body.

It didn't stack up, in fact, it seemed a right half-arsed and utterly botched affair.

A spokesperson for the boy's community had raised the alarm sometime in early April 1991. They had not wanted to bring the kid's family directly into conversation with the police due to VERY delicate politics within the camp. Old police records dismissively described the group as 'hedge monkeys' and 'houmous chucker's'. I'm not generalising, this kind of attitude was somewhat typical of parochial rural policing in the mid-eighties and nineties.

According to the files, the main contact between the Devon and Cornwall Police and the New Age travellers was a woman called Coral McCormick. Coral claimed to be from Langport in Somerset, wore purple crushed-velvet dungarees and insisted she was close family of the boy. Again, I have to say I'm embarrassed and quite frankly appalled by the disparaging comments and notes in her old police file; *fucking hippy*, *that dog-on-a-string bitch*, *cancer of the hair*, I guess in reference to her dreadlocks? And so on. I cringed when I'd read that, and concluded that the police, certainly in this case, and definitely at the Bodmin constabulary, were complete arseholes.

It was Coral who had claimed the boy would visit the Hawkeys' farm. It was Coral who'd advised the police he was mute, and it was Coral McCormick who'd spat, kicked and screamed abuse at the police when they sought to talk to the other travellers, and when they'd taken Scoob away.

Then, one day in the middle of September 1991, they'd all gone. Having been a semi-permanent fixture in the village for the best part of three years, the whole group, their buses, vans, dogs, yurts and all, had just vanished. Gone. The only report of a group even slightly resembling the troupe was offered by a retired St Austell policeman who'd been on holiday in southern Portugal in the late spring of 2007. But nothing since. Therefore and rather frustratingly, speaking with Coral was out of the question. So, right now, any potential clues or solutions were locked up within the minds and confines of this curious family. The Hawkeys.

◈

'Want a bit a ginger loaf, Doctor?' Wenna audibly licks her lips and begins the long-winded procedure of up-righting herself in her humongous, motorised armchair. Her swollen ankles retreat into the chocolate-brown corduroy seat whilst her soft, loose-jowled beetroot face is propelled skywards in anticipation of a slice of sticky cake. The prospect of a sweet treat has relaxed her. Scrunching her nose up to push her large almost octagonal glasses back into place, she looks at me and begins with a new snippet of recollection.

'Ooh, now then Doctor, how 'bout this? I remember one time, 'ims comes up to the window all bleeding from his face an' head. So, I asks him – wha's 'appened? Hard to know, see, him not being verbal. Well, he just scuffles his feet into the gravel and stares at the ground. I felt sad. I remember that the tears washed clean, clear lines down his dirty little face, like how condensation does on the fenister. Then he reaches down to the floor and picks up a flint from the ground by the garden gnomes. He tries showin' me that the rock hit him on his bonce. Lest I think that's what he be sayin'.' Wenna gives an apologetic, almost embarrassed shrug and smile.

'Well Doctor, I give him some Dundee cake, loads of almonds on it, and he proper gobbles that all up. Stops weeping too. I gives him a tissue what I keeps up my sleeve, an' motion him to wipe away his tears and blood. He looks to me for more cake…little beggar. Pa-ha,' she laughs and shuffles past the frosted-glass dividing wall to the kitchen.

I take the break as an opportunity for some light snooping and general observance of the room.

There is the aforementioned half console table, and a dining table complete with lace tablecloth and settings for three people. A mid-century sideboard hosts a boot-sale-sized collection of brown and green glass cups, saucers, plates and other vessels, they share the space with various wooden gonks holding spears and wearing tartan loincloths. The house feels damp in a humid way, and smells of a heady combination of wet towels, Bisto gravy and vanilla Shake 'n' Vac. I'm surprised they don't have a TV. There is, however, a remarkably modern DAB radio which, according to the display, is tuned to BBC Radio Cornwall.

A quick survey of the many framed photographs seems to reveal an agricultural history. Grainy sepia and black-and-white pictures of men with dogs, hay bales and ploughs. Others show women wearing cloth bonnets standing proudly next to vegetable patches and flagons of cyder. There are a couple of awkward school photos of her son, Jago. In my personal favourite shot he sports a greasy centre parting, most of his breakfast on his pale grey jumper and toothpaste round his mouth. A fine specimen.

'Our Jago was an 'andsome young man, won' he?' Wenna posits as she reappears with three slices of buttered ginger cake, which she raises towards me in triumph.

'No' is the answer in my head, but I nod in fervent agreement with her. A face only a mother could love, I guess.

It's a faded polaroid that holds my attention the longest. In it, Wenna, Edern and a young, ruddy-cheeked Jago stand proudly in front of a terracotta coloured Vauxhall Chevette estate. To the right of the car there is a picnic spread out on a rug. To the left, a man is dressed as Busby, the British Telecom bird mascot of the time. In the white space under the picture someone has written 'St Columb – 1982'. I can't say why I'm drawn to it. Maybe I like it as it almost appears 'normal'. Everything else *Hawkey* is most certainly not.

'Do you remember when you *last* saw him?' I ask, trying to resume my chat with Wenna. It's not easy, she's easily distracted, avoidant almost. Her attention deficit indicates that she doesn't feel comfortable talking about the disappearance, yet she's happy to garble on about the *old days*. She'll effortlessly witter on about Jago's school days and her old friends from the farmers' club, which I believe was a flat-roof community function pub of sorts. She talks about Pop Biddle and Jimper, and Donna from the Blue Rose as if

I know them, yet she is reduced to spewing out nothing less than nonsense when it comes to the boy in question. But I have good reason to be here and need to continue while I still have her attendance. I'd like to get some answers or at least clues to try to piece together this case.

'Can you recall when you last saw him, Wenna?'

She juts her chin forward and gives it a little scratch, 'Pop? Hmm, dunno, probably about...' she starts, but I interject.

'No Wenna, not Pop. When did you last see the boy at the window? Or anywhere for that matter? Can you remember anything that could help us understand what happened to him?'

She twiddles a particularly coarse whisker on her cheek. 'Hmm, well...no...er...Oh, my memory ain't so bright these days, Doctor...' I watch her eyes widen as she recalls a thought. 'I see him maybe a couple days after the time he's all bleedin' at the window – you remember, I just said about that matter. Then, the next time was maybe in Trebrowagh. Was a fete or something. Easter! Ess, it were Easter. They had an egg hunt. You know, 'tis famous.'

'And did anything seem suspicious to you then?' I enquire.

'Not really. He was there to do the egg hunt. He looked dirty, same as normal...er, nope...Nothing more than that.' She curtails her train of thought, grimacing to herself as if she might have given something away. 'Nope, that's it. Ne'er seen him again after the egg 'unt, so you know...that's it, I guess.' She shrugs and takes a nibble from the corner of a slice of cake.

I feel she has more to say about the encounter but is choosing to keep a lid on it. I can't quite put my finger on it, but intuition, if nothing else, tells me she's hiding something. Many things? Who knows? I'll change tack.

'I've not heard about the egg hunt, Wenna. Do they still do it?'

'Course they do. Big news in Trebrowagh. I'm at a loss to know why you ain't heard of it. You be from Launceston?'

'Truro. I live in Truro.'

'Wha? An' you don't know 'bout the Trebrowagh and St Kres egg 'unt? You'll have to visit next year, boy!'

'Yes, yes, that'd be lovely. I'll pop that in my diary. Do Jago and Edern like the hunt?' I'm not entirely sure why I asked this. I was struggling to get anything sensible from her.

'Sure, Jago loves the egg hunt. Always did, always will. He has a sweet tooth, that boy. Edern don't like crowds, so...'

I jump back to the case. 'Did Jago know the boy?'

She momentarily scowls. She straightens her back and stretches her neck a few degrees left, then right. She peers over the top of her specs, gathering her bosom as she leans forward.

'Jago don't know the boy. He never done nothin'.' She purses her lips and hisses, 'Nuffin'!' Then she starts to glaze over a little and shakes her right arm and wrist.

'You okay, Wenna?'

'No, I ain't. I got the wanderers.'

'The what?'

'The wanderers! You know, pins and needles.'

'Oh, I see. Yes, you've probably spent too long sitting with me. Shall we call it quits for the day?'

I never like to make people feel uncomfortable, and Wenna's posture, sour expression and the 'wanderers' suggest she's done talking for now. So, I force down the cloying ginger slice and try to organise next week's visit. I ask her whether I might get some time to speak with Edern or Jago.

'Edern is often sleeping in the afternoon, and Jago helps out washing up at that fancy garden centre up the road on Tuesdays an' Wednesdays, so's you'll 'ave to wait for the nummer ninety-three to drop 'im back,' she says.

I tell her I'll return next Saturday in the morning, around eleven. Her demeanour immediately improves, and she smiles again.

'Alright then, Doctor, I'll get some malt loaf ready for you.' She is content with her choice of confection.

'Sounds delicious. By the way. I'm a therapist, not a doctor...'

'As you like it, Doctor.'

Closing the front door behind me, I notice that the Hawkeys have assembled a vast gnome sanctuary on their drive. One naughty fella with a red hat catches my eye; he has 'hilariously' dropped his trousers and appears to be pulling a mooney in my direction. Overcome with childlike mischief, I pick him up and stick him next to the fibreglass goose. The resulting scene ensures that the bird's beak is now positioned behind the gnome's bum crack. I wonder if they'll notice.

Predictably, this mornings' glorious sunshine is now cloaked behind bulging and volatile slate grey clouds. As they roll over the knolls towards me, a few heavy and solitary droplets of rain make their presence known as they 'pink, pink...pink' on the car roof.

Driving home, watching the wipers dragging the drizzle from one side of the windscreen to the other, I try to process my time with Wenna. I don't really know what to make of her. She hasn't really brought anything meaningful to the conversation. I've said I like her, she's amiable. But! And there is a big but here - there's something about her I don't really trust, something doesn't sit well with me, something about her makes my guts squirm. I mean, on the face of it she seems to be a normal, relatively nondescript old lady. Her memories of the lost boy sound genuine, but they are just that, they're simply memories. There's no real sense of depth to her feelings. She doesn't attach any emotion to her stories. And yet, she reared up like an irate swan at the insinuation that her son may have had anything to do with anything. Very tetchy. Something doesn't fit. What is it? What is she hiding? Or hiding from? I won't bother filing any reports back to Truro yet, I'll hope to get somewhere with Jago next time.

Chapter 3

Trebrowagh

(Thirty-three years earlier) 30th March 1991 (Easter Saturday)

A rusted and shabby terracotta-coloured Vauxhall Chevette estate creaked for mercy as it bounced down the unmade driveway, then skidded to a halt on the gravel in front of an imposing and decrepit wooden barn. Edern Hawkey, face to the floor, skulked out of the driver's seat, his eyes fixed to the ground. Careful to avoid Wenna's glare, he sloped off into the barn.

Climbing out of the passenger door, her face reddened and blotchy from crying, Wenna snatched at the rear door handle and pulled her generously proportioned teenaged son out of the car by his wrist. Cursing under her breath and wiping the sweat from her brow, she opened the squeaking door of the car boot to retrieve the overpacked supermarket carrier bags.

'Jago, get 'ere, you lazy bastard, and give Mummy a hand with the shopping. Get here now!'

Tearful, snivelling and yet somehow market-stall majestic, in an unbranded purple and yellow shell suit he'd bought with Pascoe's Christmas money, Jago arrived at the back of the car to be met by Wenna's flying hand slapping him viciously across the face.

'Ow! Why'd you do that now, Ma?' He cowered away from her, rubbing his cheeks. 'It stings!'

'For bein' useless. Now get the shopping into the kitchen and take Edern his shitty liquor. NOW!'

'Take Edern his shitty liquor? Or do the shopping?' Jago asked, tilting his head with a cocky wry smile.

'Don't be sarcastic you little shit! And don't bloody swear!' Wenna kicked him sharply on his shin with the pointed toe of her cowboy boot.

'Nnngch! Ma, it's gonna bleed! Asides, you just swore...' he whined. Feeling hard done by Jago turned and trundled into the kitchen with the bags, three in each hand.

'Oh, stop your bloody whinging, Jago! And don't break nuffin'!' Wenna screwed up her mouth and eyes tightly as she pursued Edern into the barn.

She hated the wretched barn, and the bloody Big D peanut wall hanging which revealed parts of naked ladies with each packet of peanuts removed. She couldn't bear the tobacco smell, even more so when it was mixed with the whiff of his 'shitty liquor', which was a local potcheen he could only buy from Jimper over in St Columb Road and drank alone in his shed. But on this day, it was Edern she was particularly angry with. She was really pissed off. Pissed off, hurt, ashamed and heartbroken. He'd gone too far this time. Too far...

Jago stopped as he re-emerged from the back of the house with the potcheen in his hands. He could hear his mother shouting. She was proper reading Edern the riot act, that was for sure. She was in a blind fury; he couldn't tell if she was crying through sadness or anger. The boy stood in silence by the barn entrance and pressed his ear to the wall. He could hear a tremendous amount of chaos and commotion: the crashing of tools colliding with machines, bodies thumping bodies. Bags of peanuts flew out of the barn door.

Inside the barn, baring her gums like a rabid dog, and fists flailing, Wenna laid into her husband.

'I know about the boy, Edern Hawkey! I seen 'im in 'ere with my own eyes! What in heaven's name 'ave you been up to? Jago told me 'bout 'im. He seen you both in here, and up at the pit. What you up to? Tell me, TELL ME! Sure, Jago's dumb, Ed, but he ain't no liar.'

'You don't know nuffin', Wen! I ain't done no wrong!' Edern pushed her away with both hands in unison, but she was relentless, still she came at him, her face inches from his, seething.

'I says you're a perverted piece of shit, Edern Hawkey. A disgrace! What'd old Nell say now? Take it all away from here! GET RID OF IT! I swear, Edern, I'll call the police myself if you don't sort this mess out! GET OUT!'

Jago struggled to hear the rest of the shouting as Edern fired up an old orange Renault tractor and lumbered out of the barn and up the track, fleeing a storm of obscenities and the Big D wall hanging. As Mr Hawkey made his escape, he turned and cracked an utterly charmless smirk at his overwhelmed wife.

'hat is some pretty grubby evidence of somethin' nasty! Get it gone Edern! Don't even think about comin' back for no dinner! Dirty BASTARD!' She slammed her hands repeatedly against the barn wall. Jago scuttled around the side of the building to avoid her attention.

Exhausted, Wenna stood, doubled over, in the doorway of the barn, clutching her stomach with one hand and the doorframe with the other as she watched her husband vanish over the dusty hill. Sweat started to soak through her blouse, she felt physically sick. How could he be responsible? Her Edern. No, it wasn't true. It wouldn't be true. It bloody was. Rotten bastard.

She looked back inside at the workbenches strewn with oily cloths and tools. The air was heavy with diesel fumes from the tractor. 'Makes me shudder,' she muttered to herself, before crossing the drive and into the house, slamming the door behind her.

Jago, ever the opportunist, poked his head around the front of the barn to take a look around, glancing from side to side, and seeing that the coast was clear, he nipped out of hiding and retrieved the glamourous Big D wall hanging. It was now entirely free of peanut packets and showed a sultry Linda Lusardi dressed in ill-fitting, oily racing overalls holding a car tyre. *Looks a bit like Mother*, he thought. *A win in anyone's books.* Giving the poster a celebratory sniff, Jago followed his mother back inside, at safe distance.

◈

The thirty-year-old orange tractor rumbled up the track in a haze of dark-red dirt, then went left along Wesley's Lane and out of sight, until it could be heard no more. Edern Hawkey was heading to the top end of village. Like it or not, he had some business to deal with at the abandoned preaching pit. Actually, not so much business, in truth he had some stuff to dispose of, stuff Wenna did not want lying around at home.

Edern was not a particularly notable man. He was of average height and normal build, although manual jobs around the house and barn had kept him reasonably fit and healthy. He had mousey blond hair which was thinning on top. He wore simple clothes. On this occasion he was sporting his usual beige trousers and a green checked woollen work shirt. His leather boots were a regular dark shade of brown and he liked to tie them with thick green laces. He didn't care to speak much and undertook a few hours' paid work a week at the Westways petrol station in Tregaswith. Edern was the kind of man whose face was always facing the floor, like a human lamp post, the kind of man whose lifetime of bad choices forever tightened the noose around his neck.

As he made his way through the narrow lanes to the pit all he could think about was getting rid of the bag. He didn't care to be the cause of Wenna's fury, that woman could make even the merriest of men lose their will when she wanted.

He preferred to be left alone to his own devices, and for that matter, his vices too. Maybe he'd gone too far this time, perhaps it would be best to destroy the evidence as his wife had insisted. He knew he couldn't do it on the farm, someone would certainly find something incriminating one day. Yet he couldn't bring himself to destroy it, it was if some unearthly power compelled him to keep it. He'd hide the stuff, really well. No one ever went to the pit these days. He'd bury it there, with the other bits, that was what he'd do. If nothing else, Edern was predictable.

Bringing the old tractor to a halt in a layby a few hundred yards from the path to the rear of the pulpit, he took out a battered Golden Virginia tobacco tin from his shirt pocket, he prised the lid off, took a deep sniff of the warm tobacco, rolled a miserably skinny cigarette and stepped down from his machine. He checked up and down the lane. There was no one around. Confident he wasn't being watched, he reached under the seat of the tractor and removed an old Safeway carrier bag. It was stuffed with items of clothing, some tattered pieces of dark material, some towelling maybe, and a thin black cagoule.

Reaching the stile leading to the pit, he checked the lane again for people and traffic. He scratched the back of his neck.

Let's see 'ere, Ed...Easter Saturday afternoon, no one about, football's probably on telly down the Blue Rose. People most likely getting their chocolate and bits from the supermarket. I reckon the coast is clear...Let's get in and out, get it done, then over to Jimper for some diesel.

He curled his weathered hand over the top of the cigarette, protecting it from the breeze, he flipped the lid of his lighter, sparked the flint, lit the crumpled roll-up and crept along the overgrown pathway to the preaching pit.

❖

If you've never heard of or seen a preaching pit, they are typically large, grassy, circular manmade hollows landscaped into the ground. Originally, the pits were outdoor venues for religious sermons, allowing preachers to address crowds without the confines of a building. They were often associated with religious movements and revivalist gatherings. Invariably, they were created from existing landforms. In Cornwall, the pits were often converted from disused mining hollows. This was the case at both Trebrowagh and the nearby Wesleyan Gwennap Pit.

Sadly, by the 1990s preaching from pits wasn't as popular as it used to be, and so the Trebrowagh pit was now only a place of midnight fornications and micro raves. A location where many a schoolchild had sought and found mucky treasure – old discarded porno mags and grumble books. But it was almost always empty in the daylight hours. Except for when the summer fete was on.

◆

Scavenging around under a litter bin, Edern located and withdrew a rusted gardening trowel he'd previously hidden. He crossed the grassy pit to its highest point. Just over the lip of the top ridge he stopped at an area where someone had recently indulged in a little al fresco barbecue. Mindful not to make any unnecessary noise scraping it, he lifted the corroded cooking plate to one side, revealing a small pile of recently disturbed soil. Taking the trowel, Edern quickly dug the loose earth out and placed the Safeway bag inside, he made sure it was buried deeply enough into the ground and swiftly filled the hole back up. Having carefully covered his hiding place with the barbecue grate, he sparked up his roll-up and returned to the road and his tractor via the bin to secret the trowel back in its place. Happy he'd done a decent job, he proceeded to the petrol station to put twenty litres of red diesel in the tractor.

There's your alibi, Ed. Now you can get back to Wenna and Jago, make your apologies and get on with your bits. He nodded to himself and attempted to tidy his jacket and hair, in case *that pretty young Truman girl was working the pumps today. Now try not to get yourself in anymore trouble man. Maybe time to leave the booze a while.*

On his way to get the fuel, though, he couldn't shake the nagging feeling that he'd been seen at the pit. *Bugger!* He thought he'd heard rustling in the hedges. Had he imagined a pair of pale eyes in the dark undergrowth?

No, Ed! Stop your nonsense. Don't be such a tosser; your mind is full of worms and drink...Ain't nobody seen nothin'. He could hear Wenna's shrill voice berating him in his head. He shivered; he really hoped no one had seen him. All he knew was that he'd done some awful things. Things he'd justified because, 'Well, life 'as been 'ard', and, you know, the booze sometimes made him 'not think right'.

◈

Back at the farm, Wenna had begrudgingly let Edern in, and sent him to wash his hands. She'd cooked up some beef faggots and served them with mashed swede and carrots from their own vegetable patch. They all three sat down to eat together. This was very much against her better judgement; she really didn't want Edern in the house. She felt sick at the thought of his 'doings' and again she held her tummy as it churned with anxiety. Despondently turning and sniffing his plate, Jago screwed his nose up and pushed his dinner away, he asked for a Findus Crispy Pancake instead, a cheese and ham one. Wenna clipped him around the back of the head for being ungrateful and rude. For fifteen minutes the Hawkeys sat and ate in absolute silence with only the chinking of cutlery and slurping of gravy breaking the air. Edern tried and failed to make eye contact with Wenna, she deftly deflected his gaze by reaching for more salt or chasing a vegetable around her plate. She considered his very presence at the table compromise enough.

As usual, after dinner Jago was sent to do the washing up, which he did with as much passive aggressive clanking of pots and sloshing of water as possible. He hated it. *Every night they make me do it. I bet the other kids don't 'ave to. They probably has one of thems washdishers from Radio Rentals!*

Hearing Jago clattering and muttering away in the kitchen, and satisfied he wouldn't hear their conversation, Wenna sat back in her chair, pushed her sleeves up to her elbows and folded her arms. 'You get rid of 'em then?' She slowly chewed the inside of her mouth and narrowed her heavily made-up eyes. Though she was trying to fight her anguish, she couldn't hide her heartache as the tears began to well up. She pushed her long chin out towards the shameful man, She would not hold her tongue a minute more.

Looking anywhere in the room but at his own wife's face, Edern reluctantly forced out his despondent reply. 'Yes, Wen, all done. Stuff's all gone. Look, I'm sorry, really sorry. I swear I never meant to hurt you. None of you, not Jago, nor the Toad, and 'specially not you. I swear it!'

'Well, you 'ave, Edern 'Awkey, and ain't no amount of nothin' gonna change that. I don't believe you for one minute. You make me ill inside. 'S'gustin! I can't imagine the sickness of your rotten mind. One day they will punish you for this, mark my words, whether it be the Lord himself or the Prince of Darkness; the horror will come back to haunt you! And won't be no Wenna, Pascoe or Nell Hawkey gonna stand with you then. No, mister, this is your doin'! You are on your own!' He stared at his empty plate, he was defeated, there was nothing he could reasonably say or do.

'Go on, piss off back to your wretched shed, Ed. You can sleep in there tonight. I can't see your 'orrible face no more. You break my heart, Edern Hawkey! You break my poor tired heart, you manky stinking cur!'

Exhausted after dinner, Wenna retired as usual to the lounge and turned on the radio. She twizzled the dial to find Radio 2. She loved Alan 'Fluff' Freeman. He played all her favourite records; not that she was in any mood for pleasure. The dial was all the way over at the wrong end. Annoyingly, Jago had retuned the radio to R1 to listen to Pop Tong's Rap Selection the previous night.

Jago didn't really like rap – the truth was, it frightened him, but some of the kids at school reckoned they'd been to America and knew about it. Jago was fifteen years old and highly impressionable. He would pretend he was into rap to be cool. But Jago wasn't cool. Jago was actually a bit of a bully. The reality was, Jago got picked on at school for being 'a plank', for being 'different' and because 'his mum sleeps with her brother...'. Even at home Jago was rubbished by Wenna for being useless and lazy. And Edern didn't have much input into the boy's life whatsoever. Net result - Jago sought his revenge on weaker and more vulnerable people and animals than himself. Rightly or wrongly, this provided Jago with a real sense of justice. If Jago could redirect his misery onto another, he would and often did.

◆

Edern had returned to the safety of his barn. It was an enormous timber-clad Victorian threshing barn. The building was gable ended, at least twenty feet high and almost as long as the bungalow. Inside were two aging tractors, the orange Renault and an older blue Ford which had belonged to Old Jan Hawkey, over forty years ago, it'd long seized up and more recently had become a storage facility for dirty rags and peanut packets.

There were four sizable workbenches. Wenna's brother, Pascoe Hawkey, used to be a carpenter and had donated them after he'd sawn off his middle and ring fingers whilst making a hutch for Jago's guinea pigs, ten years back. Pascoe had got some compensation for that and didn't need to work anymore as the council helped with his disability.

Edern had a vast collection of tools. Ten different types of hammer for knocking different things into various surfaces. He had two tin boxes of spanners; they appeared rusty, but he would tell you they were as good as new, *just needed oilin'*, There were ratchets, files, screwdrivers and other apparatus that I have no real name for. Let's just agree that they were all very agricultural in design. Shelves as high as the barn roof bowed under the weight of hundreds of jam jars filled with screws, nails, tacks and bolts of every size imaginable.

One might consider for a moment that Edern's barn was rather like the Big Friendly Giant's cave of dreams in the

Roald Dahl story, the only difference here being, Edern wasn't very friendly...not very friendly at all.

Chapter 4

Jago Hawkey

May 2024

Driving through the drizzle past Castle an Dinas along the A30, I find myself wondering what, if any, use it'll be talking to Jago. He's a bit slower than most. The two times I've seen him creeping around the farm, I've found him quite awkward, he appears to lack any rudimentary social skills. I feel like he doesn't know whether to approach and greet me, or hide. He wears a vacuous lobotomised expression most of the time and looks a bit like a plain white dinner plate. He's nice enough when greeted, but I wouldn't trust him with the babysitting. Jago Hawkey is aloof, but not in a cool nonchalant way.

I've noticed he doesn't understand or know how to use punctuation. Here's a great example; I'd read the back of a postcard in the lounge last Saturday. It was perched next to a tearful porcelain clown on the mantelpiece. On the front of the card was a picture of a plum and tangerine sunset at Tintagel Castle. On the back it read:

Dear Mum wish you was ere a bird done bigs on dads head and we ate fish and chips the car was rattlin again and dad says its for the wreckers see you when I get home love Jago x

The postmark was stamped July 2005, which I guess would have made him about thirty years old when he sent it. You get the picture.

Approaching the front door, I'm amused to notice the naughty gnome has returned to his original position and gleefully waves his bulbous arse at visitors once again. I wonder, who visits the Hawkeys? I have no idea who their friends or family are; they seem to be a rather quiet and solitary unit. To date Wenna hasn't spoken about any kind of current social life.

I knock on the frosted-glass front door. It's off-white gloss, if you're wondering, with top and bottom glazed windows. I watch the pink body transmute through the distorted pane as it slowly totters towards me. She undoes three different sounding locks, a click, a slide and a sturdier clunk, before opening the door, punishing me with the stale and sweet odour of her home.

'A mornin', Doctor, come in, shoes off, sit down. I'll get you your coffee what you likes, an' get our Jago to pop in, shall I?'

'Morning. Oh yes, please. If you think he's happy to talk with me. I'd like that, Wenna. Thank you.'

Wenna invites me in, gestures for me to take my usual seat by the window and shuffles along her well-trodden catwalk to the kitchen. She must create a lot of static.

Looking through the window towards Trebrowagh, I'm troubled. The scene ought to make me feel good. It's an archetypal Cornish rural view, a cliché if you will, to the virgin visitor it is simply stunning. Gently undulating velvet green fields randomly divided by bushy hedges, the dark mauve hills of Bodmin Moor on the horizon, racing monochrome clouds tumbling across the sky, the ramshackle barn…I should love it but I don't, it really unsettles me. There's something very wrong here. Maybe it's the relentless drizzle again. I can't bear the Cornish weather. That said, when the sun shines there's hardly a better place to be on this planet.

Returning with a piping-hot cup of what she calls 'frothy coffee' and a slice of buttered malt loaf, Wenna stares at me with a menacing intensity that cuts me stone dead. Hmm, this is quite out of character. Her bulging purple head shakes from side to side, followed by her jowls. She leans in, uncomfortably close - inches from my face, the china coffee cup rattles and the coffee sloshes on its saucer.

'Now then Doctor, I wanna word with you. Listen 'ere, you bedder believe me when I say to you that Jago never done nuffin'!' she hisses. Then, having handed me the refreshments, she immediately backs away and relaxes before adding, 'He's a good boy, Doctor. He's slow, but he's kind. That boy 'as always loved his mother. Just a bit slow is all...' She pushes her glasses back into place, and gently bows, almost curtsying as she reverses towards the door.

I smile and nod in such a way as to reassure her that I won't put Jago on trial. 'Mmm, this coffee is delicious,' I tell her disingenuously. This pleases her as she turns and floats out of the room.

'Jay-go, Jago darlin', man's 'ere for you,' she calls into the darkness of the hall.

A large black dog pads to the lounge door, its head is the size of a breeze block – must be a Great Dane or similar, he looks in, sniffs and disappears into the house. I haven't seen the dog before. Weird. Weird and big. Seconds later, Jago meekly sidles up to the door.

'Hi, Jago,' I say encouragingly. 'I'm pleased to meet you; I've been looking forward to talking to you.'

Jago narrows his dark and beady little eyes. 'Mother says you a doctor, is it? Well, I isn't sick.'

'Actually, Jago, I'm a therap...Oh, you know what? Don't worry...'

The first impression one gets of Jago is that he's kind of round. Not necessarily large, just sort of egg-shaped. He's wearing a fleece-type top with the graphic of a wolf's big yellow eyes printed on the fabric. I'm surprised he's wearing a fleece as although it's overcast, it's really humid outside, it must be twenty degrees today. His trousers are muscovado brown and a bit old fashioned, made of some kind of material from the 1970s like rayon. I imagine they're hand-me-downs from Edern. They're grim. To set them off, Jago wears a pair of acid yellow and blue argyle socks – like golfers might choose, if they were feeling chipper. He reminds me of the actor Danny DeVito, his combover is similar. His complexion is challenging. His face is the colour of china clay, yet his cheeks are a deep cerise. I might say he looks a bit like a Japanese concubine, a little ovular geisha, with black teeth to boot. Okay, they're not so black, but you get the picture. According to my notes, he's forty-eight years old, the years haven't been kind to him.

'Jago, do you know why I'm here?' He looks everywhere around the room, except for at me. I notice he's twiddling the cuff of his fleece.

'Ess,' he replies, staring out the window at the back.

'Did Wenna explain that you're not in any trouble, or danger?'

'Ess.' He nods but not necessarily in agreement. It strikes me he's simply going through the motions. He's on autopilot.

'You know? About the boy?'

'Nope.' He shakes his head.

Jesus. This is going to be long and protracted.

'Do you remember a boy who disappeared around thirty years ago? Thirty-three to be precise. You'd have been fifteen. I believe he used to visit the farm here. Were you friends?'

Jago looks at me with his Mogadon face. I can see him thinking and I worry that I have somehow upset him. Now, confession time, I'm aware it's not very professional but I honestly find it a struggle to look at him. He does a curious thing whereby he licks the outside of his bottom gum. It squelches.

After a few seconds of this grotesque habit, he admits, 'Used to be the little toad come 'ere. "Ugly little black toad", that's what Mother calls 'im.'

'Why'd she call him that, Jago?'

He stares into space, trying to concentrate as he chews the inside of his bottom lip. Fiddling with his porky little fingers, he erupts: 'Cos he's dirty!' He mimics a pig snorting. His own little piggy eyes squint, barely masking his hidden contempt. 'Grubby. Grubby an' all warty – he's an ugly little black toad an' I hates him!' His face trembles, and he juts out his bottom jaw and spits the words out almost in relief. 'See...! I said it. You made me say it. I hates him, I hates him, I hates him! I blimin' HATES 'im.'

Jago has very easily become worked up. His breathing is erratic, he's snorting again. I need to calm him down. I suspect he's prone to blowing hot and cold.

'It's okay, Jago, I don't blame you. I mean, he sounds terrible...a terrible, awful toad. Did he make you miserable, Jago? Why do you suppose he was so grubby and, er...warty?'

'Mother says it's cos he don't live nowhere. But I 'spect he lived with the circus lot.'

'The circus lot?' I enquire. I'm mindful not to press too hard, but I feel as if I might actually get somewhere with him here.

'You know, thems people what lived in the vans an' that. Edern says thems was clowns!'

'Hmm...and you don't like clowns? Is that why you hated him? Because he was a clown?'

'Nope.'

'Okay, so tell me. Lots of people have an aversion to clowns. It's quite okay to be angry. What did you have against him? What had he done to make you, as you say – hate him?'

'He were always 'ere Doctor.' He sticks his bottom lip out and nods towards the window which overlooks the barn. 'Always at Mother's window getting food and treats. I think she liked him more 'un me. She always used to say she feels sorry about him, like he don't got nuffin', you know? She weren't never sorry for me. Just angry.'

I truly feel bad for him, he's almost fifty, but right now, in the midst of our conversation he's transported back to presenting as a very lonely, helpless and depressed fifteen year old. I'm beginning to understand where this is going. 'Would it be fair to say that you were jealous of him? Were you somehow upset that Wenna was kinder, more caring to him than to you, her own son? Could that be true, Jago?'

He stares at me as if I'm the fool here. 'Course I were jealous of 'im, that's why I tries to hurt 'im.' His face begins to contort as he clenches his thumbs into his fists. 'He can't speak, see, so Mother gives him stuff, nice treats and that. She don't give me nuffin' 'cept a smack or a kick or sometimes pinches!'

His cheeks redden from cerise to scarlet. Turning his head to one side, he continues. 'See, Doctor, here's the secret, I know the boy don't speak no words, I know he don't make no noises, unless it's burps an' farts an' whatnot. But I also knows he can't say nuffin' if I gets my own back on him. So...I know I can hurt him. I can smack him in silence, and ain't nobody gonna shout at Jago for it.'

Screwing up his moonlike face, and through his short, gritted little teeth, he gloats: 'I used to throw stones and rocks at the maw! I would make him hop around like a little toad. I makes 'im cry! But he don't make no sound. Not even a whimper. I tells 'im that he smells like s'gustin' dogs, and that no one likes him. I kicks 'im like Mother does to me. In his shin, and his...' Jago looks to the floor and the blood drains from his red cheeks. 'I kicks his dick sometimes...'

I catch myself grimacing. I sense it's time to cool our conversation down.

'Jago, that must have been hard for you. I'm sorry he made you feel this way. Maybe it wasn't fair that Wenna treated him differently.'

I can't stop him now though, as he continues to channel his frustration. It's not easy to describe, but he's almost, but not quite, sneering as he gathers his thoughts.

'I remember one time, the little toad is following me back from school an' the other kids are laughing an' pointin' at me. They're sayin' the canker, the crab, is my brother, that Wenna birthed it after being with a fishin' fella in Plymouth. They says we share a bed an' that we're best friends. Well, Doctor, I know I shouldn't have, but I see proper red an' picks up this big rock, see, an' I chucks it at him and tells him to fuck off!' He looks at to me as if he wants me to excuse him for swearing. 'It hit his face, at the top, and he falls to the ground. He don't move, and he is bleeding. I swear I never meant to kill 'im, but the other kids made me snap, see.' Jago's eyes well up as he shimmies his feet into the carpet.

Exhaling, but trying not to appear unnerved by this revelation, and mindful of my duties in this position, I tip my head inquisitively, encouraging Jago to continue.

'So, I goes and pushes him with my foot, you know, prod him, an' his eyes sneak open. Imagine my surprise when I see he ain't dead now! So, I tells him to go see Wenna an' she'll clean up his blood and dirt and tears. I feels proper happy he ain't dead, but so cross also that he's not dead. Understand?' His eyes flicker from side to side, left to right and back again. 'But I think at least Mother won't beat me for it, so I says nuffin', ever again, till now. You won't say nuffin' to Mother? Promise?'

I assure him that his secret is safe with me. I think I've genuinely heard enough about the bullying. I can imagine him collapsing or going into cardiac arrest. He's very stressed. 'Jago, it's okay, please don't worry, I don't want you to feel worried or panicked. Here's an idea. Let's try to think about better things. Now, I must confess I don't know much about you *Jago*. Tell me, what makes you happy these days?'

He immediately relaxes. Leaning back into the armchair, he smiles and places his hands behind his head. 'Oh, now then, Doctor, I loves workin' at the nursery. You know, the posh garden centre out by St Kres? I plants seeds and I makes sammiches. All different kinds of sammiches: some has eggs in, some has jams, an' one fella what comes there, he 'as corned beef and red onion. He must be from over the Tamar. Also, there are ladies there what point at me and smile when I asks them about how they are, and they always say, "Much better now we seen you, Jago 'Awkey." I thinks they fancy me. So, yarp, I likes the nursey work, and I like them Ant and Decs. Me an' Edern watch them in his barn. Edern's got a telly in there. We like when they do jokes on real people. They're really naughty.'

Jago has worked up quite the sweat as he wrestles to get the lupine fleece over his big round head, revealing an ill-fitting grey T-shirt with a Howard the Duck transfer on it. It reads 'Don't Duck with me...' and depicts a cartoon duck smoking a half-burned cigar. It has a rip on the sleeve. I can't help but notice that Jago's chest is, er, how to put this? Quite womanly.

I don't want to push him too far today. Wenna was deliberate and clear about his innocence, and that I shouldn't upset him. Personally, I've found his admissions rather unnerving.

'Right, you know what? I think that's enough chat for today, Jago. Listen, look, I really appreciate you talking about those things. I know it can't be easy.'

I reach for my cup of frothy coffee, which has a skin on it, so I take the teaspoon from the saucer and remove it. I can't stand this coffee, and now it's cold. Last weekend it churned my stomach to the extent that I had to down a couple of omeprazole when I got back in my car.

'Thank you, sir, I see you next week. I tell you about Edern then. Don't say nuffin' to Mother, and you got to know...I am really sorry about the boy. I have always been sorry about him, you know? About what happened to him...'

Intriguing.

He tries to give me a knowing wink, but both eyes close at the same time. He then gets up and heads into the dark hall. The black dog reappears, looks at me, licks its lips and trots away.

This place is so strange, and Jago's so bizarre, kind of gross. I wonder what he wants to tell me about Edern. I'd like to talk to Mr Hawkey myself. I have so many questions for him. I know from the Devon and Cornwall case files that Edern was well known over at the commune. Coral had reported that Edern had facilitated their takeover of the land at the back of Pop Biddle's farm. I'm led to believe that Edern was a regular visitor to the farm. I don't know why. I also have no idea if he's really Jago's dad, or if Wenna's his sister.

Yes, I look forward to getting to know Edern better.

Wenna returns to the lounge and clears the cups and saucers away onto a tray. She investigates my half-full cup of coffee and looks at me, then back at the coffee. 'Dun' you like it, Doctor?'

'Yes,' I lie. 'It was lovely, but Jago and I were having such a great chat that I forgot about it, and I let it go cold.'

She accepts this excuse and promises me a better one next time, before escorting me to the front door.

'S'pose we'll see you same time next week?'

'Ess,' I reply, slightly amused with myself.

'That'll be great. 'Ere, if you wanna talk to the old bugger, might I suggest you bring him a bag of peanuts.'

'Peanuts?'

'Sure, thems' his best you know.' Pleased with herself, Wenna closes the door quietly behind me and shuffles back into the house.

There is a sky blue lady gnome next to the fibreglass bridge; she's actually quite pretty, I don't know what comes over me, but I look around to check that no one's looking and proceed to kidnap her. Bundling the Smurf-like damsel into the car boot in the drizzle, I sigh deeply. That was all too bloody stressful. I'll enjoy getting home today. Maybe I'll stop at the Blue Rose in St Kres for a pint of Tribute and some Scampi Fries. Yes, I'll do just that.

Chapter 5

The Egg Hunt
31st March 1991 (Easter Sunday)

Easter Sunday was Jago's favourite day of the year. Better than Christmas! This morning he had risen extra early he couldn't sleep due to the excitement. Jago bloody loved chocolate, and at Easter he could and would gorge on the stuff.

The previous year he'd been sick twice by lunchtime after scoffing a Yorkie Bar egg, a KitKat egg (which came in its own mug) and no fewer than 20 Mini Eggs. The day had begun, as was traditional, with the Hawkey Easter fry-up, which always included his favourite Richmond sausages along with all the other regular bits, except mushrooms, which he hated. After breakfast, he'd consumed the aforementioned confections and finally, the point at which Jago had gone too far, his uncle Pascoe had given him a warm Cadbury's Creme Egg from his pocket. Well, Jago was like Cornwall's answer to Mr Creosote...*'Just one more Mini Egg...'* and the unfortunate youth vomited on and off for half an hour, after which his mum gave him a sound thrashing on the backside with the wooden spoon and sent him to bed. He'd cried for almost a week.

'Don't you be ruinin' it for yourself this year, Jago 'Awkey,' he reprimanded himself whilst hurriedly pulling on his new Howard the Duck T-shirt that they'd got at Bodmin market. He'd been saving it until today as it featured a giant egg with a smoking duck hatching from it. Jago thought it was very Eastery...and cool. 'Pace yourself, have one small egg s'mornin', then Mother's breakfast. Then maybe the inside of the main egg. Ess, that's how 'ee does today, Jago, then 'ee don't miss the egg hunt!' He couldn't contain his joy about the day ahead and bounded out of his room and along the hall to the kitchen, where he could already smell the sausages frying. This was gonna be a great day!

The kitchen was at the back of the house, at the end of an exceedingly long hallway, which meant it never got as much natural daylight as the lounge. The hallway always seemed dark to Jago. In the kitchen they had a free-standing cooker with a grill at head height above the electric rings. The floor was covered in a pink-and-green-chequered linoleum, and the walls were covered in a wallpaper which was predominately beige and featured illustrations of various kitchen objects such as a stove-top kettle, a slice of bread with a jar of jam and a butter knife, and an orange casserole pot. The radio was always on, throughout every waking hour. Because it was Sunday, the DJ was Richard Baker on Radio 2. Wenna preferred Derek Jameson on the weekdays. Jago couldn't care less because it was Easter!

'Happy Easter, Mother.' Beaming from ear to ear, Jago pulled a chrome and burgundy corduroy chair out from under the smoked-glass kitchen table with a clank and sat down to wait for the fry-up.

'I 'ope you ain't bin eating' no chocolate already, you tubby little shit,' Wenna sniped from the cooker.

'I ain't, Mother, I swear. I ain't got no eggs yet.' He looked expectantly at his mum, like a nauseatingly saccharine puppy waiting for a treat. He tilted his head. 'Don't s'pose you an' Edern got an egg for Jago...?'

'Course we did, my angel.' She smirked.

'Yes!' Jago grabbed the air as if he were in Bon Jovi or Whitesnake. 'Can I 'ave it, Mother? Please...'

'Course you can, my darlin' Jayjay. It's in the hens' coop out front...' Wenna cackled, cracked an egg into a frying pan and waved the empty shell halves triumphantly in Jago's direction.

Ugh. He knew she was winding him up and it deflated his mood a little. To distract himself from his ratty mother, he reached for the pile of newspapers and magazines. As it was Easter Sunday there wasn't a *News of the World*, so he took the folded-up copy of the previous week's *Falmouth Packet* and attempted to read. Jago's teacher had reported at parents' evening that reading was his forte, whatever that meant.

The headline story reported on an earthquake in west Cornwall. Apparently, houses shook, tables rattled and ceilings cracked. One local lady thought a plane had fallen out of the sky. 'Was like what 'appened in Scotland, with the Libyans,' she was quoted as saying. Others thought it was a sonic boom. The paper claimed it was 3.8 on the Richter scale and centred around the Penryn area.

Jago flicked through the pages before folding open a full-page advert for the annual 'Trebrowagh and St Kres Easter Egg Hunt – Sponsored by Trago Mills'.

''Ere 'tis, Mother. The egg 'unt! Says 'ere, there be hundreds of eggs hidden all over Trebrowagh and that kids can begin the hunt at eleven a.m. Sharp. Starting at the Methodist church, on Chapel Road.'

Last year, Jago had only found twenty or so Mini Eggs before the vomiting. This year it was his plan to take a big bag and collect the bounty for later, instead of eating as he went. He was reminded of the regrettable time his class had gone to the pick-your-own fruit farm on a school trip. Yuk. Messy.

The annual egg hunt had become quite a famous and unmissable affair over the past decade, drawing families from all over north Cornwall. One family from Bideford in Devon visited religiously every year. You shouldn't be surprised to meet an overseas traveller at the hunt either, such was the magnitude of the event. It was without question the biggest day in the Trebrowagh diary. And today it was sunny as well. This was going to be a fantastic day, Jago could hardly contain himself at the prospect.

Edern joined them at the table for a spectacular 'Hawkey Fry'. Wenna refused to look at him throughout the entire sitting. After breakfast she made herself a frothy coffee and went to the pantry to fetch Jago's real Easter egg. It was a large one.

'Biggest we could get 'ee, Jago,' gloated Wenna as she passed the giant mint Aero egg across the table. Jago felt a little bit sick at the thought of this extraordinary prize. It was if his body had had a premonition of what was to come.

'Oh goodness! Thank you, Mother, thank you, Edern. It's the best egg I ever saw. Mint too...thems is rare, least Alex Biddle says so. So...'

Jago made his excuses and left the table to get himself ready for the egg hunt later that morning. As he went, he sang a little song to himself, to the tune of the Superman theme. *'Bum, willy and eggs, Jay-go's eggs...Bum, willy and eggs – JAY-GO's eggs...'*

Things weren't so light-hearted in the kitchen.

Wenna scowled, waving a fork in Edern's direction. 'I'll take the boy up the village to the egg hunt. You can stay out of sight, Edern 'Awkey.' Wenna glared at her despondent husband. 'We'll be back by two. I expects all of them fenisters to be cleaned, an' any other nonsense from the barn got rid of. Y'ear me, Edern? All cleaned up. An' these plates an' cooking dishes.'

'But Jago does the dishes, Wen.'

'Not today he don't. You'll do them for me. For once in your pathetic life, you'll do somethin' right, Ed.'

Edern bowed his head in both submission and agreement. Wenna headed to her bedroom to do her ablutions.

By ten a.m., Wenna was ready. Show ready! She felt pretty sexy in her tight blue jeans, cream fur-topped boots and burgundy woollen housecoat. She'd put on her new green mascara in case she saw Pop Biddle or Jimper, or even Donna from the Blue Rose – anyone other than Edern. He was on her last nerve and could gladly die for all she cared right now.

She headed down the long, dark hall and knocked on Jago's door. 'You ready, Jago? Ja-go?' There was no reply. She tapped again, frowning at the poster of the footballer Chris Waddle which was attached to the door by Blu Tack and tape. 'What a silly haircut,' she moaned, looking at the mulleted young man staring back at her. Again, no reply. She turned the handle and poked her head round. 'Cooey, Jago...Jago?'

He wasn't there. Only the scrunched-up green tin-foil wrapper of a mint Aero easter egg remained on his unmade bed. 'Dickhead,' she muttered and called out for him into the house.

At the front of the farm, high on sugar, Jago was kicking an old elasticated black plimsoll around the drive and commentating to himself as he played.

'Glen Hoddle passes to Chris Waddle, he steps round Nigel Pearson, crosses to Clive Allen...' He thwacked the plimsoll towards a makeshift goal he'd made using the back of Edern's car and someone else's discarded Lord Anthony parka. 'Gooooaaaal!' He turned blindly into Wenna, who grabbed him firmly by the shoulders and turned him one hundred and eighty degrees towards the front gate.

'C'mon, you greedy little oinker...I seen you ate the Aero egg already; you better not chunder, young man...'

Jago felt just fine. Excellent, as it happened. He was off to the egg hunt, and he was certain to find the most eggs! Jago was a king for the day. They strolled to the top of the drive and turned right towards the village.

◈

The whole village of Trebrowagh was dripping head to toe in black-and-white bunting, in tribute to St Piran, the patron saint of tin miners, bumper stickers, and pretty much the adopted saint of Cornwall. There were hundreds of people out, all enjoying the sunny weather and creating a truly expectant atmosphere. The children were, naturally, the most excited. The prospect of the greatest easter egg hunt in the region – maybe the world – was too much for them to handle. Nervous energy fizzed along the streets all the way to Chapel Road.

At the modest little Methodist church hall, there were numerous stalls offering raffles, tombolas and more local games like 'Poke the Piskey'. Jago asked Wenna for ten pence for a go at poking a pixie. He handed the change over to a lady who's elongated spindly face and thin cream coloured hair caused her to look remarkably like Jimmy Savile. She passed Jago a rudimentary spear made from a broom handle, some twine and a steak knife.

'Now listen 'ere, toerag. See, I drops this 'ere piskey down the pipe, an' 'ee tries an' stabs it. You got three stabs...' She proceeded to drop a knitted elf-like character down the length of an upright plastic drainpipe, and Jago raised the harpoon in readiness before thrusting it into the ground centimetres behind the piskey as it popped out the bottom of the pipe.

'Damn,' he moaned.

'Okay, again, ready...' Jimmy Savile wasted no time in releasing the toy down the hole for a second time. Jago lunged at the right time and pinned the pixie to the grass.

'Yes!' He leapt around in the air waving his arms like his footballing hero's. 'I gots it, Mother, I gots 'im.' Pleased with himself, and much to the stall-holder's chagrin, he selected a bottle of Timotei shampoo (as directed by Wenna) as his prize. They then continued to the refreshments desk inside the foyer of the chapel, where Wenna requested a cup of tea, and Jago chose a tin of warm Tizer in readiness for the main event.

Outside, at the front of the chapel, a wide-set man with mustard-coloured trousers and a red megaphone was directing parents to organise their children into age groups. 'Kids up to eight years old must go with a parent or sibling. *You* will set off first. Nine- to twelve-year-olds will go next, and after five minutes, thirteen and upwards will go!' he bellowed.

Jago found this most unfair. All the good eggs would be found by eagle-eyed parents with toddlers who probably didn't like chocolate anyway!

The bellower continued: 'This year is our biggest ever hunt, and thanks goes out to everyone down at Trago Mills for sponsorin' the event an' supplying over a thousand eggs! That's right, there are one thousand and one easter eggs of all sizes hidden about the village. And, ladies and gentlemen, boys and girls, as an extra-special treat, and a first for Trebrowagh, there is one golden egg hidden somewhere in the village...'

The crowd cheered and bubbled in anticipation. Who would find the golden egg? What did it mean? Jago was practically wetting himself. He looked around at the opposition in his thirteen-and-over pen of eager kids. He recognised a lot of them from school. Today they weren't interested in laughing at him or bullying. They had eggs on their minds. Today was a good day; Jago thought that could be a good title for a rap tune.

It was almost eleven o clock, the kids were chomping at the bit. 'Five...four...three...two...one...gooooooooooo!' Megaphone Man roared operatically with the voice of a miner in full song, and a sea of parents and toddlers crashed through the church gates onto Chapel Road like a human tsunami. Jago prayed that they wouldn't find the golden egg. God, it was so unfair! Families scattered in every direction, stooping and scooping up mini eggs as they went. Jago was getting twitchy and wanted to ask his mum if the eggs would melt in the sun. Wenna, however, appeared to be chatting with Pop Biddle over by the bar and ignored her son completely.

More mayhem ensued as the master of ceremonies began his countdown for the nine- to twelve-year-olds. By now Jago was hyperventilating. *These kids are the ones to watch – thems is quick, right good at finding eggs, I bet.* The sense of injustice was overwhelming, and the colour began to drain from Jago's cheeks as he expelled a mint-chocolatey belch.

To make matters worse, at the back of the pack Jago spied a boy in dark, tatty clothes, his face unwashed and his head hanging low. *It's the Toad! The dirty kid from the circus.* Jago's cheeks refilled, now with the blood of hatred. 'Grrr, it's the 'orrible toad. Why's he 'ave to be 'ere? He 'as no right!' he grumbled to himself.

A young voice piped up from the remaining group. ''Ere, Jago, your brother's over there – he's gonna get all your eggs.'

Another kid pointed to the Toad, adding, 'Yeah, he's gonna give 'em all to your mum.'

A third joker continued, 'Just like Edern does...'

'Ignore 'em, them's idiots,' Jago shook his head as the countdown began for the final egg hunters to start.

The Master of Ceremonies raised his megaphone one last time. 'Five, four, three...'

'Arrgggggggghhhh! FOR FUCK'S SAKE...'

Over at the stalls, a young child had just speared Jimmy Savile through the foot. It'd pierced her pumps and dug right into the top of her foot. The St John's Ambulance people ran across the start line to the screaming stallholder. And, with an air of defeat, met with equal dismay, the loud-hailer guy informed the thirteen-plus group that there would be a short delay whilst order was restored.

Jago kicked the stone wall in front of him. 'Ughhh. NOT FAIR!'

Chapter 6

Edern Hawkey
May 2024

Now, I'm no counterfeit Columbo or second-class Sherlock. I hadn't been sent here to solve the case of a murdered aristocratic authoress, or to piece together a series of unconnected poisonings. I was simply here to get to know and interview this peculiar family. To understand if their tenuous relationships with the missing boy may eventually help lead us to discover his whereabouts or potentially ratify the general consensus that he was dead.

In time I'll report back to HQ at Truro any conclusions I make about the Hawkeys. If anything is untoward, I'm sure the powers that be will flex their legal muscles accordingly. That's Devon and Cornwall Police's prerogative. But I must admit, on a personal level, I'm getting drawn into the story. I guess what I'm really seeking are any admissions of guilt, any chinks in their armour, just to satisfy my own presumptions. Maybe I'm starting to wonder if they really were involved. If any one of them was, I'd certainly be picking Edern out of any given line-up. To be perfectly honest, I'm enjoying playing the *secret policeman*, and I'm particularly interested in talking to Mr Hawkey.

I arrive at the farm at eleven o'clock as usual. The clouds have temporarily broken apart and the early summer sun is beginning to warm the ground and wake the plants. Bluebells shake the overnight rain from their heads and gently turn to face the warmth.

Wenna and the big dog greet me as I get out of the car. 'Mornin', Doctor.'

'Morning, Wenna. Lovely to see you. How are you? All of you?'

'Bin better. Jago 'as some pain in his back and his…you know. His rear end.'

'Sciatica?'

'Good heavens, Doctor, no! Just a pain in the top of his bottom. Probably all the sitting around he does.' She snorts as she laughs at herself. ''Ere,' she continues, 'I tells Edern you be comin' over today. I said I'd send you over when you gets here. He's in his barn. Go over. Pop in an see old Ed. I'll fix you coffee and a cake after.'

I thank her and turn towards the barn. It really is a big building. Foreboding, in its way. I find it strange that he's always in his barn, like it's his secret lair. No, I don't like it at all. Makes me want to wash my hands. Nevertheless, I'm here to see him, and see him I will.

I knock on the side of the barn wall as I enter. 'Hello…hello, Edern…'

The beige and bent old man looks over the top of his brown acetate spectacles and slowly unwinds his crooked back as he stands. 'Go away, not interested. I'm seventy eight years old, I don't be needing your business. Nor my Wenna, nor our Jago.' His voice is strong, deliberate and direct, it defies his age. Edern is pottering at the back of the barn. He's fiddling with an oily piece of machinery. A vehicle part perhaps. It's not my area of expertise.

'Listen, I understand that, Mr Hawkey, and you're not obliged to say anything to me. It's not a legal thing, I'm just trying to help close an old case about...'

'I know, 'bout the boy,' he sneers and curls his top lip. 'Wenna tell me. Says you're okay, she says you're kind. I 'spect you're just bloody nosy.'

'Well, I guess it must seem strange, a little unexpected, a tad nosy if you say so, but ultimately, Edern, the reality is simple, that boy went missing, he somehow just vanished off the face of the planet. Nobody gave a damn back then. The story is too weird, how can a child disappear in plain sight? I don't believe it, we don't believe it. There are people out there who believe there should be some form of justice, at the very least, some answers.' He blows his rubbery lips out at me and huffs for wasting his time.

I try to divert him. 'What are you making?'

He raises two surprisingly bushy eyebrows. 'Making? Not makin' nuffin'. This 'ere's a carburettor, makes your engine run right. This one's from my old Renault tractor. Clogged up with all years of crud.' He taps the carburettor on the workbench whilst apparently unblocking it with a pipe cleaner.

'Oh, some maintenance, I see. A bit like my job here, Edern. I'm just trying to repair something that got broken years ago. It's similar...'

He purses his soggy lips, forcing a thousand wrinkles to line up across his face. 'Ain't nuffin' the same. You're talking skollyon, total rubbish! Why don't you bugger off back to Launceston or wherever it is?!' he retorts, seeing straight through my schtick.

Edern's dialect is thick, I'm going to struggle with this. But, ever prepared, I reach into the pocket of my jacket and withdraw a couple of packets of Big D peanuts. I glibly raise an eyebrow. 'Fancy a bag?'

He carefully places the carburettor back on the bench, his face relaxing and his hooded eyes widening. 'Don't mind,' he replies.

I walk towards him at the back of the barn. He's very suspicious of me, he bears his teeth like a rescue dog in a pub.

'Here you go, Ed, a little dickie bird told me they were your favourite.'

'Used to be, can't get 'ems no more. Where be you findin' 'em?'

'B&M bargain store, in Bodmin.'

'B&M, eh? I should ask Jago to nip down there for me then. Didn't know they was still on the market. Thank you.' He's finally warming up as he rolls a dry roasted nut between his thumb and forefinger. He pops it into his mouth, his eyes look to the heavens, and he's transported back thirty years. 'Mmm, that is proper lush, a taste o' heaven.'

He taps a small handful into his palm and scoffs them. His shoulders drop, he rolls his head across his shoulders and he almost, not quite, but almost, cracks a smile. He's definitely softening. He looks at me through his eyebrows.

'Listen here, whoever you are. I don't really know so much 'bout the boy. He was always with Wen, you know, at the fenister. She gives him titbits. Odds and ends, you know, biscuits, cake and the like. I think Jago likes him. They sometimes go out into the yard or the fields, playin' hide and seek an' wotnot. One year Wenna gives 'im fifty pence penn-bloodh money. Dunno why she knew it was his penn-bloodh – his birthday, yer know. He don't got no words, but she can be spiritual an' that.'

'Edern, you knew the folk over at the commune, right?'

'Not s'much. They turned up 'ere in 1988 or something. They was a travlin' circus, I think. Lady what had bad, dirty hair asks to stay in our fields. There's maybe ten to fifteen vans and a couple of lorries. One fella has an old yellow American school bus, can you believe? I can't let 'em be 'ere. The field don't drain nice. It's the clay, see. I says to the hairy lady, I can speak to Old Man Biddle. He owns farm 'cross the other side o' Trebrowagh.' He continues in his somewhat rambling way: 'Biddle sorts 'em. Don't know what thems paid, but they seem to live there for quite some time.'

'I understand you would visit the commune, Edern. Did you do some work over there maybe?'

He rubs his right thumb into his left palm and looks around the barn. He's an unnervingly shady man.

'Yarp, jus' bits. Tinkering. Helped with the lorries and stuff. I worked over the garage in Tregaswith, 'Westways', so I knows a bit 'bout engines.' He wipes his hands on his brown trousers, adjusts his glasses and looks away from me and back to his carburettor. 'Asides, I don't care much for talkin' now. So that is that. Thank you. Good day.'

I've lost him again, I'll leave him to it, he's never going to tell me anything useful anyway. My plan is to pop back again tomorrow if possible. I'll try to get further then.

'I understand, Edern, you're busy. I'll pop back tomorrow. I'll grab some Big Ds for you later, I've got a date in Bodmin tonight.'

He looks up, flashes the quickest and most disingenuous of grins, and then goes back to his work with a muffled grunt. As I reach the door he pipes up, ''Ere...'

Ooh, perhaps a morsal of sense is on its way...

'Yes, Edern?'

'Don't s'pose they sells thems nuts stuck to the picture of naked ladies, does 'em?' He smirks and winks.

I shiver, *what a dirty old man*. 'I'll check for you, Ed,' I lie, and roll my eyes.

I leave the barn and cross the driveway towards the house. Wenna cheerfully waves at me out of the window.

'Cooey, Doctor. You see Edern?'

'Yes, we just had a quick chat. Thank you. Jago any better?'

'Bit better, Doctor. He's havin' a lie down. Now my shingles is playin' up; makes seeing things all a blur, but all okay, I be used to it all these days. You want that frothy coffee?'

'Yes, great, I'd love that.' I'm not really satisfied with my time with Edern. I'll press Mrs Hawkey further.

Wenna catches me surveying the gnome garden as she eventually gets to the front door. 'Oh yeah! Here's some news...Rosie's gone, Doctor!' she reports.

'Rosie?' I know exactly whom she means.

As we head to the lounge, Wenna explains the mystery. 'Rosie, she's one of Edern's princesses. She be a blue gnome, Smurf-like. She's run off. Jago swears blind he ain't touched 'er, and I certainly isn't in the business of takin' gnomes from myself. She's been there twenty years can you believe? Just left. Vanished. Weird.' She shrugs; she's genuinely puzzled.

I seize the opportunity. 'Just like the boy we're interested in?'

'S'pose so...' My words are like water off a ducks back. 'Ere, 'ow's Edern? Anything to say about anything?'

'No. Not really. He says he didn't have anything to do with the boy. He recalled that Jago and the boy were friends – said they'd play together – hide and seek and that sort of thing. He didn't claim to have much to do with him. He more or less suggested that the kid spent most of his time here with you. Helping you out with baking and washing.'

Wenna's frown becomes a scowl as she folds her arms high across her chest. 'Did 'ims now? Edern 'as a selected memory.'

'Selective.' I can't help correcting her.

'Whatever, selected, selective, I dunno. But I knows he used to have that boy visit him in the poxy barn over there. Says he's teaching him woodwork and engines and bits. A long time I believes him.' She deliberately scans my face and continues, 'then Jago sees summat, an' he comes runnin' and tells me that he seen the boy all tearful, torn trousers and wotnot...' She stops short of getting into a panic. 'He's never changed! Nuffin' a do with Jago, mind. Jago dun nuffin', Doctor. Nuffin'.'

An overwhelming sense of distress fills the room as Wenna starts taking short breaths in but letting none out. Her face becomes blotchy, her eyes start to bulge, she appears to convulse, and she audibly passes wind as she grasps her generous waist with both arms. *Shit! She's having a heart attack! No, no it's a panic attack*, I reassure myself as she slowly finds a natural breathing rhythm.

'You okay, Wenna? Wenna, can you hear me? Let me get you a water. Do you take any medicine for these attacks?'

She shakes her head and wags a finger rapidly to say no to the medicine but desperately gestures in a drinking motion that she wants water, whilst still catching her breath. I jump up, head to the kitchen and open a couple of cupboards in search of a tumbler. Nothing but cleaning fluids and dusters. I try the pantry door; there they are; a shelf of blue glass tumblers with knobbly bottoms. Then, something very surprising happens. An extraordinary discovery. A game changing scrapbook of evidence. I notice the back of the door is collaged with newspaper clippings...

'TREBROWAGH – KIDNAP' reads the title of one article. 'UNREST AT BIDDLE'S FARM' reports another. I scan the door; there must be thirty to forty different cuttings. A brief once over and I'd say all of them either directly or tenuously pertain to the case of the missing boy. *Fuck!* My heart is now the one wildly out of control. *What the fuck?! What are these people up to?* A half-page grainy black-and-white photo shows members of the hippy commune. There are at least fifteen young adults and a handful of children. Some are wearing stripy jumpers; one lady appears to be wet nursing a child who looks to be about eight years old. In the centre I recognise a rather more attractive woman with dreadlocks. She's wearing a Levellers t-shirt and has raised her middle finger. It's Coral! She's quoted under the photo as saying that unless 'the boy' is returned unharmed, there will be no rest in the village...The bottom has been torn away, so I can't get the full story. If you ask me, she looks feisty – I wouldn't pick a fight with her. *Bloody hell!* I did not expect this.

I'm about to move on to the next picture when a loud bark booms out behind me. I jump out of my skin, I turn to see the black dog in the doorway. It's long flappy jowls drip with slobber as it barks again, a deep sonic boom of a bark that passes through my sternum.

Jago appears at its side. 'What you doin', Mr Doctor?'

Busted. I've been caught prying. Reaching for a long glass on the shelf, I tell him about Wenna's attack.

'Don't panic, Jago, your mum is having a funny turn in the lounge. I'll get the water; you go and check on her, please...chop, chop.' I know he's clocked me reading the articles, but the Wenna story should put him off the scent. I still sense a great presence behind me. Jesus, that dog is massive. It's the hound of the bloody Baskervilles. I take the cue and quit being Poirot in the pantry, close the door and head to the tap to fill the glass for Wenna.

Back in the lounge, Jago is crouched down by Wenna's giant chair. He's stroking her blubbery nougat-like arm. Thankfully she's returned to her normal colour and appears quite calm.

Jago snarls at me, 'What you dun to 'er, Doctor? Why she be in a panickin' way?'

'I be jus' fine, Jayjay. Mans was just talkin' w'me 'bout Edern, and I gots flustered is all.' Wenna moves his hand from her arm and looks to me. 'Thank you, Doctor, for fetchin' the boy and this nice water.'

Jago flares his nostrils in my direction: 'He's been starin' at the pantry door, Mother. Him's nosy, I tell you that! What were you doin' in there, mister? Readin' 'bout us 'Awkeys' I spect.'

I feel my hands getting clammy, I've got myself a bit cornered here. 'Well Jago, as I explained to you out in the kitchen, your mum was having a funny turn, so I rushed to get her a water. I don't know your house very well, so I checked a few different cupboards for a glass. I don't know what I could've done differently to be honest.'

'You see 'em old bits of newspapers I s'pose?' Wenna asks me.

'I did, Wenna. I don't want to stress you out any more than I need, but I will say I was quite surprised by the content...incredulous in fact. It strikes me that someone here had a rather unhealthy interest in the case of our missing little boy, wouldn't you say? Who was that?' I'm more than a bit surprised, actually I'm really hacked off, to discover that after weeks of nurturing a trusting relationship with them, Wenna especially, that the Hawkeys are most certainly hiding something. I'd been caught discovering their enigmatic door pastings, I have no alternative but go on the counter-offensive. 'Okay, you two. Let's stop the games. What do you know about this case? Spit it out. You Know more than you're letting on. I'm certain of that.'

Wenna rocks backwards in her chair and grimaces. Her eyes dart around the room; she attracts Jago's attention, and I catch her shaking her head at him. I think she's shocked that I've been so direct. 'I promise you Doctor, I tells you everythin', sir.'

Hmm, this is a shift, she's never called me *sir* before. She's perturbed.

'Well, that's not completely true, is it, Wenna? Until just now, you have failed to mention that you'd made a door-sized collage from old newspaper clippings about the missing boy. It's a bit suspicious, wouldn't you say?'

She looks down at her hands, transfixed by her own yellowing fingernails. 'You is not right, sir. We were interested in the story is all. You don't live here, nothin' never 'appens in Trebrowagh or St Kres. So when it did, we just thought it was exciting. You know, like a proper mystery, like Miss Marple and wotnot.'

They think I'm an imbecile. 'Wenna, I can't accept that. I won't accept that...You've told me that he was a regular visitor to the house. You've told me you'd treat him to cakes, Ryvita and drinks and such like. You cleaned him up and wiped away blood and tears. Edern told me you'd once given him some birthday money – something I very much doubt you'd do unless you cared about him. You clearly had your own strange little relationship with him. In a way you treated him like a member of the family. Wenna, he trusted you.'

I turn to Jago. 'And you, what else can you add to this, Jago? You told me you were jealous of him; you admitted to bullying him, chasing him, kicking him, even throwing stones at the boy!'

Wenna scowls at Jago as he pulls the sleeve of his grotty brown cardigan over the back of his hand and uses it to wipe a tear from his cheek.

'You promises me you ain't tellin' Mother 'bout that. You a liar!' he huffs, and mocks spitting at my shoes. Disgusting.

I'm not finished with this, but must remind myself that I am here in my capacity as a psychologist. I gather my thoughts and temporarily squat down beside them both, like Jeremy Kyle.

'Okay, listen to me, both of you. I understand you might be worried, but I'm acutely aware that you are both covering something up.' Wenna and Jago stare at each other, as if activating some secret code. 'That said, I don't believe for one second that either of you had anything to do with the case. Wenna, you must forgive Jago for hurting the boy. He was, I believe, at a difficult age, and he felt that you paid more attention to, and were more affectionate with, the boy than him. That's fair to say, isn't it, Jago?'

Jago nods, still snivelling into his silver sleeve.

'But I ask you to find the strength in your hearts and the words in your minds to help me understand what happened to the boy from the commune in 1991. Please. Please...anything.'

They don't say anything. Nothing at all.

'Nothing? No words? Really?' I bite my bottom lip and shake my head in disbelief. 'Wenna. Could you imagine for one minute how you'd feel if it'd been Jago who'd disappeared? How would you react if you knew your neighbours knew where he might be, but wouldn't tell you? Can you think about that? I put it to you that you'd have lost your mind.'

'Oh, Doctor. It ain't that easy.' She wobbles her head and her jowls follow. She focusses on the hellfire carpet below her and very quietly she says, 'I'll have a word with Jago and Edern tonight. Come back in the morning Doctor, I'll make you coffee, we'll have a sticky flapjack, an' Old Wenna'll see if she can help. Promise.'

◆

On my way back home I stop in St Columb as I have to send a parcel from the post office. I get there at twelve forty-five, but it's closed. I try the door but it's locked. I can hear a couple of male voices inside, so I call through the letterbox, 'Could I come in, please? I need to send something.'

A particularly grumpy-sounding man calls back, 'We're closed.'

Hmm. I check the sign on the door; it says, "Closed 13.00-14.00".

'It's only twelve forty-five. Your sign says you're closed at one...'

'Don't care what it says, we are closed,' comes the predictable response.

'Okay, fuck you very much!' Some people are very rude.

So, a quick google and I find myself heading to the post office in Summercourt, a bit further down the A30 from Trebrowagh. The postmaster there is charming, with an equally wonderous name: His name badge reads - Mr Bliss. He has a glorious smile and dark, trustworthy eyes. He's wearing a thick jumper with a large anchor motif on the front. He agrees to send my package with Parcelforce 48, which is perfect, I have to pay cash as the Wi-Fi is down, which is not so great. He's a little puzzled when he asks what my parcel is and I respond, 'Cake.'

No real reason to mention this other than to recommend that you don't bother with the post office in St Columb.

Chapter 7

The Egg Hunt, part two
31st March 1991 (Easter Sunday)

The master of ceremonies, the rotund gentleman in the mustard coloured corduroy trousers with the megaphone, raised the loud hailer to his mouth and gleefully roared, 'GOOOOOOOOO!'

Jago had had his eye on an egg across the road. Its yellowy-gold foil had been glinting in the sun from underneath a neat hedge behind the red letterbox. He'd had his eye on it for the longest few minutes of his life. It was certain to be his first egg of the day.

He rushed forward but realised too late that his right leg hadn't followed his left. He just managed to push his arms out in front of his body as his shoelaces were pulled taut, causing him to fly face first into the gravel, grazing his chin on impact.

The rest of the egg hunters stopped their stampede at once and turned towards Jago before realising that some joker had tied his laces together. The kids laughed and pointed at the very embarrassed Jago lying on the floor.

'Haha, well done Linford Christie!' called out one of the group. The trip had torn the sleeve of his new Howard the Duck t-shirt. He was well and truly gutted. Looking up, he saw one of the cheering crowd, a girl from his year, reach behind the post box and collect the yellow Jelly Tots egg he'd been eyeing up. Double gutted!

Still, he thought, *you gots a plan, Jago 'Awkey, an' you gonna stick to it*. With that, he sat up, untied the laces of his Hi-Tec Silver Shadow II trainers, retied them correctly, dusted down his jeans and t-shirt, got to his feet and turned left up Chapel Lane. Away from most of the crowd.

He scanned the stone wall along the road, immediately locating two medium-sized, plain, unbranded Easter eggs. He popped them into his Safeway carrier bag. *Good start, Jago*. He gave himself a thumbs-up. Before the race, Jago had reasoned that the one thousand and one eggs could not all be in the village centre; some of them had to be further out, and in more obscure hiding places. He was correct.

The day before the hunt, members of the parish council and a representative from Trago Mills had spent over five hours hiding eggs in all corners of Trebrowagh. Naturally, a great percentage of them were near the chapel, for the little kids to find. But for the expert hunter like Jago Hawkey, a prime selection of the treasure had been hidden further afield. Jago found his third egg, a Walnut Whip in a blue packet, in the 'Free Veg' trug at the front of the house of Montague Hawkey (no relation apparently). Alex, the Biddle kid, found one enclosed in a jam jar tied to a piece of string down at the stream out by the Newquay Road, which seemed like miles away. Others were found in trees, under cars, next to gnomes, anywhere and everywhere. This was truly a marvellous hunt.

◈

Back at the chapel, Wenna and Pop were getting on famously. Pop had bought her half a pint of cyder and a packet of Hedgehog crisps. They were lying on the lawn, flirting with each other and talking nonsense in the sun. Wenna had always cursed the fact she'd been forced to marry Edern. She'd always preferred 'dear' Pop.

'Bloody Jago...' she tutted.

The St John's Ambulance chaps had managed to negotiate their vehicle through the village, which had proved difficult due to the road closures and the throng of egg hunters. The lady from Poke a Piskey was driven in shame and at a snail's pace out of Trebrowagh and over to A&E at Newquay Hospital on St Thomas' Road. Her husband – who, incidentally, looked like Bobby Ball – begrudgingly took over the stand, dragging his own treasure island map tombola with him.

◈

As Jago methodically worked his way around the outskirts of the village, he began to wonder whether his plan was working. He'd only collected seven eggs so far. *Fair dos though, Jago, you has found a Black Magic egg – that is probably the most* *expensive egg you can get. That is usually the one that grown-ups get, so...*He convinced himself it wasn't all bad.

Somewhere in the near distance, a police car siren grew incrementally louder and louder, before the blue and white panda car tore around a bend in front of him and blasted right past, leaving a trail of dust. He could see the petrified passenger hanging onto the roof handle for dear life as it sped by. *Bit quick that*, he thought as he followed it up the road until it was out of sight.

As he returned his attention to egg hunting, he caught sight of someone rustling in the woodland across the road. *Hmm, 'tis the dirty toad.* He screwed up his nose. *What's it up to in there?* The boy was jabbing a long stick up into the branches of a huge old tree. It was one of four very mature oaks in the village. Jago was probably about two hundred metres from the boy. *He must've gots an egg in there. If I gets there quick enough, I can steal it from him.*

He stepped up his pace, put his hand to his mouth and called out, 'Toad, little toad...Ugly little black toad...Gimme your eggs. Give 'ems to Cousin Jayjay.' Jago was jogging now, which was probably as fast as he went. 'You dirty little toad. Why you pokin' about? What you lookin' at?'

Ignoring Jago, the boy continued to prod away at the branches of the oak. With Jago fast approaching, he threw his staff into the foliage, and in doing so dislodged a small, conker-sized, gold-coloured egg. The boy deftly caught it as it fell, and he clasped his hand tightly around the treasure and scurried off deeper into the woodland.

'Oh goodness me, oh fuck it! He's got the golden egg. The canker has the blasted golden egg! I hates him so much. I'm gonna catch him and I'm gonna kill him! I'LL KILL YOU, TOAD!' Jago screamed.

He pushed past the Bestwell twins, who tutted and said they'd tell on him. Of course they would. He chased the Toad into the woods as fast as he could. His Safeway bag ripped open on a bramble, and he was forced to let go of his bounty. Without time to stop, he glanced back to see the twins salvaging his lost treasure. *Pesky, stinkin' girls!*

The boy was disappearing deeper into the trees, and he leapt across the stream which trickled through the woodland. Jago had never run so fast; he was wheezing and puffing, but he was not going to lose the chance of getting his hands on the golden egg. What was it worth? Could he exchange it for money or prizes? Thoughts of prizes whizzed through his tiny mind. *Maybe a radio-controlled car, like Bigfoot or the Lunch Box...Maybe a mountain bike! I bet it's a Raleigh Lizard...No one would laugh at Jago on a Raleigh mutha-fuckin' Lizaaaard! What if it's just a bit of gold? Maybe I sells it for five hundred quid...Oh God, Oh God, Oh God, I needs that egg.*

He continued his pursuit for what seemed like infinity. He pictured himself running through space and time – past stars and planets and dinosaurs and exploding volcanoes. This was the longest Jago had moved continuously in his whole life.

After less than one hundred metres he had to stop running; he literally couldn't run another step. He was knackered. He couldn't see the Toad anywhere. He'd lost his own eggs and now he'd lost the chance to get the golden one.

Shitting hell, Jago, you've lost him. You're a fat fuck, Jago Hawkey, an' a failure. Don't you dare go back to Wenna empty-handed. He sat with his head in his hands; he pulled his shoelaces tight and kept pulling them tighter in anger, so it hurt his foot. He hoped they'd snap! He was furious, so hurt, so ashamed. Jago had completely lost control of himself and was a snarling, snivelling mess thrashing about on the ground by the time the boy reappeared in front of him. Holding the golden egg out as a peace offering, the boy tried to smile, as if saying, 'This is for you' – a token of friendship.

Seeing the golden egg glinting in the boy's hand, Jago felt as if all his dreams had come true. Looking up through the leafy canopy, he grinned like a lunatic and pictured himself popping a wheelie on his new mountain bike in front of Mr Gurd's SPAR shop and outside the school. Without thinking, he reached to his side and picked up a broken length of branch. Jago jumped to his feet and swung the wood behind him, before striking the boy around the head with all his might. There was a sickening crack of bone shattering, as the boy crashed to the ground releasing his precious egg. Jago was possessed and continued his attack, bringing the branch down across the child's ribs with an audible snap. 'That'll tell 'ee, DIRTY. UGLY. LITTLE. TOAD!' he hissed loudly with each kick to the lifeless wretch lying on the forest floor.

As Jago slipped out of his fury, he looked down at the crumpled mess of a kid left crippled on the ground and felt a cold sweat all over his body, then a rumbling from his tummy. Acidity filled his chest, he felt weak, he belched, he took a breath, then vomited what felt like a bucket's worth of thick, minty, chocolatey puke all over the boy's bloody and broken body.

'Yuck! Oh bugger,' he spluttered and spat out the rest of the sticky sick from his mouth. He picked up the golden egg, wiped his mouth and checked around the woodland to see if the Bestwells had seen anything. If there were any people in the world guaranteed to tell tales, it was the 'crawly-bumlick' Bestwells. He was drawing his breaths quickly now.

Nope, you be safe now. Toad don't speak. Toad is scared to make stories about you, Jago. Get back to the chapel un' get your prize. Deciding he may find more chocolate eggs by going back the way he came, Jago turned and headed back towards the village.

Immediately forgetting about the pain he'd just inflicted on the boy, Jago crept out of the woods onto the walled lane. He was trembling with excitement. His walk became a trot, then a canter, and soon enough he could hear the hubbub of the village.

Everyone gonna be so jealous 'bout Jago. Feeling incredibly pleased with himself, he started humming his favourite *Superman* theme. 'Who's got the gold egg? Jago does. Who's got the gold egg? JAY-GO does.'

Never in the history of humankind had there been such a happy fifteen-year-old. He was actually skipping towards the chapel field when a second police car sped past him, bringing him crashing down to earth in another cold sweat.

Damn you, Jago! What have you done to the Toad? You most probably has killed it now. Why did you kill it? You squashed him... He stopped running and began to panic.

'Police comin' for you, Jago!' bleated Old Monty Hawkey, leaning against the gate on his driveway, as Jago passed by.

Hows' he know? 'Not funny, Mr 'Awkey!'

What if they were coming for him? After all, he had just murdered the circus boy and stolen his golden egg. He would most definitely be hanged. He needed a plan, a good story. He decided that he'd return to the village and try to find a couple of chocolate eggs on the way. Then he'd go to his mother and tell her he'd got the golden egg. He'd tell her he'd found it down by Montague Hawkey's house. He'd say that he'd given his chocolate eggs to the Bestwell twins as they didn't have any. Then he'd go to the deacon and show him the egg. The deacon would give him his prize and then they would quickly go home, because Jago would tell his mother that he felt sick, sick from eating all the chocolate. Hmm, the Toad? The Toad wouldn't say anything. *He can't say nuffin', alive or dead, so...Okay, you'll be fine, Jago. All fine...*

As he reached the village, he sensed something wasn't right. He couldn't hear any cheering and the music had stopped. Hushed murmurings could be heard from chattering groups and families. Oh God! Had someone seen him kill the Toad? *No. Pull yourself together.* It was just his mind playing tricks.

Jago slipped the golden egg into his jeans pocket, and seeing his favourite teacher, Mrs Hardwicke, he ran over to ask what was wrong.

'The egg hunt is off, Jago dear.'

'Off? But I got the...' He reached into his pocket, but stopped midway. 'Oh, nothin'. Er, why's it off?'

'One of our kids, er, Davy Yellen, I think. He found something disturbing down by the preaching pit.' She looked much paler than normal. In class she'd always been so bright and bubbly. The big numbers on her massive digital watch read 12:20. 'The police are down there, and as far as I understand they have called off the egg hunt, Jago dear. Until they can be sure about what Davy found...'

'JAGO! Get your fat arse 'ere now!' a relatively inebriated Wenna slurred from the chapel garden across the road. Jago felt very down, the wind taken from his sails. He weaved through the dispersing crowds to his mum.

'Jago, they stopped the 'unt. They says we all gots to go 'ome.'

'But, Mother, I 'as the gold egg.'

Wenna clipped him around the head. 'Stop your fantasies, young man. Come on, let's get back to Edern and I'll make a nice lunch.'

Jago was mortified, but at least he had the egg. It was gonna be worth all the upset. He wriggled it out of his jeans and showed Wenna.

'Bugger me! You ain't so useless, Jago, gimme it 'ere. Let's see what this is all about...Deacon! Cooey, Deacon.' She summoned the deacon over, as he was the principal organiser of the hunt. 'Sir, Jago gots the golden egg.'

She proudly passed the precious prize to the man, carefully presenting it to him on her palm. He gently picked it up between his thumb and forefinger and held it up to the sky. He reached into his cream linen blazer for his spectacles to conduct a proper examination.

'Ummm, yes, hmm, nice, I see, ummm...' He was impressed. 'Jago Hawkey, I do believe you've found the very first Trebrowagh golden egg!'

Jago at once felt more upbeat. His thoughts returned once again to his prize, his mountain bike! His fame...his fortune. 'Yippee! What's it worth, Deacon? What's my prize? 'As I won a bike, Deacon? Say, say...'

The deacon turned to the over excited lad and proudly beamed. 'Even better than that, Jago my boy', he patted him on the shoulder, '*You* will have your name etched into the egg as this year's golden egg finder. That makes you The Winner. Be sure to come next year and try again. Well done, Jago Hawkey.'

And that was that.

Chapter 8

Thick as Thieves
May 2024

As usual, I'd arranged to meet Wenna and Jago at eleven a.m., having called ahead yesterday to check that everything was still on. She assured me there would be a slice of Dundee cake and a nice fresh pot of tea. The weather is finally improving, I'd go as far saying it was almost hot. I have the window down as I drive down the track to the house. The driveway is always longer than I expect, and without any rain of note for a few days, the dried mud surface is judderingly rutted. Every nut and bolt in my car squeaks in submission.

It's now precisely eleven a.m. The wooden gate is shut, which, in my brief experience of the Hawkeys, isn't normal, and there is no sign of the battered silver Vectra estate. *Well, I think, I doubt they'll have gone far? What if I spooked them when I found their weird scrapbook on the pantry door? Maybe they've done a runner. Ah you wouldn't leave your dog would you?*

I get out of the car and untie the fraying blue rope which is keeping the gate closed. I can hear the dog barking from inside the house. I pull up where I normally would, just to the side of the barn, next to the gnome enclosure. I turn the engine off and open the door to enjoy the sun. Believe me, it's been a rarity this year. I leave the radio on and began scrolling through my phone. Just idling. On Radio 5 Live, Nicky Campbell is inviting guests to whinge about their miserable experiences of long Covid. On Instagram, a Boxer dog called Newt with no snout and a curly tongue gets swiped at by a cross-eyed mongrel called Picasso. *What a time to be alive*, I laugh to myself.

Five minutes seems an absolute age when you're waiting for someone, so I decide to have a stroll around the farm. Firstly, it's not really a farm. Thinking about the old black-and-white photos in Wenna's lounge, I can imagine it was a functioning farm once upon a time. Today, the Hawkey estate consists of the chalet bungalow, which I guess was built in the 1950s and extended upwards with dormer windows in the 70s. Opposite the house is Edern's barn, which is considerably older than the house and has the largest footprint on the land. I suspect it dates back to the nineteenth century. The drive is cratered, a pitted landscape similar in colour and form to photographs of the moon. And they have a field. The field must be at least two hectares – like two and a half football pitches – and were anyone to get planning permission to build on it, it would be worth a small fortune. At the bottom of the field is woodland, then countryside opens out into wider plains which stretch tom the umber heights of Bodmin Moor, somewhat hostile and on the horizon. It's not an awful place by any means, the Hawkeys have simply never cared to realise its full potential.

Hmm, weird. Eleven fifteen a.m. and still no one. Waiting and doing nothing has convinced me I need the loo. Perhaps I can sneak round the back of the barn. As I walk around the front of the building, I impulsively try the door handle. Not the big barn doors, the regular wooden door with blistered green paint. It opens. My heart skips a few beats and becomes irregular as I enter Edern's eerie palace of exile. I'm conscious that I can still hear Radio 5 Live in the background, so reassuringly I know I'll hear their car coming down the drive if it ever does.

Nothing has changed since I was here last week. The weeping carburettor lies on its side on the workbench next to the empty Big D peanut packet. Both the orange Renault and blue Ford tractors are where they have always stood. Everything is normal, except for the lack of Hawkeys.

At the back of the barn, Edern has fashioned a kind of small corner office. It's a bit like a ticket kiosk, with a large service window and a relatively pointless flimsy door. I look inside. It smells of Swarfega. There is a desk with two chairs behind it. One is a swivel and recline blue cloth 'manager's' chair; the other is a vintage wooden school chair with the strips of wood on the seat, the kind that used to make your legs itch.

On the desk is one of those old televisions that are as deep as they are wide. Aha! Edern and Jago's telly room. I bet there's some more evidence of their covert interest in the disappearance in here somewhere. I check the three drawers: nothing but receipts and books of carbon copy paper. The desk is surprisingly clear, except for an old Kit-Kat mug filled with pens and a compass for drawing circles. A large cork pinboard on the back wall of the office has nothing of significance on it either. There is a faded photograph of a younger Wenna next to Edern in what looks to be a pub or 1980s flat-roofed function room. They seem close. He has his arm around her and appears to be presenting her proudly in front of some dark furniture, a plywood bar and Bordeaux-coloured velvet curtains. He has more hair and a sturdy set of bushy sideburns – he looks like a cross between Fred West and the fellow from *Emmerdale*. He makes my skin crawl.

It's now eleven twenty a.m. I've got to go and find the toilet. The loo is outside, around the back, facing the field. I carefully leave the barn as I found it, leaving the door unlocked.

Looking up the drive, I see there is still no sign of them, so I sneak around the side to the privy. It's genuinely an old brick shithouse. A rusty, heavy bolt keeps the door closed from the elements. It screeches as I wriggle it free. Inside, I'm greeted with more Hawkey collaging: this time the three walls are adorned with hundreds of magazine cuttings of naked women – not kidding, wall-to-ceiling nudity. This is someone's work of art. They're probably very proud of themselves. A false widow spider tries to put me off from entering any further but quickly scuttles off as I lift the seat.

Reaching for the hanging flush chain, I notice a stack of newspapers on a deep shelf above the cistern. I almost missed them, they were stuffed so far back towards the wall. I dare myself to reach through the cobwebs and grab them. Just as I pull the papers down, I hear the crunching of gravel in the distance. *Shit, they're coming back!*

With the papers under my arm, I dart back to the car and dive in, before the silver Vauxhall Vectra comes into sight. Phew. I shove my treasure under the car seat and casually lean against the roof of the car as the Hawkeys pull up.

'Mornin', Doctor, sorry we's late. Edern 'as lumps in 'is pipes, we had to go to Newquay and see a specialist.' Wenna struggles to free herself from the passenger seat, her bosom getting caught up in the seatbelt.

'Not a problem, just got here myself,' I lie.

'Oh, 'tis a good thing then. I says to Edern an' Jago that you probably has gone already. We're glad you're still 'ere,.' She lies back to me.

I look each of them stoically in the eyes, they are all vacant. 'Listen, I feel like all three of you are probably getting tired of me coming here. I don't blame you. Can we, all four of us have a sit down to help me get to the bottom of this? I promise you, after today I'll head back to the Devon and Cornwall HQ and tell them I don't think we should continue to bother the Hawkeys anymore. I'm just really troubled by the collection of news about the case that you have glued inside the pantry door.' I look to Edern. 'Mr Hawkey, tell me about the cuttings...'

'I dunno what you mean, Doctor. I just 'ad a camera in me arse an hour ago. I can't think proper.' He fidgets with his trousers, pulling them away from his bum.

Wenna concurs. ''Tis true Doctor, they put something up 'is bum so he don't feel no proddin' and wotnot. Makes him sleepy.'

I ignore her and continue, biting my lip somewhat: 'Okay, Edern, I'll spell it out for you. What I mean is, there are thirty to forty odd cuttings from newspapers back in the 1990s glued to the back of the pantry door. They all, and I mean *all*, have something to do with the little kid from the commune who went missing back then. What I'm asking you, Mr Hawkey, is why you have collected them? And why, even more bizarrely, you've kept them for thirty years? Could you honestly tell me that you wouldn't find it highly suspicious if you were in my shoes?'

Continuing to scratch his behind, Edern stares across the drive at Wenna. 'Why's he in your pantry, Wen? I told you he was a nosy bastard.'

She shrugs and looks to Jago. 'I dunno, Ed. Jago and Brutus catches him in there. He was fetchin' me a water.'

Jago turns back to his dad/uncle. 'You sticks 'em up, Edern! You always made me cut them out the papers. An' thems mucky ones for the loo, too.' Brutus barks in collusion with Jago from the house.

'Right!' I look to the heavens for some divine guidance with these fools. 'But why are they there?'

The three of them all look back at me and in unison ask, 'What?'

I shake my head incredulously. They are going around in circles. It's infuriating, such classic avoidance. I think they were undeniably involved. In fact, my intuition tells me they are absolutely guilty – but guilty of what?

Wenna takes control. 'What? Thems old bits of paper? Them's nothin', Doctor.' She puts her hands on her hips. 'Jago had a news project at school when he were fifteen years old. So 'appens that were the news then, the boy runnin' away and wotnot. So, we just all collects bits from papers and sticks 'em away in the cupboard...so...'

I put my hands together before my face in a prayer motion. 'But, Wenna, it's not that simple, is it? You, all of you, knew the kid. You all knew him quite well. So, it strikes me there is more to your collection than just a passing school project.'

Jago tries to confirm the story: 'Yeah, you could go and ask Mrs Hardwicke...'

'What?' I'm about to lose my shit. 'Who is Mrs Hardwicke? Why would I ask her anything? What about?' Over in the house the dog, sensing the temperature rising, is now growling.

'She's the teacher what made the newspaper project,' Jago added.

'Jago, she's probably dead by now!'

'Nope,' says Edern. 'Seen her up St Kres two days ago. Buyin' wine with her fancy lady. They was cuddlin' and wotnot.'

'Will the three of you stop talking such nonsense!' I'm getting quite irritated.

'Cornish wine apparently,' Wenna adds.

'Bubbly! Luverly bubbly!' says Jago.

'I likes a bit a bubbly. Do you, Doctor?' Edern asks.

They're absolutely mental! They're clinically insane. What is wrong with them? I feel like they've all been on gas and air down at the general hospital.

'NO, EDERN! I DO NOT FUCKING LIKE A BIT A FUCKING BUBBLY!'

They stand silent and in shock. The dog's barking could be heard in the next village! I slam my car door shut and walk over to the three idiots in the drive.

'Do you understand how serious this is? Do you understand why I've been visiting you? It's not a bloody game, Edern. I've come here to investigate what happened to a poor, innocent boy in this village in 1991. That boy had no way to defend himself. He was mute, he was shunned by his own community most of the time, he spent a lot of time here, with you. All of you. I know Wenna tried to look after him. I think I understand why you took your aggression out on him, Jago. But I do not understand what you're hiding, Edern, I do not know what happened to him. My job is to get to the bottom of this incredibly sad story.'

'You're gettin' a bit shirty, mister.' Edern's face straightens out as he cracks his knuckles. 'I won't 'ave no one shout at my Wenna an' Jago. Not so professional, Doctor. I'm gonna have to phone your superior. I be proper complainin' that you been aggressive to us 'Awkeys.' He puts his arms out to Wenna and Jago, gesturing to bring themselves close to him.

I really didn't mean to snap at them, but they are so thick. Their dialect is thick, their demeanour is thick, and somewhat commendably they stand together – thick as thieves. But they really have driven me mad! I bet those papers I nicked from the toilet are about the boy, I just know it.

'I'm sorry for raising my voice, Edern. It's pure frustration. To be fair, I've spent over a month visiting you. I've been understanding, patient and honest with you all. Look, we're not looking to charge anybody. The case is over thirty years old. It's closed. We won't prosecute anyone now anyway. My job is simply to try and find any scrap of information that the police may have missed back then, to help bring some kind of closure to the tale.' I pause to calm down. 'So, Mr Hawkey, sir, with all that in mind, is there anything you would like to tell me that you remember that may be helpful? Anything at all? The tiniest morsel of information? An insignificant memory...?'

'Nope.'

The dog is going berserk. 'Will someone shut that sodding dog up!' I'm losing it...Taking a deep breath, I look into Edern's eyes, long enough to make him uncomfortable. He's lying. He knows I can see he's lying. He's pathetic. He's seventy-eight years old and still acts like a child. He makes my blood boil, but I slowly retreat to my car. I open the boot and reach in and withdraw the blue lady gnome. I look at them smugly and smirk. I parade the gnome in front of the old man and his face drops to the ground in abject horror. I take the gnome and place her in the middle of the driveway. All three of them are fixed to the spot in disbelief.

I get back in my car, reverse back a little into the drive and lower the electric window. 'Well, thank you for your time. Now watch this, you total and utter inbred, half-witted weirdos! *This* is for the boy...' With that, I put the car in gear, spin the wheels, chucking gravel and dust in their direction, and run over the Smurf. The front of the car strikes the gnome, and the little tart is smashed to smithereens. Their horrified faces in my rear-view mirror are a picture to be treasured. *Wankers.*

I know! It was not professional, it was downright immature, but do you know what? Damn them, all three of them.

I smack myself on the forehead. *That went well then...*

I have no idea how I could feasibly return to the Hawkeys' now. But I know enough. I know they are withholding some very dark secrets. I decided to head to the Blue Rose and have a look at the papers I found in the outside toilet. And a well needed pint.

Chapter 9

The Egg Hunt, part three
31 March 1991 (Easter Sunday)

Energy in the village had flattened out to little more than a chronic hum. The crowds had started to disperse, but many families continued to mill around by the cyder tent and village hall, in the hope that maybe the hunt and festivities would resume. That was doubtful.

Down at the preaching pit, extra police officers and CID from Truro had cordoned off all the roads, paths and public bridleways within a quarter of a mile of where young Davy Yellen had made his discovery. Every few minutes another vehicle with flashing blue lights sped through the village; three panda cars and two others, completely unmarked. There was a real sense of unease and cynical speculation amongst the villagers.

Some suggested a dead person had been found, others muttered about body parts being discovered. Alex Biddle told his dad and Wenna that an unexploded World War Two bomb had been unearthed. Jago, grateful to discover the police weren't after him, thought this was exciting! Truth is, it was all a cloud of chaos, and very few people knew what was really happening or what had been discovered.

At the pit, forensic police officers were carefully and methodically scouring every inch of ground for clues and evidence to help them understand if there was any importance to the discovered Safeway carrier bag. It looked from afar like the scene in *E.T.* where the alien is dying, surrounded by a crowd of people in lab coats. Little white plastic tents had been erected over points of interest, and people in overalls and masks held quiet conversations with men in dark suits. Not your average sight in Trebrowagh.

At the other end of the village the Bestwell twins had made their own grim discovery. The boy had somehow survived Jago's brutal attack and, covered in blood, he'd managed to heave his broken body out of the woods and attract the attention of the girls. At first, they'd screamed and fled at the sight of this monstrous carcass dragging itself out of the darkness. Then they'd realised it was the kid from the commune who didn't speak.

The girls knew him from primary school. He'd started two years ago but didn't continue on to secondary as his selective mutism was a problem for the teaching staff, apparently. Also, nobody really knew how old he was, so guessing when he should attend big school was difficult. The consensus was that he was ten or eleven.

They rushed over to him and could see he was in agony. He was bleeding from his head and his hands from where he'd tried to protect his face from Jago's attack. Rachel was the first to his side. He was in floods of tears, his face blackened from dirt and dust sticking to the tears, blood and vomit. He tried to show her his left leg. The lower half, from the knee down, was pointing in a hideous direction.

It was possibly broken, Rachel thought. She beckoned her sister over.

'Ruth, you need to go and get Ma and Pa. I'll wait here with him to make sure he doesn't panic. He needs to know everything will be okay.' She leaned towards the boy and whispered in his ear, 'Everything will be okay.'

He tried to smile, grimacing through the agony of his leg and a scorching pain in his chest.

'Go quickly, Ruth. Run!'

Ruth, who'd only ever left her sister to use the bathroom (and that time someone had stuck chewing gum in her hair, and she had to go to the school nurse to get it cut out), ran as fast as she could up the lane to seek help.

Jago, who was sitting with Wenna and Pop Biddle outside the village hall, was quick to notice the singular twin darting through the crowds. A cold sweat came over him. He knew straight away why she was on her own...

'Ma, I feels sick. I think I ate too much chocolate. Ma, can we goes 'ome? Please?'

'No.'

'Mother. Ten minutes ago, you said we 'as to go 'ome cause the hunt were all finished...'

'NO! No, we cannot go, Jago. I just got settled talkin' to lovely Mr Biddle 'ere; I 'as no intention of going back to the house for all the afternoon.' She was starting to feel quite merry after a couple of pints and was finding it enjoyable talking with someone other than Jago and Edern. 'Mr Biddle 'ere says he wants to show me some intrestin' graves round the back of the church dreckly, so you stays just 'ere, Jago, and when I get back, maybe we goes 'ome...' With that she tottered to her feet and followed Pop towards the chapel.

'Oh Ma!' Jago winced, he knew he couldn't stay there. He assumed the Bestwell girl had seen him attack the Toad. He guessed she was rushing to snitch on him. *Little tell-tale-tit*, he thought. *Right then, Jago. You got to sneak back 'ome, make out like no one knows you bin 'ere. Tell Edern you been home all morning playing football or some such.*

He felt sick. He began to sweat uncontrollably. *What if they did see me do it? I 'opes he still be alive. Oh God! I know I is always unkind to the Toad, but dear Lord Jesus, please don't let me 'ave killed it! Please, Lord. I never meant it. Oh Lord...no!*

He started weeping; he couldn't stop the tears. He was going to spend his whole life in prison, he just knew it.

◈

Ruth was completely out of breath by the time she reached the crowds in the village. She looked around desperately for her parents as instructed by her older twin. There were so many people there. Where were her mum and dad? She saw Mrs Hardwicke and approached her.

'Miss, Miss, please, Miss,' she whimpered. 'Have you seen Ma and Pa?'

'Yes, dear, they're over by the cyder tent, talking to Coral and Scoob. What's up, Ruth? You look like you've seen a ghost. Where's your sister?' It hadn't occurred to Mrs Hardwicke at first, but nobody ever saw the Bestwells on their own. This was odd, quite unsettling.

'Rachel sent me to get help, Miss...' Ruth gasped for air. 'The commune boy...I think he's dying in the woods! Please help, Miss.'

'Ruth, slow down, tell me what you mean. Let's go to Mum and Dad.' Mrs Hardwicke gently took the girl by her trembling hand, and they threaded their way through the crowds towards the tent.

Ruth almost tripped over her words as she rushed to recount her story about how she and Rachel had been collecting eggs down at the bottom of the village towards the woods. That they'd seen the commune boy looking like he'd been attacked by the beast of Bodmin itself, and how Rachel had told her to come for help, and that she'd seen Jago Hawkey running into the woods and dropping his chocolate eggs...

'Right, let's try to calm down sweetheart. We need to tell Coral and your parents. Let's go. Oh, hang on, I just saw Jago with his mother five minutes ago; I'll go and ask him if he saw anything,' replied Mrs Hardwicke.

Mr and Mrs Bestwell, quite reasonably, feared the worst as they watched Mrs Hardwicke approach at pace with only one of their precious daughters. But it was Coral and Scoob whose faces swiftly turned from merriment to horror as Nadia explained in her panicked fashion everything she'd witnessed in the woods.

'It looked like he'd fallen from a tree, or been hit by a car, or attacked by an animal.' She was racing to get her words out. 'He's in a terrible way, sir, ma'am. He needs help, maybe an ambulance.'

'I'll call the police, Coral. You lot hurry ahead and make sure he's okay.' Mrs Hardwicke spread her palms in her teacherly manner and tried to sound reassuring.

'NO POLICE!' Coral cried as she raced away from the village with Ruth, her parents and Scoob. Mrs Hardwicke was surprised by Coral's aversion to the law, but nodded in agreement anyway, and set about looking for Jago Hawkey.

Jago peered over the top of the chapel's stone wall and watched the Bestwells, Coral and Scoob disappear out of view. He had to get home. He was shaking, terrified of what might happen to him. He saw his teacher approaching, his hands trembled, he saw black spots in front of eyes, his fingers tingled, his lips went numb, his heart raced and that was that, he couldn't fight it. Jago fainted and collapsed to the ground.

Luckily for Jago, Mrs Hardwicke had not seen the boy and had entered into a conversation with the deacon about the twins' story.

Jago was probably out cold for a minute before being woken by an absolute soaking as Wenna launched half a pint of sparkling perry into his face. He was slumped against the wall.

'What 'as 'appened 'ere, Jayjay?' his somewhat flushed mother asked as she staggered from side to side.

Looking around to try to understand where he was, Jago wiped the booze from his eyes. 'I dunno, Ma. I was just' looking down the road an' then I feels all flimsy an' passed out.'

'Right! Is that so? Well, you've wrecked my day out! Why can't you ever do anything right, boy?! Let's get you home and cleaned up. Edern is not gonna be happy when I tells him you spoiled everything again. I am proper disappointed in you, young man!'

She grabbed the neck of his t-shirt, dragged him to his feet and pushed him all the way back to the farm. 'Another Easter ruined by you and your greed! You never think 'bout no-one but your 'orrible self.'

◈

At the preaching pit, detectives had begun bagging up the pieces of evidence they'd found. However, at this point they really didn't have a clue what the items were actually evidence of. What they did know was that something gruesome had happened. Somewhere. And to somebody.

The Safeway bag contained three tea towels with traces of blood and faeces on them. There were items of a child's clothing, probably a boys', maybe aged between eight and eleven years old. There was a plain black t-shirt, a pair of torn black jeans and a couple of odd socks. They were all very dirty. In the same hole in which the bag was discovered, police also found a bloodied screwdriver, several pairs of used disposable blue rubber gloves and some screwed-up balls of carbon paper. By the side of the hole, they'd retrieved the discarded butt end of a roll-up cigarette.

Police officer Jacob Merlyn had been first on the scene, as usual. So, this was his crime scene. He'd set up the cordon, he'd called in forensics, he was going to get to the bottom of this. His first hypothesis was centred around the 'hippies'. Jacob Merlyn despised hippies, especially the ones over at Biddle's farm, and they hated him. In fact, there weren't many folk who liked Jacob Merlyn.

Physically, he was brutishly large, taller than six foot, ruddy of cheek and thick of hair. His hands were like shovels; his huge woolly arms, like a great ape, hung to the floor. There had never been a man more devoid of a sense of humour than Jacob Merlyn. He'd twice been cleared of involvement in money laundering and was affectionately known as 'PC Persil' or 'Detective Daz' behind his back. He didn't understand why. One thing was for sure: he was not a very trustworthy member of the force.

After only one hour since they'd begun their search of the site, Sergeant Merlyn asked his forensics officers if they'd found everything, and curiously they all agreed that they had. Making sure everyone was busying themselves accordingly, he took it upon himself to have one last look around. He located the hole where the bag had been found, checked nobody was looking and surreptitiously dropped a brown-paper packet into the void.

He then instructed the other members of his team to begin packing up. He sent an officer up to Trebrowagh, to tell the deacon that the pit area was out of bounds, but should he wish to resume the egg hunt and festivities, he may. Jacob was always keen to be seen to do the right thing; it kept the nosy parkers at bay.

The forensics officers meticulously loaded their vans with the bagged and labelled evidence, and their scientific equipment before leaving for Truro, and their laboratories. The other police officers left the scene and dispersed back into the Cornish countryside, all except for Sergeant Merlyn and his ever so slightly simple associate.

'Jed,' he grunted. 'Those white coats are bloody useless half the time. Do me a favour and do an idiot check of the pit. I'll tape the area up and we'll get back to HQ in time for tea.'

Jed agreed and scurried meticulously around the green steps of the preaching pit like a scent hound pursuing a fox on Boxing Day.

Already back in the patrol car, Jacob was watching his deputy's futile searching and was now ready to 'retrieve' the last piece of evidence.

'Find anything, Jed?'
'No, sir.'

'Go and check the hole, boy.' Jacob rolled his eyes and waited for Jed's eureka moment.

'SIR! Oh my God, sir...there be drugs 'ere, sir. In a packet right at the bottom of the 'ole.'

'Is that so? You'll make a great detective one day, young Jed. Let's see what they missed then...'

Jed passed him the package and Jacob feigned surprise as he carefully unwrapped what must have been at least half a kilo of weed.

'Well, well, well, looks like we scored a goal here, Jed. I think we should pay a little visit to the commune, don't you?'

Jacob Merlyn was only too aware that Scoob dealt a little bit of marijuana around Trebrowagh and St Columb. Nobody cared too much. It was small scale and difficult to prosecute. But if he could somehow tie this in with the glut of grisly findings this afternoon, he might have an exceptionally good chance of setting the grubby little hippy up! He turned his police radio to silent and they headed to Pop Biddle's.

◈

Coral had instructed Scoob to go back to the farm to get the car, as she expected the boy might not be up to walking the distance.

Arriving at the scene, Coral gasped to see the extent of the boy's injuries. He was in a far worse state than she could have imagined. She fell to her knees by his side, her hands trembled as she scooped his bloodied head into her chest.

She stroked his face to calm him, explaining that Scoob would be here soon, and they'd get back to the commune and make him some dinner, and he'd need some time to recover but that all would be okay.

She spat into the sleeve of her tie-dyed blouse and started to clean the boy's face of dirt and drying blood. Through all the pain and discomfort, he looked up into her eyes as a son to his mother, and he smiled; he knew he'd be okay with Coral and Scoob.

Mr and Mrs Bestwell praised Rachel for staying with the boy. Coral thanked her too and told the twins they were always welcome at the commune, their parents too. The Bestwells were grateful, if a little nonplussed. Returning the hospitality, they made clear that if they could help in any way they would. Coral asked if they might wait until Scoob arrived.

Scoob never did arrive.

Act II: Injustice, faith and hope

Chapter 10

The Blue Rose
May 2024

The Blue Rose Inn is less than two miles down the road from Trebrowagh, in the picturesque hamlet of St Kres. I'd like to describe it as a dark, foreboding and treacherous place, where fishermen, smugglers and builders rubbed shoulders and shared stories, dealt drugs and came to blows. Where a stranger is welcomed as a plague by suspicious eyes across the bar. But I cannot, for there is not a more welcome and friendly village pub in all the county of Cornwall. Well, maybe that's a little over the top, but I like the place and have, so far, always been guaranteed a superb bowl of cheesy chips paired with a pint of St Austell Tribute. But stop for a second, about the chips. I'm compelled to tell you about them. It's not just a bowl of chips with cheese melted on top of them – that wouldn't be worth a mention. Lend me your ear, this is important, *these* chips have been hewn from local potatoes and deep fried at least twice in beef dripping. Then, in my educated opinion, they've been sautéed with finely sliced shallot or maybe a white onion.

After that, I would assume they've been transferred to the enamelled individual roasting tin and smothered in a heart warming mixture of English mustard, Cornish Yarg, mature crunchy cheddar and a dash of Worcester sauce. Finally they're grilled to bubbly perfection. Wash them down with the citrusy pale ale and you, my friend, will struggle to find a greater refreshment in any establishment throughout the realm.

There is a lovely coolness inside the pub today compared to the stifling midday sun outside. It's early, so I'm able to get a comfortable cosy window seat and enjoy the perfect balance of warmth through the glass and the cool air circulating across the flagstone floor. Hanging opposite me, just to the side of the fireplace, is a framed, tattered poster from 1987 advertising an evening with Brenda Wootton here at the Blue Rose. If you don't know her music, give 'To the Sea' a listen and hear Cornwall come to life in your ears. Her voice, like a siren's song, could bring to wreck any ship on those rocks. Devastatingly beautiful.

I order a pint of Tribute and lay out the old newspapers across the table. The pale ale is a perfect remedy for the stresses I've just endured at the Hawkeys'. They're such imbeciles, they assume everyone else to be fools and play them so. Wenna with her pseudo-bumbling ways: cake, tea, weather, frothy coffee and more bloody cake. She knows what she's covering up. I could read the fear of betrayal in her aging yellow eyes. She would never be disloyal to Edern. Even in old age she is as devoted now as she was in those old, brown 1980s photos. Maybe she is frightened of him. If she is, she'd never let it be known.

Wenna Hawkey is the ideal foil for covering Edern's darkest perversities. If you ask me, they all have blood on their hands. Jago is too conniving to be dumb. I'd like to accept that he's the village idiot, but no, he's too weird, too obsequious and cunning to be a natural fool. He's strong too. It might surprise you, but I've seen him lugging tractor tyres around the drive, and despite his rotund appearance, I suspect he could land a good punch on any man who should provoke his ire. And his dad? Edern is clearly his father. It's there for all to see: the same deep-set piggy eyes, the wonky tooth; they even smell ripely similar. I find it so strange the way he calls him by his Christian name.

Edern Hawkey may be old, but his brain is still rose-thorn sharp. Sharp and cantankerous. I would describe him as a very distant and tortured soul, angry at his younger self, a man trying to attain some kind of inner peace for his sins before he accepts the grave. I won't allow him that luxury though. He doesn't deserve that.

I take a long sip of the golden pale ale. It's blissful. Pulling the pile of newspapers closer, I can see that there are all sorts of papers and documents here: letters received, letters opened and letters unsent. There are official police orders and myriad cuttings alongside five different regional newspapers and one *Daily Express*, dated July 1991. I opt to peruse the pages of that one first.

Not much to report really. A Labour MP was sentenced to sixty days for refusing to pay his poll tax. Pablo Escobar was also in jail, and Bryan Adams was at number one with that ball-achingly boring Robin Hood song. The back pages were interested in the Wimbledon final on Sunday, Stich vs Becker in an all-German affair. It takes me the time to eat a bag of scampi fries before an article grabs my attention: 'NEW AGE TRAVELLER DIES IN CUSTODY'. It continued:

The police watchdog is investigating after a man died in custody whilst awaiting trial. The Independent Office for Police Conduct (IOPC) launched a probe after the man collapsed while in police custody in Bodmin, Cornwall before he later died. Stuart 'Scooby' Dowie (27) of no fixed abode, previously of Gloucester Road, Bristol, was pronounced dead at the scene by paramedics. The coroner at Truro recorded death by misadventure. Police have made no comment due to an ongoing internal investigation.

Below the report is a colour photograph, the exact same photograph as the black-and-white one on the back of the pantry door at the Hawkeys'. Under the picture, Scoob is named as the suspect. Alongside him is his partner Coral, and a short sentence describing how their son had recently disappeared, and that they were desperate for his return. *Obviously.*

Coral must have been beside herself. She would undoubtedly have held the police accountable for this. And it says *they* were the lost boy's parents. I'm surprised by this. The Hawkeys never told me this. Why would they though? No reason to. I wonder what happened in that jail, and why?

The photo appears again in a copy of the *Falmouth Packet*. This edition was a published a week later than the *Express*. The report on Scoob's death went a little further, suggesting that he'd been a 'kingpin' drug dealer, and that Devon and Cornwall Police had devoted many months to bringing him to justice. The piece also added that he was due to be charged over certain other crucial pieces of evidence found at the location of the drugs bust. It didn't say what the charges were but speculated that other items of evidence may be related to an ongoing missing person's case. Again, his death in custody was not expanded upon. But he was dead, that was clear.

My gut reaction to Scoob being guilty is that the whole thing stunk. Can you imagine a kingpin drug lord counting out his millions at a New Age traveller site in north Cornwall? The 'missing person's case' was clearly the boy; the timing couldn't point to any other case. Yet the *Daily Express* had intimated that Scoob was the boy's father. He may have been caught dealing a bit of weed, but I can't imagine why or how he'd be involved in his own child's disappearance. Still, nowt so queer as folk...I decide I'll get another pint and delve deeper.

An old fella with curly, dark hair, enormous, long ears and a leathery face stares at me through pale grey, squinting eyes from the other side of the pub. I shiver as someone steps over my grave. I smile back at him, he raises his eyebrows, nods and reverts his gaze to his ale.

A third paper only had Scoob's death notice listed in the announcements section, unless I'm missing something. But here it gets interesting. Page five of the *Cornish Times* dated Wednesday the fourteenth of April 1991 led with the following:

HAWKEY'S PORKIES – Father and local family man Edern 'Big D' Hawkey of Trebrowagh was released yesterday from police custody in Bodmin. After nearly 48 hours of questioning related to the disappearance of a young person, Police Sergeant Jacob Merlyn announced that he was releasing Mr Hawkey, and that he was to face no further questions relating to the missing boy from the Biddle farm commune. Speaking to the Cornish Times, *Sergeant Merlyn said: 'We are currently questioning a second suspect in this case and no longer consider Mr Hawkey of interest to our enquiries. Naturally, we will update the media at the proper time when our investigation is complete. Right now, we ask all members of the community to stay vigilant, advise us of any pertinent information, no matter how trivial, and rest assured that we are continuing to do whatever it takes to find the missing child.'*

Of course! Edern had been a suspect. I knew he had. The article continued, relating frustrations from within the hippy commune that he'd been released. There were claims that he was a drunk, a chauvinist and a liar. One man named Sprite was quoted:

'Edern Hawkey is guilty as sin. He's a habitual liar, his family had an unnatural way with our lad, and we believe he has committed murder. Now Bodmin Police have one of our own in custody, and we know this is an injustice. He [Edern Hawkey] is

manipulative and dangerous. He has somehow lied his way out of trouble, and we demand justice be done. Local police forces from Newquay and Bodmin have consistently bullied and dogged our community since we set up camp three years ago. We believe the police may be complicit in this. We have a right to be here, and we have a right to be safe. We do not trust Sergeant Merlyn, and we just want our kid back. Safe.'

Blimey, Sprite didn't hold back did he? I wonder what kind of storm this created back then? Bet you the police were pissed off. I'd have pursued that guy's story. In my mind the trouble with these local papers is that the quality of journalism is always a bit entry-level. No one ever proposes an opinion or frames a story; they just safely report facts and quotes. The problem with that is; people read an article and are very quick to forget it. People just don't care.

I decide to look at the other ephemera which Edern had sandwiched between the newspapers. Backing up the piece on Edern's release, I find a letter on Bodmin Police-headed paper dated the third of April 1991. Signed off by one Sergeant Jacob Merlyn, it warned Edern Hawkey not to go anywhere near the commune but accepted that he was to face no charges relating to the boy's disappearance and was free to leave police custody. They must have had reason to bring him in, in the first place. What had it been?

There are a handful of photographs, mostly Polaroids. A couple show a picnic scene with Edern, Wenna and a young Jago – he's in a pushchair. One is an amusing photo, as the parents stare straight at the camera lens but Jago, who is quite frankly too big to be in a pushchair, appears to be off balance in some kind of struggle to escape his restraints. I imagine he probably rolled the chair onto its side in the seconds after this photo was taken. There is also an envelope containing Premium Bonds. Edern must be keeping them to himself, I think. Next, an old Ordnance Survey map of Bodmin Moor and a street map of Bourne in Sussex, which seem like peculiar things to hide but bear no clues.

I've saved the bundle of letters until last – they're tied together with a length of green ribbon finished with a bow – and I decide I'll settle down to look through them after lunch. I push the papers to one side to make space and go to the bar to order a bite to eat. I opt for the 'Wrecker's Burger': *'Our biggest ever burger, 100% local grass-fed beef mince and Cornish Yarg – garrotted to leave you crashed on the rocks'.* Funny how there's always a misspelling on a pub menu. Anyway, the lady behind the bar is pleased with my choice and recommends I have it medium rare. I accept. The grizzly old man is staring again.

'Who's that fella then?'

The landlady looks at the chap and back to me. 'He's no 'arm. That's Ol' Man Biddle. Pop's bin there in that seat there 'bout twenty years.' She chuckles and scuttles to the kitchen with my order.

Pop Biddle! Brilliant. What are the chances? It hadn't occurred to me until now that some of the characters from the Hawkeys' tapestry of tales truly existed, let alone that they're still alive and well.

The landlady informs me that lunch will be about twenty minutes. That's perfect; I'll introduce myself to Mr Biddle and see where that might lead. He's clearly aware I'm heading for him, and he shuffles on his stool uncomfortably. He makes some strange audible clicks which seem to be coming from the back of his nose.

'Name's Biddle, Bryan Biddle, you can call me Pop, and I ain't done nuffin' wrong. I used to keep a puma, but he got away years ago, so...'

'Pleased to meet you. I'm guessing the puma thing is a joke?' I reply. He winks. 'Can I buy you a beer sir?'

After a couple of raises and drops of his very bushy eyebrows, some scratching of his thick white sideburns and a few nasal clicks, he agrees. His beaming smile pushes up his purple cheeks, they are demarked with spiderwebs of fine broken blue and red veins. 'It's Pop, I ain't used to bein' no 'sir', and yes you can. That'd be luverly of you, young man.' He gestures to the landlady to come over and motions swigging a beer, the international sign language for 'I'd like a drink, please'. 'Jug 'o the usual please, Donna. This 'ere fella's buyin'. Thank you, young man – care to join me?'

I find this opportunely convivial of him and couldn't have hoped for a better scenario. 'Yes, please. I've just ordered some lunch, so I've got a few minutes. Also, if it's not too much to ask, I think you may be able to help me out with a little investigation I'm working on...Perfectly understandable if it's not your thing...'

'Go on...' Pop takes his jug of beer from Donna and takes a long sip through the froth.

'Well, you'll forgive me – I've been sent down by Truro, I have a bit of a grim job to do. I'm trying to piece together some information about people, places, times et cetera. It's an old, unsolved mystery. I understand there was a case in the nineties surrounding a child who disappeared from a hippy commune. No one ever found out if he'd been killed and disposed of, or kidnapped, or he simply ran away. Do you remember this story?'

Donna looks over her glasses at the old chap and gently sways her head from side to side as if trying to warn him not to talk about it.

'Ah, Donna, 'tis thirty year ago now. Don't make no difference what anyone says. He's long gone...' Pop says calmly across the shiny oak bar. He turns back to me and silently mouths, 'Kidnapped', slowly and thoughtfully closing his eyelids as he does.

Donna tuts, turns on her heel and resumes the task of polishing the glasses as they come out of the dishwasher, putting them back on the overhead shelves with a clink and a clank. Pop twiddles his thick sideburns and takes another seemingly endless drink from his pint.

'You be asking 'bout the lost Toad of Trebrowagh, I 'spect. Am I right?' He glances at Donna, ensuring she heard him.

I nod. I'm pleased: finally, someone here doesn't appear to be messing me about.

Pop's forehead troughs as he starts to frown. 'I don't s'pose his name really were 'Toad' – just what folk round here called him. Dunno why. Probably a nickname at school or summat. Come to think of it, his people at the commune never used a real name neither – always darlin' or luvver or wotnot; maybe they even called him Toad – affectionately, mind.' He slowly moves his face towards mine. He's very close; I can feel his body warmth, his breath, sweet with the smell of beer, his eyes search my souls as he asks, 'Don't suppose you'd know his name? Would you young man?'

I shrug and shake my head. He withdraws, relaxes into the raised back of his bar stool and continues.

'Well, anyhow. I owned the farmland what the travellers made their community on. I rented it to them. Fair price too. Nice people mostly. They'd help me about the farm – bit of fencin', harvestin', even a bit of lambin' in springtime...I never 'as no trouble with 'em. So, when all that business happens with their man dying at the police station, and their boy goin' missin', and the feuding with the 'Awkeys, I was quite surprised. Got all a bit bothersome.'

Farmer Biddle could easily be a caricature of any generic rural man of the land. Now easily into his seventies, he perches on his stool strong as an ox. Glowing golden brown from a life in the fields, his face is like a crumpled, old, tanned leather boot crushed for years under newer shoes in the hallway of life. He wears a cream and brown checked woollen shirt with the sleeves rolled to the elbow, dark-green corduroy trousers which are thinning at the knees, and a battered pair of black, well-used wellington boots. His gnarled shepherd's crook is balanced against the bar top. Pleasingly, his demeanour is seemingly merry; I believe that Pop is at peace with the world. Curled at his feet is a slender and obedient tri-coloured Border Collie. She is asleep. Pop's end of the bar is a tranquil and lovely part of planet Earth.

He resumes his story: 'Police says that the hippy fella disposed of the kid, but that never made no sense to me...He'd already been taken in before the lady raised the alarm that her boy is missin'. You know it were her husband what died – or was knocked off, at Bodmin police station? What was 'is name, Donna?'

'Snoop, I think,' she replies.

'Nah, weren't Snoop...Hmm, Spud or something, I don't remember. Anyhow, he got rumbled with a big amount of that marijuana, they takes him into custody, and within forty-eight hours they says he's dead! SCOOB! That's it, his name was Scoob.' He calls over to the landlady, 'Scoob was his name.'

'Oh yeah, that's 'im. Scoob,' she agrees.

'Anyhow,' Pop proceeds, 'this smells fishy to me. Scoob weren't no drug dealer. They all smoked a bit round the fire and wotnot. Sometimes if I were around, they'd give me a wheeze too. I quite liked it, most relaxing. But they was peaceful people. You ask me, it was that Sergeant Merlyn that dun 'im in. I always says that, din' I, Donna?'

'Yes, Pop, you always said that Merlyn dun 'im in.'

'He were a nasty piece o' work. Always on my land complaining that there was too much noise, or there was a car nicked someplace, or rubbish had been dumped over St Columb way. Ask me, he had it in for the hippies. Then there was the thing with Jago 'Awkey...Remember that, Donna?'

'Oh yarp, nasty business that...'

'I used to have a bit o' fun with his mother, Wenna 'Awkey back then.' Pop gives me a wink and lowers his voice. 'She were a proper goer...' He chuckles and gets back to his story. 'So, one day, I reckon it's the day of our annual Easter egg hunt up in Trebrowagh, me an' Wen is havin' a few cyders in the sun when her boy Jago comes over all bouncin' and braggin' about findin' a golden egg. Turns out the parish has hid this special egg in the woods. Jago comes up and says he's found it down Chapel Lane or something. Anyway, long story short, the kid from the commune who don't speak has been found all beaten half to death. He somehow gets across to his mother – Scoob's partner, Coral – that it's only bloody Jago 'Awkey who bludgeoned him about the head and ribs to steal the golden egg...left the little sod for dead. That right, weren't it, Donna?'

'Yes, Pop.' She rolls her eyes.

'So, the hippies all pile in on the Hawkeys' farm, threatening Edern and Wenna about wanting money cause of what Jago done. Sort of compensation I spose. They get all pushy and smash up Edern's barn windows. Jago says he ain't done nuffin', and course Wenna always believes her little Jayjay...' He scoffs to himself. 'The injured kid's mum won't have nuffin' 'a do with the police, so it all goes quiet. Least for a few days. Their boy don't talk, so no one knows what really happened...'

Donna pipes up from across the bar: 'Remember them twins, Pop? They said they'd seen Jago Hawkey near where they found the poor little lamb.'

Pop's eyes widen as the memory is restored. 'Oh yeah, the twins did say they'd seen Jago nearby. True. Next thing we hear is that the kid had gone. Disappeared off the map. Vanished into thin air. Well, the hippies, especially the mother, is fraught with anguish. They is especially upset cause the police is back at their camp with forensic scientists and wotnot. The police says they don't have much to go on, but they believe that the fella in custody is to blame. Next thing is, he's dead. Strange business...Anyway, that's all I remember.'

He takes another sip of his ale, wipes his mouth with his shirt sleeve and concludes his monologue. 'I think to myself, this is all too much for a peaceful fella like me, so I has no choice but to ask them to vacate my farm. I give them a few months to get sorted. Then one day they were gone. Portugal, last I heard...'

The bell pings from the kitchen, signalling the arrival of my burger. I thank Pop for his time. He puts out a giant trowel of a hand and grips mine. Squeezing my hand hard, he looks into my eyes and whispers, 'Edern Hawkey...'

He releases me, finishes his pint in one gulp, grabs his crook and softly taps the sheepdog. 'C'mon, Wen.' Tail wagging, she immediately jumps to attention from her slumber, and the pair of them leave into the blinding spring sun.

Sitting down, I realise there's a lot to digest there. And I've not even started my 'Wrecker's Burger'.

Chapter 11

Kidnapped

1st April 1991 (Easter Monday)

The misty and peaceful dawn was shattered at six a.m. by the sound of smashing glass and shouting. Half a brick bounced off the windscreen of Edern's Vauxhall Chevette and collided with a faded yellow and blue garden gnome, leaving the car window cracked and the gnome faceless.

The fracas had woken a dog, which was now howling and barking in a spirited frenzy. Voices were coarse and shrill through the crisp morning air.

'COME OUT! WE KNOW YOU'RE IN THERE...!' Cried one.

Another, in a rich Somerset accent, called through the letterbox, 'WENNA, WEN-NA 'AWKEY! Get down 'ere...Your Jago has tried to kill one of our own! Come out, face the consequences...'

'Come out, you disgustin' April fools,' yelled a third voice.

'We want Jago! We want answers...' The calls were incessant, and angry.

Edern nudged Wenna in the ribs to encourage her to check what all the commotion was about. She grunted resentfully, wishing she'd stayed in her own bed. She crossed the darkened room, which was cast in a brown light from the sun penetrating the tobacco-stained net curtain. Peeking around the edge of the curtain, she was horrified to see one of the New Age travellers taking a swing at the barn door with a small wooden chopping axe.

'Edern!' she whisper-shouted. 'Edern! Thems hippies is smashin' up your barn! An' your car is all broke! Edern, get up! There's about ten of them.' She hissed at her dozing husband, 'ED! Get up! For shittin' hell's sake.'

Edern rolled out of bed in his sleeping vest and grey cotton boxer shorts. He yawned, coughed and joined Wenna at the window.

Scratching around at his nether regions as he pulled the curtains open, Edern was startled to find himself face to face with Coral from the commune. On the shoulders of a burly-looking man, she was thumping the window with her fists, her face wild-eyed with incandescent rage and her orange dreadlocks flailing like bullwhips with each thump. It was if Medusa herself were there at the bedroom window, and for a moment, Edern truly felt like he'd turned to stone. Behind Coral, a crowd of angry young men and women were smashing everything in sight. They were using sticks, stones, garden furniture, anything and everything to cause as much havoc as they could. Edern gestured to Coral that he was coming out. She spat at the window, he watched her face distort as her saliva dribbled down the glass.

'Dirty cow.' Edern turned to his wife and raised his eyebrows. 'We seems to be under siege 'ere, Wen. What do you s'pose this is about?' he asked calmly as he pulled himself into his usual brown trousers.

'Dunno Ed, They're crying about Jago – dunno why though. What stuff did you take up the pit, Ed? What 'as you done? You done summit awful with their lad? This better not be your fault!'

'Shut up Wenna! No, I ain't done nuffin'. I'll go see what's up. Now go sit with Jago. Don't be letting him out, sounds like they want to hurt the boy. Wen, ya hear me? Wen?'

She nodded and went to Jago's room. Edern walked down the stairs from the dormer and along the long hall to the porch. At the front door, he closed his eyes and drew a deep breath to calm himself; he really didn't want his temper to further fan the flames of this riot.

The second he opened the door he was under a full-on attack. Coral leapt into the dingy hallway and made a grab at his throat with both hands. He instinctively pushed her to the ground. She lay on her back and kicked him with both feet before scrambling up and pushing him straight back.

'What in God's name is happening here?' he yelled.

Coral jumped on him, raining punches onto his face and chest. 'Your boy Jago tried to murder our boy!' she hissed and spat squarely into Edern's eyes.

'Ugh! You dirty bitch!' He shoved her off his body, careful not to fight back as he could see a crowd of people circling behind her. He wiped his face with his forearm sleeve and looked for a less angry rioter to talk with. 'You,' he snapped, pointing to a meeker-looking lad in ripped jeans, a Pop Will Eat Itself t-shirt and natty waistcoat. 'Would you kindly tell me why you're all here smashing up my property, before I get my Wenna to call the police. What in St Piran's name is it you want?'

The meek lad looked flushed but put on a cloak of bravado and approached Mr Hawkey. Jabbing a spindly and long finger in Edern's direction, he began to explain. 'Yesterday afternoon, at the egg hunt, our little man was brutally attacked. The boy's no harm to no one. The twins from the village found him in the woods at the end of Chapel Lane in a right sorry state. Left for dead he was. The twins says they seen your Jago run into the woods, and back out – like, five minutes later. Our kid don't speak – he's a selective mute, see. However, Mr 'Awkey, the boy does draw pictures. Damned fine pictures. So, guess who he draws when we asks him who done this to him? Can you guess? Go on, have a stab, Mr Pervy...Have a fuckin' guess!'

Edern pushed the man's hand away from him and squinted his angry bulging red eyes. 'You're suggesting our Jago had something to do with bludgeoning your dumb kid? That's what you're proposin', is it? Is it? I tell you what, you streak o' piss, if I finds out you've got this wrong, I'll fucking clatter you. All of you.' He stared intently at Coral, who was weeping and trying to speak, but nothing would come out, so she scowled back at him.

'WENNA!' he shouted into the hallway. 'Wenna, get 'ere now, woman!'

Wenna appeared behind Edern seconds later, her messy mousey hair tumbling over a hastily-put-on pink dressing robe. Her face looked tired, dry and blotchy from yesterday's cyders with Pop, and a few more when she'd got in. She was in no mood for this hippy nonsense, that was for sure.

'Wen...' Edern began. 'This fella 'ere, that looks like he needs a beefburger or a good slice o' cake, says that Jago attacked the dirty toad kid at the egg hunt yesterday. You know anything about this?'

'No, Ed, not our Jago, he was good as gold yesterday. Spent the afternoon with me. We played some fete games – you know, like tombolas, that "Poke a Piskey" thing and wotnot...'

Coral found her voice and screeched back at Wenna: 'You lying, fat slag, you was with Pop Biddle all afternoon getting right pissed up! I never seen you with Jago, not even for a bloody second.'

Edern frowned at Wenna and was about to question her when the timid lad, now growing in confidence, piped up again.

'Our boy was all smashed to pieces, Wenna. Right now, we got him resting in the big yurt. It's gonna take weeks for him to recover, he's so weak. He drew us pictures of a golden egg he found in a tree, then he shows us that Jago beat him up with sticks and stole the egg. Your son almost killed our boy to steal his treasure. Now we demands an apology from Jago and two thousand pounds compensation for fixing the boy. If not, we'll fuck you all up! We'll start by burning all your fucking shit down, you manky, incestuous tossers!'

Without a second thought, Edern clenched his left fist and let fly. The crack of the man's jawbone breaking was loud enough to be heard over in St Kres. He fell to the ground like the proverbial sack of potatoes, onto the gravel drive, in a heap, screaming as he tried to hold his face in shape. Edern erupted with a primordial roar directed at the rest of the mob and rolled his fists at them like a 1950s comedy boxer. The veins in his neck were almost bursting as he bellowed, 'Get off my land! GET THE HELL OFF MY LAND!'

'Not unless you pay us two thousand compo,' shouted one of the bawdy contingent.

'WHAT?! Fuck's sake! For what? Jago ain't done nuffin', you can't prove otherwise, now fuck off my farm! NOW'

A waifish girl of about eighteen who'd thus far been quiet picked up a rusty pail and threw it through the kitchen window with an almighty smash. This brought a bewildered Jago out of his sleep and to the bedroom window. At first nobody noticed him. He rubbed his eyes, and as the scenes of carnage in the drive became clear, the horror of yesterday wrapped around him like a rain-soaked cloak. He shivered and felt sick. He began to cry. He wished it would all go away. Then something hit the glass, followed by shouting from below.

'There he is! Up there!' The pale girl threw a handful of gravel from the drive at the window.

Edern could feel his temperature rising. He reached for his heavy walking staff, which was in its usual place by the door. Growling as he lost control of his temper, he charged at the travellers, swinging the stick freely at anyone in his way.

'Call the police, Wenna, and tell them we're under attack down at Hawkey's farm. Tell 'em to get here quick!'

Now, if there was one thing the traveller community despised more than the Hawkeys, it was the police. They didn't trust them, they were always in some kind of conflict with the law, and only the last night Coral's partner, Scoob, had been arrested at the camp for possession of Class B drugs. He was, at that time in custody over at Bodmin nick. The last thing they needed was anything to do with Sgt Jacob Merlyn and his corrupt constabulary. It wouldn't help them, and it certainly wouldn't help Scoob's case. So, on Coral's orders, they scarpered on foot across the fields. Edern caught the slight young woman across the spine with his staff as she ran. She fell but gathered herself up before he could strike her again.

Coral turned back to Wenna and Edern from a safe distance and shouted through cupped hands: 'You ain't heard the last of us. Jago, he's a dead boy walkin'...You all are! FUCK YOU!'

Exhausted, Edern dropped his staff on the ground, wiped the sweat from his eyes and pushed both arms out in front of his body as he leant against the barn wall, heaving heavily to catch his breath. Looking around the farm, he could see that at least three different windows had been broken, his car was damaged, and there was an extensive casualty list amongst the gnome guard. He looked across the drive to Wenna.

'Go get the boy, right now.'

Wenna, who knew not to disobey Edern when he was in one of his black moods, turned on the shiny heel of her slipper and disappeared inside to fetch her terrified son.

Jago had secretly locked himself in the pantry and was crouching in silence in the dark kitchen cave. Wenna called throughout the house, but he wouldn't answer. He couldn't answer. He knew he was in serious trouble. He knew if Edern got hold of him, he would be beaten black and blue, or even worse...His only solution was to hide; he would stay there until his parents died if he had to.

Edern had already accepted that Coral and her people were probably right, and if truth be told, he could easily believe that Jago had it in him to attack the Toad, especially if he had something to gain. He was also acutely aware that the police had found the clothing and items he'd hidden at the pit. He needed to act. Now.

He thought back to the times it had happened. *Fuck's sake Ed.* He could only count twice from memory, but he had been continuously blind drunk on potcheen for many days when he'd abused the boy. Of course, he felt remorse, but, he argued to himself, he'd not been able to control his urges through the wretched booze. The Toad had been hanging around the farm for a while by then, mostly by Wenna's side, helping her hang out laundry or doing a bit of weeding with her over at the herb garden. One late afternoon the boy came into the barn and seemed to be showing interest in the broken bathroom cabinet he'd been repairing. He remembered how strange he found it that the boy didn't speak – *what an odd thing, it must have been so difficult for him*; he recalled how he liked the smell of the boy – *like biscuits and raw meat, not unlike dogs*; he had been attracted to how dirty he appeared, and how soft his skin was. Edern was convinced that he'd been in love with the ugly little toad, he found him fascinating, to the point he couldn't think of anything else. That is why, he reasoned, he'd made love to him. He needed to feel close to the boy. He had never meant to hurt him, he'd assured himself time and time again. He was adamant in his mind that they were in a consensual relationship.

He snapped out of his thoughts suddenly. He knew what he needed to do. Tears welled up in his eyes, *this gonna be tough Ed.* He'd go now. He quickly crossed the drive to the open front door, he reached in, grabbed his car keys and his ripped green-and-brown-checked work jacket, put on a grubby red Old Milwaukee beer trucker's cap, and unlocked the Chevette. Without a second to consider saying goodbye, he slung his things in the back of the car and sped away up the drive in a cloud of dust and gravel.

Relieved, Wenna listened as the car disappear into the countryside. 'Jago, Jayjay, you can come out. Dad's gone. For now.'

Whimpering and snivelling, Jago unlocked the pantry door, and, head bowed, he shuffled to his mother, tentatively put his arms around her waist and squeezed her with all his might. He would not let her go.

Of course she knew he was guilty, but she loved her son more than anything. She knew Edern would do the right thing for them and sought to reassure Jago accordingly.

'There, there, my darlin' Jayjay, everything's gonna work out jus' fine. Mumma promises.' She stroked his head tenderly.

◈

As he accelerated towards Biddle's farm, Edern began constructing his plan. He would certainly get there before the angry mob who'd left the farm five minutes ago and would be now rambling home across the fields. He didn't expect many more travellers to be left at the camp. He figured someone would be nursing the boy, but it was still before seven a.m. on a bank holiday, so there shouldn't be many folk around or awake. He figured he could sneak into the big yurt and somehow encourage the boy to come with him. Then his idea was to take him out into the depths of Bodmin Moor and get rid of him. That way no one would ever be able to link him to the rapes, nor Jago to the beating at the egg hunt. *Because,* Edern reasoned, *there won't be no prime witness. Those hedge-monkeys will be at least twenty minutes makin' their way back, and they still think I'm at home clearing up the mess they made.*

He hurtled down the narrow and winding Toldish Lane. He could park at the back of the farm and make his way over the stile to the camp without anybody noticing. He pulled up behind the two derelict silage towers and checked no one was around, before tying a black bandana around his nose and mouth and putting on a pair of Day-Glo-orange sunglasses Jago had found in the pub car park. He reckoned he only had ten minutes to get the Toad before the risk of being caught presented itself.

At first Edern jogged, he'd have to be swift, no question about that. He passed the drainage tunnel, where he used to hide as a youth, and climbed over the stile onto Pop's land. He slowed a little, the world was eerily quiet; the mist was beginning to lift, but the long meadow grass soaked his boots and trousers as he strode through.

He ducked in reaction to the loud snap of a branch triggered by a deer bolting into the undergrowth. He was on edge. His heart was racing and he began to question whether he was doing the right thing. In his mind he pictured himself in a courtroom, Wenna and Jago heartbroken as he was sent down for life, for rape and child abuse. No, he wouldn't let that happen, and this was his only solution. *Dispose of the evidence – the boy is the evidence*, he told himself over and over as he trudged stealthily towards the camp.

Now there was only the barbed-wire sheep fence between him and the yurt. He carefully snipped the wire, and it snapped back, curling up with a metallic swoosh. He waited a few seconds and, seeing that nobody had been disturbed, he ventured into the camp. He crouched down behind an old Routemaster bus. He could only hear the deep breathing of sleep. Keeping his body low, he snuck between the parked cars and tents. There was nobody around, to his relief.

He pressed his ear to the outside of the yurt, there was nothing, no sound at all. He sneaked up to the entrance and peered through the flap. It was still dark inside, with only flecks of golden daylight seeping in between the stitches which bound the fabric. In the centre of the tent, next to a gently smouldering wood burner, was the Toad. He was asleep on a raised bed of pallets, blankets and animal hides. At the back of the yurt, Edern could just about make out the shape of a man under blankets sleeping on the floor; luckily, he were facing away from the entrance, so Edern crept in and approached the boy. The sleeping man stirred momentarily, mumbling something about tea.

Thinking quickly, Edern whispered to the man from across the yurt, 'Jus' gonna take 'im for some air. Coral wants him showered early...I'll get the kettle on.' The man grumbled, pulled his blankets over his head and fell back into his slumber.

Edern looked down and gently shook the boy. 'C'mon, son, carefully, we're gonna go grab some air,' he said quietly. The injured child instantly recognised the smell of potcheen and tobacco on the man's breath. He wriggled and squirmed in resistance, but Edern gripped his wrists firmly, and with menace, pulled him to his feet and out of the yurt. The boy thrashed defiantly, to no avail, his abductor was too overpowering, and in no mood to be discovered.

As he slipped out of the yurt door, Edern, with the child in a kind of bear hug, calmly called back to the sleeping man, 'Back in a mo.' The dozer only managed a mumble in reply.

Edern did not say a word as he hurriedly half carried and half dragged the bewildered child through the camp, over the fence and stile, and back to the car. He opened the whining back door of the Chevette, lifted the kid up and sat him in the boot space. He stared at the boy's savagely beaten face; he couldn't take his gaze away from the injuries. It was truly horrific. Both his eyes were bruised, purple and blackened from Jago's attack. His lip was split and swollen and only just only held together with dark dried blood. A bald patch on the right side of his head showed that a clump of hair had been freshly pulled out. He had a splint on his leg kept in place with fresh bandages. He was a heartbreaking sight.

'Jago done this, did he?' Edern stoically asked. The weak boy stared through Edern's soul. 'Well, I'm sorry for what he done. I'm sorry for what we both done. Truly. I have been plagued by demons all my life; they make us do things we don't mean to do. But right now, young man, we're gonna go for a short drive, go and see Bodmin Moor. My way of apologisin', I s'pose.'

The boy sat dead still on the lip of the car boot. Any colour left in his face had drained away and he was struggling to catch any air, taking a succession of quick, sharp breaths. He couldn't move; as much as he tried, he felt as if he were glued to the spot. Edern pushed him gently but firmly back into the boot. He then took the boy's hands and bound them together tightly with very coarse and dry fishing rope. He shut the door down, checked his surroundings, turned the ignition, which heart stoppingly faltered first time, he tried again, and the engine choked into life. The two headed north east to Bodmin.

Edern checked the rear view mirror as he pulled away. He could not see the boy behind the rear seats, but he could hear him kicking and struggling. He looked back at himself and saw a monster in cheap sunglasses. He dared not take them off; he did not care to look into his own wretched eyes. Smacking the steering wheel, he cursed the booze and his bad luck, and Jago, for his part in all this. But for now, he was away, and not a soul had seen him, he was convinced of that. *Time to dispose of the evidence, Ed. It has to stop Ed!*

Chapter 12

The Beast of Bodmin
1st April 1991 (Easter Monday)

They drove in absolute silence. No radio, no talking, no nothing. Edern needed to think. He had to choose the best place to do it. If there was one place Edern knew well, it was Bodmin Moor. Most people thought they knew it, but in truth didn't know it very well at all. At its highest points it was a desolate seemingly lifeless granite moor like Dartmoor in Devon. Similar in its bleakness, polarising beauty and proliferation of neolithic standing stones and circles. At lower altitudes, free range cattle and ponies had made their homes amongst the boggy marshes, streams and spinneys. Compared to the coast and large mining settlements, the moor was a lonely place where only a few had ever sought to make their home, its boundaries demarcated by smallholdings and family farms rewarded with nature's rich bounty of abundance provided by nutrient-rich soils and vast open skies.

As a child, Edern had spent long summers on the moor with his brother, Pascoe, at their aunt's cottage in Bolventor.

They had been fascinated by Arthurian legend and there were myriad locations on the moor shrouded in this folklore. He thought it somewhat fitting that he should take the child to one of the mystical places on the moor tied to these stories. Perhaps his final resting place should be Dozmary Pool, where he could lie with the Lady of the Lake and wield King Arthur's sword Excalibur in the murky depths for eternity.

No. He reasoned that although it was still early, there would likely be ramblers or student historians trudging around the lake on a bank holiday. Then a terrifying tale came to him, he shivered as, he recalled the story of Jan Tregagle and his eternal task of emptying of the lake with a broken shell and his bare hands! *Damn you Jan!* He wouldn't have his little boy haunted by such a harrowing spectre. He knew where to do it, they'd trek over the marshes to King Arthur's Hall. It was far, but not one soul would see or bother them out there.

It was only just past seven thirty as they swiftly passed through Bodmin town and out across the moor on the A30. The calm and crisp dawn was giving way to a changeable morning. Cumulus clouds were visibly bubbling up over the higher ground, forcing blinding beams of sunlight to illuminate the occasional patch of mauve heather or cast elongated shadows from behind tors and rocky outcrops. Every so often a singular large raindrop would land on the windscreen, displacing the dust from the previous dry days in a puff.

Within minutes, the sky had merged with the granite horizon, and those clouds which had formed only seconds before, burst in the mightiest deluge. The wipers of the car sloshed from side to side on their fastest setting and still managed to be completely ineffective. Edern had to slow down to stand a chance of seeing more than five metres ahead. He chastised himself for not predicting this. It had been so warm, sunny and muggy. *Of course there would be torrential storms.*

Lightning lit up the blackening sky in front of them, turning from white to blue to orange as it tormented itself through the atmosphere. Thunder rumbled, almost undetectable to human ears but noticeable throughout one's body. The Toad, still bound, bounced around in the boot of the car, looking up through the rear window in a state of fear and shock. He tried to free his hands from the rope, but they were bound too tightly; he could feel the stifled circulation make his fingers tingle, in a bad way. He slumped back into a ball and accepted this was a one-way journey. Staring up at the turmoil in the sky, he might have imagined that the gods were waiting for him. The heavens were so angry. He kicked at the glass of the boot door in frustration.

'Pack it in! You'll hurt yourself. You won't get out here. We'll stop soon. I promise.' Edern tried to stop the boy's protest, but he persisted, kicking on through the pain of his shattered knee. He kicked and kicked the window relentlessly, until eventually the rubber seals gave way, and the glass was sucked out onto the A30, where it smashed on impact with the tarmac.

'Fuck's sake!' Edern hit the brakes hard. He had no choice but to take the next turning off the main road. He could barely see two hundred meters in front of him. It was diabolical. A quarter of a mile up the narrow lane they pulled to a standstill on the gravel drive of an ancient church. St Catherine's, in the tiny moorland hamlet of Temple.

'You'll pay for that! Smashing up Edern's car!' He slammed the steering wheel. Repeatedly. 'State of this bloody car!' The windscreen, damaged by the brick this morning, and now the rear window had gone. 'It's a deathtrap, and it's letting in a month's worth of rain per minute.'

Edern turned the engine off, put on his cap, fastened his jacket and after struggling with the door handle, he leapt out of the car. Opening the passenger door the kidnapper grabbed a khaki canvas tool bag and slung it over his shoulder. He then moved around to the rear of the car, where the boy was thrashing about in the boot as if he were fitting. After taking two or three deep breaths, Edern leant in. 'C'mon, my dear, we'll go inside, get dry and make our peace with God.'

He pulled the wriggling child out through the windowless boot lid, dragging him into the rain and down the narrow path, past the gravestones, to the shelter of the church vestibule. Edern knocked on the heavy, water-stained oak door and waited. No one came. He twisted the iron door handle, which turned with a rusty screech, and the door creaked open.

Inside, the small church was clearly devoid of people, yet someone must have recently been in as candles flickered throughout the building and there was a delicate scent of campion hanging on the damp air.

Edern took two embroidered prayer cushions from a pew and laid them in front of the altar. He pulled the boy to his knees next to him and whispered, 'Now is the time to make your apologies to the Lord. If you ever think'd you done a bad thing, or told a lie, then you says sorry now and the gods give you a safe passage to the next place.'

◈

The boy trembled as tears streamed down his dirty face. He bowed his head and closed his eyes. He expected this was the end, but he had nothing to apologise for. He'd only ever led a simple life. He'd chosen never to speak as he'd hated the way other people had spoken and shouted at each other when he was very young. He could clearly remember those poltergeists arguing and throwing pots across rooms. He began to weep as he held his bruised ribcage tightly.

In all his short life he'd never hurt anyone; he'd always enjoyed his solitary adventures. The church felt so alien to him. There at the altar, in front of the three brightly coloured stain glass panes, he recalled how he'd found a love of the darkness when he was quite young while waiting in the woods at night to see and hear the owls and badgers and foxes. The nighttime didn't worry him like it did other children. He felt there was an entire world of animals that were usually too scared to come out in the daytime but could live freely in the dark without fear of being attacked, he was one of them. He'd learned that the most dangerous animals – people – were mostly out in the daylight.

He couldn't understand why his hands were bound with rope, nor why the man had taken him from his home. But it had been a lifetime of not speaking, so despite his feelings, it was impossible to try to communicate with his captor. He felt useless; he felt as if he were in trouble for something he hadn't done, yet there was no way of helping himself. However, he did as he was told. In his mind he apologised for sneaking biscuits, he apologised for hiding from his mother when it was a dinner he didn't like, he said sorry for losing his dad's tools after fixing his bike. That was it. He truly couldn't think of anything else. He was innocent. Pure, almost. He looked up at the image of Christ healing his followers in the stained glass Christ looked back at the boy, and humbly he nodded.

He had often thought about how it was so unfair that people – society, would cut down woodland for their fires and to make their homes. He found it difficult to accept that nobody had asked the owls if it was okay to move into the forest, nobody ever asked the deer in the fields if they minded being eaten. No, because they couldn't answer back, so people - *man*, just like the beast next to him, always took what they wanted. He decided to pray, not for himself but for all that could not speak. The trees, the insects, the fish and animals. He knew that as sad as his mother would be that he was gone, she could be proud that he had listened to her all his short life. A bittersweet smile cracked across his battered face and his heart beat with pride.

◈

Next to him, Edern grumbled about things not being his fault, how booze did it, how things would have been different if Wenna had loved him. Essentially, in his mind everything had been someone else's fault, and therefore forgiveness should be his right. He continued to ask forgiveness for what he was about to do.

'Dear Lord, I asks you to understand that I ain't done this for no reason. My son, Jago, he ain't no angel, I admit that. But his life bin 'ard. His mother used to beat him and say unkind things to him. I never had much time for him as I was workin' away. He gets laughed at by all the schoolkids cause they see him different like. He's a dreamer, he wants to fit in, but he get things wrong. I know what he done to this 'ere toad was unkind, but I can't let him be in no trouble about it. And as I've said before about me an' the Toad...I love him, and he loves me. So you understand, Lord, that I must do this for love, for your love, dear Lord. Thank you for listening and understanding. Amen.'

With that he stood up, his apologetic expression replaced by a look of stoic resignation. 'C'mon, poppet.' He motioned to the boy to stand.

The boy looked up at him as if asking for forgiveness, his eyes dark, tearful and wide with fear. Edern couldn't stomach the child's expression and so, removing the black bandana from around his neck, he spun the boy away from him and blindfolded the kid before marching him out into the downpour. Edern put the canvas bag back over his shoulder, tightly grasped the child's hand and led him northwards, out onto Bodmin Moor.

◈

Back at the Hawkeys' farm, Jed Bosanko, the young policeman from Bodmin, arrived to see the mess in the front yard. He knocked and the dog barked. Jed didn't like dogs – a long haired Jack Russell called Bandit had bitten his leg when he was a paper-boy a few years back. Wenna answered moments later and was both surprised and delighted to see a man in uniform at her door. She swiftly attempted to tidy her hair and loosened her dressing gown around her chest.

'Mornin', Jed, what you be doin' down 'ere? We never called you. Something up?'

Jed felt intimidated and out of place, squirming as he spoke. 'Morning, Mrs 'Awkey, you be well, I hope? I was, er, just doin' some rounds really. I was hoping to speak with Mr 'Awkey. He about?'

'No, dear, he's gone out. Went off before the rain, probably gone to fix a tractor somewhere or summat. Can I help, Jed?'

'Well, it's a bit, er, it's a bit sensitive, see...'

Wenna recognised Jed was weakening and connived to turn the conversation around. 'Go on, Jed, spit it out lad. I'm the boss about these parts – s'pose you tell me what you want with Edern.'

Pulling his blazer tight and fiddling with his buttons, he did his best to appear official. 'Well, I dunno if you heard, but yesterday when the egg hunt were on, we made a discovery down by the preachin' pit. The Yellen kid from St Kres, Davy, found a whole load of old rags and child's clothes. The forensics told us last night that they suspect someone has, er, oh, cor...oh, Mrs 'Awkey, 'tis gruesome. I'm sorry to say this. The forensics say people been having relations with kids or something!'

Wenna frowned at the young officer. 'So...Go on. What does this 'ave to do with us Hawkeys?' She narrowed her eyes as she watched him fidgeting uncomfortably.

''Tis just routine, Mrs 'Awkey. We wanted to know if anyone seen anything. Just that we 'ad a report. You know, of Mr 'Awkey's orange tractor up that way on Saturday, and we just wanted to check that he were just going about his normal business. That's all.'

Wenna shook her head. 'Course he was officer. I sent him out to get Jago an Easter egg, one of thems mint Aero ones.'

'Ooh, yummy,' Jed slurped.

'Then he goes over to the petrol station to get his red diesel, so that's why he took the old tractor out. Then he came back for dinner. We 'ad faggots and swede – home made. So, unless there's anything else, Jed, I got to get lunch on, for when he comes back...'

'Oh, okay, well, thank you for your time, Mrs 'Awkey. No more questions. If you could ask Mr Hawkey to pop into the station when he's free, we'd appreciate that.'

'Will do, Jed. Thank you, bye.'

Jed took a second look around the yard; it was a real mess. ''Ere, what happened out here Mrs Hawkey? Looks like a tornado came through...'

Completely straight-faced, Wenna replied, 'It did, Jed, just before the rain.' With that she closed the door in the young man's face.

※

Edern knew exactly where he was heading. He understood how to negotiate the marshes without sinking; he knew the pathways and which side of the waterways he should be on so as not to be forced into the dead end of a meander or the unpassable mazes of gorse.

The rain had stopped for now and, typically, the sun was breaking through the storm clouds, casting its striking light across the moor. Both Edern and the boy were soaked through, and the wind chill froze them to the core. The sun was a very welcome stranger. It had been at least an hour of hiking before Edern saw the stones of King Arthur's Hall rise out from the mound ahead of them. They were almost there. So, this was it. No one would find the remains here for weeks or months – or ever, if the harrier hawks and crows got there first.

King Arthur's Hall was a megalithic enclosure high on Bodmin Moor in the shadow of Garrow Tor. Academics hypothesised it was a Bronze Age ceremonial site. There were fifty-six large granite rocks arranged in a rectangle surrounded by a raised bank of earth all around. Edern believed that this site had once been part of Camelot and was therefore a fitting location for the final resting place of his young knight. In his experience, nobody ever ventured out this far onto the moor, and if you did, then unless you knew the moor, you'd not likely get back.

Edern turned to the boy. He could see he was exhausted; his body had already been broken even before this final hike. He was completely limp as Edern picked him up over his shoulder. Suddenly disturbed, a bevy of larks took flight as the two strangers climbed to the top of the mound and descended to the pasture of the open-air hall below. Edern looked around the site as he threw the boy to the ground, all his 'love' now gone. It was perfect, miles from anyone or anything. A site so remote and, its name aside, so unremarkable. *This is it Ed. Here's the spot.*

Too broken to move, the boy lay face down in the cold, wet grass. Edern stepped on his back to stop him moving and fumbled about in his bag for the crack hammer he'd brought. A forced lungful of air was expelled from the child's chest as Edern knelt on his shoulders and held the child's face into the ground. He raised his hammer above his head and roared. 'I WISH YOU NEVER BIRTHED ME, DEAR OLD NELL,' his cries carried across the moor. Three hawks circling high above them let out their shrill chwirks to each other; they were ready to dine.

Sweat merged with tears and ran down his weathered face. Edern was about to bring the hammer down on the boy's skull when the bluish-black cloud above him exploded into light, as a biblical electrical storm ignited.

'NO! You won't do this Edern Hawkey! Damn you, Jesus! I won't do it.' He looked to the louring sky and screamed at the top of his voice, 'I WILL NOT DO THIS, WENNA! I WILL NOT.'

Defeated, the God-fearing kidnapper jumped to his feet and spitefully kicked the boy sharply in the ribs. 'You go! You go forever. I will kill you if you ever come back to Cornwall to haunt us Hawkeys. I don't know what prayers you told the Lord back at the church, but he must have forgiven you. I cannot take your life now. Today you are the luckiest boy in the world. I hope one day you will forgive Edern Hawkey. His only sin was to love you.' The child rolled in agony at his feet.

Returning the hammer to the canvas bag, Edern clambered out of the pit. At the top, he turned to look back at the tortured body writhing below. He rifled through his baggage and removed what appeared to be an Ordnance Survey map, then took a biro from his jacket pocket and impatiently tried to scribble something down on the wet paper. When he'd finished, he chucked it down at the broken boy.

'I wrote a name on the map. If you find her, you may be safe.' Then, as callous as only he could be, Edern Hawkey left the site. He moved swiftly and silently across the moor so as not to attract attention. He knew the kid didn't stand any chance of survival: he was severely beaten up from Jago's attack; he was blindfolded, bound with rope, soaked and freezing and hungry; and he had no idea where he was. *This is the best outcome*, Edern thought to himself. He hadn't killed anyone, and the boy who had no voice could simply have run away from home and got lost on the moor, where he would have perished. *'Tis a dreadful tale.*

The skies were as capricious as ever by the time he got back to the car; Edern Hawkey truly believed they were angry with him. He stopped short of approaching the Chevette, as a neat and tidy lady had parked next to him and was carefully moving a stack of laden cardboard egg trays from the back seat of her car to the roof. Instead, he walked purposefully past the church and continued down the lane until he reached a fork in the road. A red phone box stood on the centre of the grassy triangular verge. Edern rummaged in his pocket and found a ten-pence piece in his change. The phone box smelled of beer, cigarettes and urine. He picked up the receiver and wiped the mouthpiece with the corner of his jacket. He listened for the gentle purring of the dialling tone, put the coin in the slot and dialled a three-digit number. He used his cuff to wipe a pane of the steamed-up windows, to see that nobody was nearby. The phone answered.

'Bodmin seven-two-five, Jacob speaking...'

'S'Edern. Meet me at the inn. I need to talk, it's time to cash out.' he said softly down the line.

'Lie low for a couple of hours. I'll see you there at one o'clock, I trust it's worth it...'

Edern put the receiver down and returned to a hidden position behind the church. He waited there until the lady had left, then got back in his car. He'd find a layby, somewhere secluded, and catch up on his sleep for a while, then he'd head to the rendezvous.

Chapter 13

Extortion

'I have honestly not eaten such an enormous and excellent cheeseburger in my life.' ***** 7 May 2024 – TheQuietOne83 (6 reviews)

I was moved to leave a Tripadvisor review. And, to paraphrase Samuel L. Jackson in *Pulp Fiction*, that was a tasty burger, like, an absolutely sublime burger! If I may, I'll briefly run you through it. For starters, their description on the menu doesn't even begin to do it justice. True, the beef tastes very fresh, and I've no reason to doubt it's not from the neighbouring field; Without question, that beef was freshly ground in the kitchen today, probably to order. It's lightly seasoned with crunchy sea salt and cracked black pepper and just the faintest hint of smoked paprika. The mince has been flattened to about fifteen millimetres, a nudge over half an inch, and judging by the charring, it's cooked over a naked flame. But it doesn't stop with the patty. The delicious bun is a welcome return from the saccharin trend for sweet, shiny brioche eggy cake, they've gone back to a classic white-bread cob topped with sesame seeds, a few of which catch and brown as it's toasted. The beef sits on a nest of tart and sweet pickled cabbage and is shrouded in the same Yarg, Cheddar and mustard concoction as the cheesy chips. Finely diced sweet white onion, two rashers of crispy applewood smoked streaky bacon and a delicately spiced burger sauce speckled with chopped gherkin top off this incredible hot sandwich. It is a masterclass. Totally different, yet absolutely on a par with the grilled fresh mackerel and hispi I had down the road at the Mariners in Rock last summer. Perfection. The Royal Mint should put a picture of this burger on the back of twenty-pound notes! I'd say it's a national treasure.

Donna collects my plate, and I tell her how much I enjoyed it. It's very agreeable here. I can see myself settling in for the afternoon, so I enquire about the possibility of finding somewhere local to stay. Donna tells me the pub has an Airbnb cottage, run by her brother-in-law, fifty yards down the lane, but usually they only rent it out for weekends, and full weeks during the high season. She isn't certain if it's occupied now; she figures it will be vacant as it's a Tuesday. Feeling confident, I order another beer, and the landlady goes off to check the availability of the cottage.

I hope I can stay here. I have a vague plan in my mind concerning the Hawkeys and it'd suit me to be nearby. Back at my table, I resume sifting through Edern's collection of papers. Now is as good a time as any to read the letters. I organise them by the date on the postmark. There are four in total. The first letter is addressed to Mrs W. Hawkey:

Dear Mrs Hawkey,

I write as one mother to another. When we visited you on Monday, we were extremely upset as our boy had described in his own way how your son, Jago, had beaten him up the day before, at the easter egg hunt. We took him back to the commune and started to nurse him back to health. Now he has gone! He has run away.

We believe that you Hawkeys have frightened him away or done something more sinister. He used to draw horrifying pictures of Mr Hawkey and Jago, but happy scenes with pictures of you in, Wenna.

I need your help, Mrs Hawkey. I need you to be honest with us and tell us anything that may have hurt or worried him. We are going out of our minds here and fear he might never be found nor come back. We ask that you let us know at once if you see or hear from him or have any idea where he might have run away to.

We also expect you Hawkeys to pay us a compensation to help us fund finding him. We believe it is the fault of both Jago and Edern that he has gone. We don't care to involve the police at this stage, but we will talk to them if you don't pay us £2,500 in cash.

Yours faithfully,
Coral McCormick

The next letter, dated a week later, is addressed to Edern this time and lacks any pleasantries, and is more a note than a letter.

Edern, you arsehole!

We sent that last letter to Wenna! NOT YOU. What kind of person intercepts their loved one's personal post? Your controlling ways have not changed at all, it seems.

We asked her to help with the money as we believed she'd understand. We knew you wouldn't because you're a belligerent piece of shit! She cared about our boy, but you have undermined me yet again. We just need to find him, then we'll be gone. Forever.

I am furious, Edern! If only that boy would speak! I have taken the time to write a letter telling her EVERYTHING! Now if you don't bring £2,500 by Saturday, we will personally deliver that letter to Wenna BY HAND.

Do the right thing for once in your shitty, self-obsessed life. Don't forget, Edern, I know Wenna is your sister. And never forget…There's that other little matter…

C.

Ha, his sister! There it is! The confirmation of what we all knew but never said! The rumours of incest are becoming undeniable. I turn the letters over as Donna approaches. I'm not sure why, it just seems proper.

'Right then sir, seems the girl can get the room ready by four this afternoon. We needs it back Thursday by eleven a.m. That suit you?'

'Oh yeah, great. Sure, that's excellent. How much will it cost, please?'

Donna bit her bottom lip. 'Well, 'tis May, so...er, a hundred and twenty-five pounds a night. Two fifty, plus thirty-five pounds for cleaning, so two-eight-five all in,' she replies, unable to look me in the eye.

Extortionate, I think. 'Great! I'll take it,' I accept.

Still, a nice little break. And a good base to finally sort this Hawkey business out.

'Could I have another ale, please, Donna? Pop it on my room.' She raises an eyebrow at me, as if I've not yet earned the right to use her name, but she silently nods in agreement and makes her way back to the pump to pour another jug of the good stuff.

Back to the Hawkeys. So, they are siblings. I mean, it was hardly Cornwall's best-kept secret, but it's still quite fascinating. And Jago? Is he the overripe fruit of their love? I bet he is. Such odd people. I wonder what the effect of this must have been on Jago growing up. Putting my academic hat back on; I'm aware that Freud expressed the belief that many cases of hysteria had a basis in childhood incest, and if I recall correctly, findings in a 1998 paper by psychologist Doctor Pamela C. Alexander, demonstrated the propensity for insecure attachment among incest survivors. He absolutely presents in those ways, the mood swings, his clingy behaviour with Wenna.

I must investigate this more. In many ways I feel sorry for Jago, but equally I have reason not to. And what was the 'other little matter' Coral wrote about? This is all beginning to get interesting.

The third envelope is once again addressed to Wenna – *By Hand*. The manilla envelope smells burnt, and the paper inside is brittle and begins to crumble as I remove it. There is a Polaroid photo at the bottom. It is almost impossible to make out, but I can work out that it's Edern with a girl. The picture is quite gloomy, and there seems to be a fire behind the couple, probably a campfire. He has a full red and brown beard, but his eyes give him away. She is a much younger, red-haired hippy girl, no older than twenty, I guess. She's wearing a white Aran sweater and blue jeans, and her eyeshadow is an alluring dusky midnight blue. They're hugging each other whilst raising a couple of cans of Heineken towards the camera. They seem quite happy. On the bottom it reads '***Glastonbury 1981*** – ***CND***'. On the back someone has written '*I love New Order + I love you xxx*'.

The letter has been burned and then extinguished, leaving the bottom – and probably the most juicy and important parts – lost to history and locked away in only two people's memories.

Dear Wenna,

I'll give you this letter personally. The last one we sent you was nicked by bloody Edern. In it I asked for your help. We need money to help us find our boy, who, as I'm sure you're aware, has gone missing. I said last time that we didn't think his time spent over at your house was too healthy for him, and now we're left believing that you or your family have had something to do with his disappearance.

Although he chooses not to speak, he describes his experiences and thoughts through drawings and acting out. I know it was Jago that beat him near to death last week. But what is far more disturbing are the drawings he done of your Edern. I do not need to fully describe them, only to say they show what appear to be disgusting acts and abuse!

We do not want to go to the police about these problems. Instead you will pay us £2,500 to keep quiet and move out. We will go far away.

You may or may not know this, Wenna, but some of us knew Edern from years ago. He went buy the name Jules or Big 'D', over at the CND commune in Somerset in '80/81. Here's a photo of him and me, before we found out he was a sodding police informer! A fucking grass! That stopped everything. But by then it was...

And that's where it ends. Damn. I have to struggle to read the last paragraph through the charred staining, so to be fair, it may not be verbatim, but the gist is about right. There's nothing on the back and no stamp on the front of the envelope. I don't imagine it ever got anywhere near Wenna.

This has been quite the afternoon. I'm done with it all, I need a break. After gathering the bits together, I settle the bill with Donna, and we arrange for me to meet someone from housekeeping at the cottage at four. I'll go for a walk, clear my head and try to fit these puzzle pieces together. Thinking back to this morning, I'm pissed off with myself. I really messed up with my histrionics at the Hawkeys'. I ought to go back. I doubt they'd be pleased to see me. But now I have more questions to ask than ever. I'll have to go back.

Outside the pub I'm immediately hit by the heat. It's like getting off the plane onto the tarmac in a foreign country. The sun is hot, leaf-curlingly hot. I cross the car park of the pub. There is a little gap between the trees, and I can see out to the fields, where heads of corn weave in and out of each other in a futile search for shade. The farmer will no doubt be pleased though, it has been very wet, even by peninsula standards, and any dry spell is likely heaven sent.

I grab my old Panama hat from the parcel shelf of the car and sneak through the trees, then carefully over the barbed wire fencing. My hat is of great reassurance to me, it's a wonderful comforter. Over the years of owning it I have worn a small tear at the front from years of pinching it as I take it off or put it on. It's probably a bit grubby for Glyndebourne but would surely be welcome at Glastonbury. It's a good hat. Every few meters I hear kernels of corn pop due to the intense sun beaming down on the crops. Most pleasingly though; it is surprisingly still, not even the faintest breeze. Down here at the handsome end of the country I've grown used to the perennial southwesterlies blowing in laden with heavy rain from the Atlantic Ocean, but today I could be in the south of France such is the warmth and tranquillity. The ground is still squidgy underfoot though, and infuriatingly, my baseball boots are not waterproof. Squelchy! I hate that.

At the far side of the field is a dry and chalky unmade lane. I accept the invite and follow it, passing a fully functioning farm on my way. An old boy and a couple of ruddy cheeked lads wave with suspicion at me from the shade of a giant yellow combine harvester. A handful of courting mayflies dance around me as I continue, and a herd of cattle flick their tails and eye me up for a trampling. I'm pleased to report it's doing the trick, nature is beginning to soothe my mind. I often find a solitary walk is a great time to assess everything, to take a reality check. I started to organise this missing person's story in my head:

The burnt letter, which I suspect was from Coral McCormick, made it clear that she was accusing Edern Hawkey of the sexual abuse of a minor. She also claimed that Jago had beaten the boy up. So, I figure, if Edern had been guilty, these two accusations would have been reason enough to get rid of the boy. His son would surely have been in trouble for attacking the child. Why didn't they ever report any of this to the police though? What is clear though is that If the kid was the only witness to any of this, then Edern had to get rid of him. A no brainer.

At some point the police were interested in Mr Hawkey; I've seen Edern's release form. That doesn't necessarily mean anything though. The last letter, the hand delivered one claimed that he'd been a police informer. That might have been enough to get the little snitch off the hook with a bent local constabulary.

I know he was responsible, my gut reaction concurs, but as I said at the beginning of this story, there is truly little evidence. The boy was the only solid evidence, and he was lost. I guess Mrs Hawkey could reveal the truth about Edern, but why would she? They'd got away with it thirty three years ago. She knows now, as she did then, that there's no proof he did anything. She's seventy-three years old. All she has to do is bake cakes, make dinner and wait to die. No need for that idiot Jago to make a fuss about it, he's probably still shitting himself about being in trouble for the Easter egg fight he started. Pop Biddle told me in a roundabout way it was Edern, but he didn't say what he'd done. No one is going to tell me anything round here.

The fact the commune decamped decades ago just makes matters more frustrating. I wonder where that lot went? They were so convinced of the Hawkeys' involvement. To the extent that they found it reasonable to try to extort money in return for silence. I fail to understand that part. What a strange amount for a life. What shut them up in the end? Why their aversion to the police?

And around and around in endless circles the thoughts go never quite tying up. At some point I stumble upon a footbridge. I can hear the thunder of a large road nearby. Climbing the bridge, I realise I'm traversing the new A30. Almost immediately on the other side of the carriageway, glowing out of the ground in front of me, I spy an enormous white scar in the earth. One of the St Austell kaolin mines. Vast grey clay holes, mined over hundreds of years. In places the pits can be over a hundred metres deep. To put that in perspective, imagine three Nelson's Columns on top of each other. At the bottom, vivid blue and green lakes have formed. The pit is huge. So big, you can hardly see anything else. The circumference must be at least ten miles around. Tall pyramids from excavations rise out of the mines. I've heard them described locally as the Cornish Alps, which always makes me smile. So very Cornish! People could disappear forever down there in this extraordinary other worldly landscape.

The sun is relentless, and I can feel my neck burning as I sit dangling my legs over the edge of the precipice. I'm looking forward to my stay at the cottage, truly, it'll be quite the treat to stay away from normality for a while. I'll eat at the Blue Rose again, although for a split second I consider the McDonald's. Nah, the pub is great. Maybe craggy old Pop will be back. Hope so, he's quite the character.

At four p.m. I meet a girl from housekeeping at the tiny stone cottage. It's one end of a thatched terrace and is tragically quaint. A heavy modern stable door opens onto a flagstone-floored lounge and kitchenette. Stairs divide the room and rise, left to right, up to the small and pristinely white bedroom and bathroom. Any available surface has been adorned with some maritime-themed objet d'art, including porthole mirrors and naval bunting. Twee, but lovely. I like it anyway. I thank the girl, ask her to book me in for dinner at six p.m. at the pub, and collect my bag from the car.

And the fourth letter? I'll sit down in my little cottage, pour a tea and read through that just now.

Chapter 14

The Fourth Letter

To my Wenna,

I don't know how to say these words to you. I ain't so smart at writing. You have always been here for me. Ever since we was little kids playing out in St Columb woods or on the moor at Nell's house. You'd never let me get in trouble and you always looked after me and Pascoe. I have done some things that are bad in my life, Wen. I spose I need to write them down. I hope with all my heart you won't leave me on my own.

When I was workin' away when Jago were small, I met a girl. She were too young for me. We didn't mean nothing to occur, but we got close. One thing led to another an' we just sort of got together. I want you to know I never loved her like I do you, but I feel such shame and guilt every day – it never goes away.

I said to you that I was working for John Deere as an engineer on thems tractors, but truth were that I were being paid by the police to work as a kind of spy. Undercover sort of thing. So, I were pretending all those days that I were a hippy. I lived on a commune near Glastonbury, between Langport and Street. They was anti-establishment. They didn't want nuclear weapons or power. They didn't get it. They was protesting about that Hinkley Point power station up in Bridgwater. That Margaret Thatcher didn't want no one disrupting stuff down there, so the police came to some of us farmers and says we can get loads of money if we moves in with the communists and get information on the troublemakers. We weren't makin' enough money to provide for our Jago, so I says, yes, I'll do it. A few of us did. Some never did, because of their families and wotnot. But I figured you wouldn't care as long as we 'ad enough money.

Now a lot of the same people who knew me by the name Jules have moved in at Pop's farm. It's been over ten years since I informed on their people, but they know it was me. They threaten to burn our house and hurt you and Jago. I must give them money every month, so they don't do nothing. Jacob can't help cos the police weren't s'posed to work like that. He says it weren't legal to go around catching people out.

I also needs to tell you something else. I been so terrible, Wenna. The drink made me do it the first time. I need to write this down, cause Lord knows I can't say such words aloud…I been having relations with their boy. But I really cares about him, an' I know that if could speak he would tell you he loves me. But I got to get rid of him. I'll chuck him in the clay pits. Then myself too.

Wen, I don't know what to do! I am not well. I want to be free. I wish I weren't born never.

Please forgive me when I'm gone.
E.

❖

May 2024

I feel sick. He is the vilest creature imaginable. How dare he ask for forgiveness? How fucking dare he?! Well, it's a shame he never did throw himself into the pissing pit. This arsehole had lived a life of incest with his sister, had been a police snitch and a rapist – at best. And here, in this cowardly excuse for a letter he had the audacity to ask to be forgiven for his actions.

He clearly never sent this to her, as the envelope is blank and has never been sealed. I wonder how much of this man's evil Wenna knows about. Probably a fair bit after all these years. Probably everything. Complicit old cow.

Well, that's that. I have everything I need. All the evidence points to Edern Hawkey. I'll visit the Hawkeys this evening, but first, dinner. I'll go to the pub. I need a pint. I really need a pint. Am I drinking too much? Maybe, but it's my only release. I like it.

The Blue Rose is heaving this evening. Donna is behind the bar, as always. She's been joined by a young woman and a village lad. The beer barrels are emptying fast. It is still very warm inside and out. Scores of thirsts to quench. Every bar stool is taken, and every person has to speak louder than the next to be heard.

Wonderful! Pop is there in his seat, dog at his feet and jug of ale in hand. He is talking to a man who looks to be of a similar age but much frailer and balder. He looks happy though, in a red-faced kind of way. In the far corner a gaggle of girls are drooling over a chap in a blue gilet who seems to have won the jackpot on the fruit machine. They are all shouting their drink orders as the machine regurgitates an endless stream of one-pound coins.

Donna had reserved the seat I was in earlier, which was kind. I put the cottage keys and my Panama on the table and go to the bar to get a beer and the menu. I squeeze in between Pop and his companion, making apologies as I do so.

'Sorry, Mr Biddle, just gonna grab a pint,' I reassure him.

'No bother, young man,' he replies. ''Ere, this is me old pal Jimper. He knows Edern Hawkey.' He gestures to introduce his friend. 'Jimper, this polite young man works for the police, and he's been nosin' around at the Hawkeys',' he says, giving me a knowing wink.

I don't really know how to react to this. He was perfectly helpful this afternoon, but now he's got his friend here as backup, he's ambushed me. Politely, I offer my hand to Jimper.

'Pleased to meet you, Jimper. Actually, I'm not a policeman, I'm a psychotherapist and...'

He wipes the beer froth from his mouth, smiles and shakes my hand. 'You'll be the one needin' a therapist if you spend too much time with the 'Awkeys. They has twisted and dark secrets. Strange folk.'

I think about the letter I just read and can completely concur with Jimper that a) they do keep a lot of messed-up secrets locked up over on that farm, and b) I would love to see my therapist now. I seriously miss her. Things are getting a little overwhelming.

I turn to Pop and say, 'Listen, Pop, something's troubling me. Why did you whisper Edern's name to me earlier?'

His bushy eyebrows come together as he narrows his eyes and stares straight into mine. He looks at me for what seems an eternity, checking out every crease and pore of my forty-four-year-old face. It feels very intrusive; the energy is quite magnetising.

He leans back away from me but keeps my gaze. He takes a long sip of his beer, never once releasing his stare, and says, 'Edern Hawkey is the one you want. I see that. You know what he did. I know you know…He is an answer, but not the whole answer.'

He raises his eyebrows and turns back to Jimper as if I was never there and resumes his conversation about the slipping timing belt on his van.

I take the hint and order a pint of Guinness for a change. 'Would you pull that straight through, please?'

Donna almost scowls at my incomprehensible request. 'That's just wrong!' she claims as she shows me the sparkling clean branded pint glass. 'You can't just pull a Guinness straight through. T'ain't right!'

'I'd argue that it makes no difference whatsoever to my pint, just takes less time, and has the added advantage of giving me more time to watch the little bubbles descending instead of fizzing upwards.'

'Skollyon! It ain't right, mister.'

'Maybe it the Guinness that isn't right. Do you pour two thirds of any of the other barrelled beers and leave them to settle for five minutes?'

'No. Course not.'

'So why do it for this one? You're just wasting your own time. There must be over twenty thousand beers in the world, but this is the chosen one? Oh, special dispensation where a pint of the black stuff is concerned?'

Donna hands me my pint. It has been ready for over a minute. I pick up a copy of tonight's menu and head to my table. Donna rolls her eyes. 'Weirdo.'

I'd love that 'Wrecker's Burger' again, but you can't have the same thing twice in one day, can you? I mean, you can, but that's just not done. But then again, I don't live at home anymore, I can have what I want. I'm a grown-up. I pick up the menu to try to feel inspired by the other offerings. It all looks good to be fair. The Padstow crab and asparagus risotto sounds tempting, and so does the Bodmin spring lamb chop with minted Cornish new potatoes and buttered rainbow chard! A lot of the other mains are a bit 'beige', but you know, it's a pub. I ask myself what I'd choose if it were my last supper. The condemned man's final luxury. It's obvious: I'd have the cheeseburger. I always said it'd be the cheeseburger. I catch the barmaid's eye, and she signals she'll be a minute, so I put the menu face down cross my arms and lean back – the universal sign that one is ready to order.

I have to organise my evening visit to the Hawkeys'. It's so convivial here that I really can't be arsed to go there, but Pop's 'Lynchian' utterings and the letters, especially the last one, have given me no choice. I'll go straight after dinner and sort this out once and for all. That thought fills me with dread, but I reason I have a job to do, and like anyone else in the world I have to do it.

The barmaid comes to the table. 'Sorry, sir, we're proper busy 'anight. All the specials is gone already. What can I get you?'

'I'll have the *Wrecker's Burger*, please.'

Chapter 15

The Vicar of Temple
1 April 1991 (Easter Monday)

In the most bucolic of all the moorland hamlets, the Reverend Maria Sherrington had only been inducted at St Catherine's Church two months ago. If they were honest with themselves, many of the parishioners had not at that point fully adjusted to having a lady vicar in Temple. However, Maria had leapt at the chance to leave London and to embed herself in a countryside parish. She'd been highly commended for her charitable work with disadvantaged children when she was the vicar of St Mary the Virgin in Lewisham. The diocese of Truro had recognised in her a kind, hardworking and modern ecclesiastical approach that they liked, and handed her the keys just weeks before Lent. She was in her element.

◈

The rain had been on and off all morning, and violent thunderous electrical storms came and went within minutes of each other. Maria called this weather changeable and thought it typical of a bank holiday. Gratefully there wasn't a service today, but she liked to keep the church doors open for anyone who wished to find a moment's solace. This morning she'd opened early, lit some candles and collected an abundance of Cornish daffodils and campion to put in vases to liven the little chapel up. Ducking across the narrow lane from the rectory to the church and back between deluges, Maria felt at peace and was grateful for her lot.

As a matter of due course, at precisely eleven a.m. every day, Maria would plunge the filter of her cafetière, remove a warmed croissant from the oven, sit at the round pine kitchen table and lose herself in the distant views of the peaks of Bronn Wennili and Rough Tor all those miles across the moor. The view was never the same, and this morning it was one of the most entertaining she'd witnessed. The black and blue sky heaved with rainclouds, the lightning illuminated features she'd never seen before, and the rain washing down the window further distorting the surreal landscape.

As she stared into the distance, she became aware of a dark shape moving slowly and uncomfortably through the rain. *'Tis the beast of Bodmin*, she thought, amusing herself. *Probably one of those ponies or cows, or an escaped pig.*

But the shape kept trudging towards the rectory, maybe only two fields away now.

'Oh my word, it's a person,' she put her hand to her mouth. 'Now what kind of a fool would be out in this weather? A farmer? Most likely, a hiker possibly? No! This is a small person, a child, why are they moving so oddly?'

Without hesitation, she moved to the kitchen door, put her yellow mac back on, grabbed a cloth cap from the hat stand and ventured out across the sodden garden to the gate for a closer inspection.

'Hello!' she called out across the fields. No reply. She waved her arms to catch their attention. 'Hello, are you okay? I'm the vicar here. Are you okay?' No reply.

She was beginning to see the figure more clearly. The bedraggled mess of a child was dragging himself towards her through the drizzle.

'Wait there, I'll come to you,' she called, and made her way through the long, wet grass to the boy. 'Wait there!'

He collapsed at her feet and rolled onto his back. Paralysed with exhaustion, he looked up at her and motioned with his hands that he didn't speak. She bent down by his side, shocked to be faced with such plain tragedy. Maria noticed he was clutching a map, it was soaked through. She carefully took it from him and gently pulled him to his feet. Then, putting his arm around her waist, she led him slowly across the fields and back to the rectory kitchen door, at the back of the house.

He dug his feet into the ground as she tried to direct him inside. She understood by the way he tried feebly to pull away that he was absolutely terrified.

'It's okay, you're safe. Everything will be okay. I'm going to get you some water, then you can have a glass of squash if you like. We'll get you clean and dry, and then we'll get you home, okay? It will be okay...'

He baulked and shook his head. He couldn't go home. Edern had made it clear that he'd kill him. He very nearly had. As much as he wanted to see Coral and Scoob, he was, in that moment, too horrified and afraid to ever return. He took the soaked map back from the vicar, careful not to tear the wet paper he opened the first fold up and showed her the name that Edern had scrawled at the top. He tapped the name with a dirty finger.

Maria looked at the map, then the boy, then the map again. 'You don't talk? Can you write?' He shook his head and shrugged his shoulders. 'How on earth am I supposed help you?' she asked the heavens and the child simultaneously. He pointed to the name on his map again, but she didn't take much notice this time.

She ushered him into the kitchen and pulled a chair out from under the table. From under the sink, she produced a first-aid box. 'We'll need to dress all your wounds again. Their soaked, you'll get them infected. I think I have some bandages and antiseptic. First, though, I'm going to ask you to take a paracetamol, in fact take two. It'll help take some of the pain away.'

Maria poured a pint of water from the tap and passed it to him with the tablets. He gulped it down in seconds, spilling half of it down his muddied jumper.

'You must be dehydrated. I'll get you something else.' She proceeded to pour him an orange juice, and his eyes lit up.

Maria frowned. Looking him up and down, she couldn't draw any conclusions about who he was, why he was here or what on earth had happened to him. Yet here he was, soaked, lacerated, gnawed ropes hanging from his wrists, his lip bleeding, and he did not speak.

She thought she should call the police and hand him over to them. They'd be sure to get him home; someone would be missing him, and he was in a very bad way. Maybe she should call a doctor? But a nagging voice in her head held her back from phoning either.

Her mind taking her back to her childhood. She'd been three years old when she and her sister had been evacuated from their parents' home in Stepney, East London, that was in 1943. They were sent to live with a family on a large farm in rural East Sussex. She loved it there, they were always busy collecting eggs or feeding the cattle. But then, when the news came that their parents had died when their home was flattened during an air raid, Maria and her sister were separated, and she was sent to a convent in Bexhill on the south coast. She was captive there until she was thirteen. It had been traumatic. The experience scarred her for life. Bullied and abused by the nuns, and denounced as a liar when nobody accepted her cries of rape directed at 'Godstowe' the groundsman. She had vowed a peaceful retribution for the price of her childhood by never letting any child in her care suffer the same systematic neglect at the hands of apathetic authorities again. And this, of course, was why she'd been ordained and had devoted most of her working life to caring for those darling underprivileged children in South London.

No, she would do what was right. And at this moment in time, that meant she would care for the boy herself, for a while. If in a few days or weeks a reasonable solution presented itself, she would act accordingly.

She looked to the heavens above. 'Well, Lord, you have me stumped today. Why have you sent this poor wretch? What am I to do with him?'

She turned back to the boy and eyed him up and down. 'To start with, we need to get you cleaned up. Then I want to dress your wounds for you. I believe I can help you feel a whole lot better. Follow me.'

Following Maria, the boy hobbled up the stairs of the cosy rectory, to the bathroom. 'I'd like you to have a shower. Take as long as you like, you must be chilled to the bone. Whilst you do that, I'm going to make you a yummy hot chocolate. Would you like that?'

He shrugged, she wasn't sure if he'd ever had one. She handed him a dressing gown from the top of a pile of freshly laundered bedding and guided him into the bathroom. She turned the water on, and the room began to fill with steam.

'When you've undressed, pop the dirty clothes here on the landing and I'll get them washed and dried for you. Okay? The water may sting your cuts and bruises at first, but the pain will wear off, and it will be good for you. I promise everything will be okay. Okay?'

On hearing the bathroom door lock, Maria collected his laundry and returned to the kitchen to prepare the hot chocolate, make herself a tea and put the washing machine on a quick cycle. She took the time to cross herself in front of the crucifix above the stove and addressed the corpus.

'He must be hungry? How long has he been out on the moor? Hours? Days? Looks like weeks. How does a boy find himself so broken and battered? I must confess, I am challenged by his lack of speech.' She tickled the face of the crucified wooden Jesus... 'Oh, you tricky little man...What am I to do with him?'

Maria made her way into the kitchen. She had a quick rummage through the fridge and cupboards and realised that she had practically nothing to offer a young boy to eat. Yesterday had been terribly busy at the rectory, as she'd thrown an Easter picnic, and it appeared that the villagers had eaten her out of house and home. She had some yellow courgettes that 'Green-fingered Jim' had brought over, and a jar of anchovies.

'Oh dash, this won't do at all. He'll starve. I know what we'll do, Maria.' She proposed to herself. 'You've had a busy Easter, you deserve a treat. We'll go out for lunch. Yes, we'll go for lunch at the inn.'

The boy eventually appeared in the kitchen at the foot of the stairs in the dressing gown she'd lent him. His hair was dripping on the tiled floor. But he was clean. Maria watched on as he smiled whilst he ran his fingers through his soaking hair and repeatedly sniffed his hands and inspected his fingernails. Maria could smell that he'd used the pine-scented shower gel she'd received last Christmas. She smiled back at him and handed him a long nightshirt to put on while his own clothes were being laundered.

'Pop in there, get yourself properly dry and put this on.' She showed him to the lounge across the hallway. 'When you're done, we'll have that hot chocolate and try to get to know each other.'

◆

He took the shirt and closed the door behind him. He was amazed at how clean the house was. It was also very warm. He scrunched his bare toes into the soft carpet and shuffled around in circles, it was simply perfect. There were several sheep hides in various shades of cream on the sofa and he felt warm inside as he rubbed his face into the sweet smelling wool. He had never seen the inside of a house like this. Yes, he'd been in Wenna's lounge and kitchen, but the Hawkeys' house was cluttered and smelled like gravy. He shuddered at the thought. This place felt calm and was filled with aromas of lavender and biscuits. It was also noticeably quiet; he could hear the vicar stirring some teacups in the other room, but other than that he could only make out the heavy drops of water falling from the chestnut tree leaves onto the gravel drive and either a dove or cuckoo cooing, he couldn't decide which it was. He dried himself and his hair as well as he could with the towel and pulled the nightshirt over his head, before making his way back to the kitchen.

◈

Maria put her mug down on the kitchen table and placed her hands on her hips. 'Well, now. Look at you. An angel, you must have been sent from heaven,' she said, delighted. 'I expect you'll be rather hungry. All I have is half a croissant, which you may have now, but nothing else. Well, a courgette, but I doubt you'd want that, would you?' He scrunched his nose up. 'So, I thought it might be a nice treat for us both if we went to the Jamaica Inn for a spot of lunch. They have fish fingers, or a salad perhaps? I wonder, do you like a ploughman's? You know, bread and cheese and pickles?' He nodded enthusiastically. 'Then it's a deal. But first I'd like you to help me out...'

Maria produced a pencil and a few sheets of plain paper from a drawer in the Welsh dresser and put them down on the table in front of the boy. 'In my experience, children love to draw. I imagine that you're very good at drawing. Something tells me you're very creative and a possibly even a great artist,' she said encouragingly. He smiled again and tried to take a sip of the hot chocolate, but it smarted as it was still too hot for his torn lip. 'So, young man, maybe you can begin by telling me your name.' He looked at her inquisitively. 'With your pencil...Write your name down if you can,' she continued.

Nervously, he picked the pencil up and restacked the paper in front of him. He began drawing while the vicar put a bag together for their outing. Checking back to see what the boy had produced, she was surprised to see he'd drawn, quite intricately, a rather ugly and forlorn-looking warty black toad.

'Your name is Toad?' she asked. The boy made an inverted smile and nodded. Careful not to upset him, she continued: 'And you like your name? Many people don't like their own name you know. I hated mine at school. The nuns teased me for my holy name. But I must say I've never heard of anyone called Toad. Well, apart from Toad of Toad Hall.'

She took a step back and looked at him. He was quite sweet all in all. His hair was a bit unruly, but no, there was nothing she thought remotely amphibious or warty about the wee chap.

He reached across the table for the map he'd been carrying. He looked at the top and pointed to the name written on it. The ink had run, but it was still just about legible. Maria wrote it down on a blank piece of paper, then she opened the map up. It was an Ordnance Survey map of Bourne Old Town. The word 'FILO' was written next to a hand-drawn circle which appeared to highlight the location of several houses at the top of the High Street. She didn't have a clue what it all meant, yet she guessed the boy wanted to get there.

'Do you need to get there? Is that where you were going when you found me?' He gave her a thumbs-up with both hands. This was silly, Bourne was the other side of the country.

She had heard of Bourne of course; she'd grown up not far away when she was at that dreadful convent. In fact, she was certain she'd been there. She recalled going to an organ recital at All Saints Church there once. And a weird pagan festival where a man had dressed up as a giant tree and been chased by more small treelike men, while the entire population of the town cheered them on and became inebriated over the course of an afternoon.

'Well, maybe that's what we need to do, we should go there. Do you know the person who's name is written on the map?' He turned his palms up and shook his head. 'I wonder if she's a relative?' She looked up, 'I know it seems like madness Lord, but, okay, well, Easter's over, and I have a few quiet days here in the parish, so I'll take you there, I promise. I believe you have been sent to me for a reason. I do not yet understand why, but time will tell. We'll work this out. Together. Now, finish your drink, and I'll get your clothes out of the dryer and maybe some newer boots for you. Your feet look the same size as mine. I have some spare walking boots that would suit you. We'll grab some lunch, then we'll get you to Sussex, no matter how long it takes.'

Chapter 16

Collusion
1 April 1991 (Easter Monday)

The Jamaica Inn was one of the most infamous pubs in the county, made famous by Daphne du Maurier in her novel of the same name. Its history was steeped in more debatable stories of smuggling, than of rum, and sadly by the nineties it was little more than a tourist trap out on the A30, high up on Bodmin Moor. It even featured a museum of taxidermy: an enormous collection of stuffed animals in complex dioramas, such as an animal courthouse and school classroom populated by baby squirrels.

Maria and the boy pulled into the car park just after one p.m., luckily, just in front of a Rambler coach brimming with sightseers. They made their way inside the vast, cold tavern and chose an empty booth. The booths consisted of two high-backed, pew-like benches of dark wood facing each other across a sticky table.

Maria left the child with her bag and keys and crossed the room to the bar to collect drinks and a menu. He followed her with his eyes, distracted by how the shards of sunlight projected through the small, mullioned windows illuminated millions of pieces of dust floating in the atmosphere. They reminded him of the stars on clear nights back at the commune. He marvelled at how, the longer he looked, the more of them he could see, floating in their peaceful and chaotic way. They swirled and orbited each other, yet somehow their energy always kept them from colliding.

He noticed that the barmaid seemed to know Maria very well as they chattered away. The vicar looked over her shoulder, offered a neat and friendly wave, and smiled at him. Thinking about it, she didn't look much like the kind of vicar he'd imagine if he was asked to draw one. She didn't seem old fashioned – you know, like vicars were. Also, she was...a she. A lady vicar. He liked her. She made him feel safe and warm. He was fascinated by her moss-green eyes, and the streak of white which fell against the rest of her dark brown hair, it made him happy how it matched her collar. Natural quirks pleased him.

Presently, the heavy oak front door flew open, and in poured a sea of tourists, picking things up, tapping cabinets and screeching chairs across the stone floor as they commandeered every seat in the house. Every seat except the booth directly behind the boy's head. Two men had already been surreptitiously hunkered down there before Maria and the boy had arrived. They were deep in conversation, their tone was sombre, and they kept their voices down.

Maria returned with two lemonades and two menus. 'Here you go, young man.' She offered him a glass of fizz.

'Now, I don't imagine you can read so well, so might I suggest that we choose something hearty, fill you up, you know, a big meal. The drive to Sussex is going to be a long journey, and you already look very hungry.' He was, and the thought of food made his tummy rumble. 'How about sausage and mash? Do you like the sound of that?' He shook his head and scrunched up his nose. 'Fish and chips?' He gave her a thumbs-down. 'A cheeseburger? Says here it comes with bacon, a portion of French fries and a side salad. That sound good? You must eat your salad.' His eyes widened and he rubbed his tummy with both hands. 'Marvellous! A cheeseburger it is. In fact, you know what, young man? I think I'll join you. What a great choice.'

She rubbed her palms and joined the back of an exceptionally long queue of holidaymakers.

The boy pressed his ear up to the back of the booth. He could just about hear the two men speaking. He doubted anyone could catch their conversation above the racket of the coach party, but his hearing had become finely tuned over the years; it was, he thought, his most trusted sense. He could make out every word of their sinister discussion. He detected that they were both very local; the mid-Cornish drawl was an accent he'd listened to all his life. They definitely weren't holidaymakers. And he thought he recognised the first voice he heard.

'...I just need you to 'elp me out 'ere. I proper done some dreadful things...'

'Well, I'm not sure how I can. They're watchin' my every move down there. You know, since that bit o' cash went missing from them dealers in Launceston,' replied the second man.

'Now listen 'ere, Jacob Merlyn, I 'elped you all thems years ago down at Bridgwater. You got promoted cause of what we found out for you. C'mon, man, I jus' want this to disappear.'

The boy froze. His heart raced. *NO!* No, no, no...That voice, the same that had terrified him for as long as he could remember. The tongue of the man who had only hours earlier wanted to kill him was inches from his head, and he didn't even know it. He gulped and clenched his fists. Surely he was safe in here? He gripped the table. The vicar would keep him safe. She had to. There were so many people in here. They'd see if something bad happened... wouldn't they?

Maria turned and gave him a thumbs-up, blissfully unaware of the danger he found himself in. He wiggled his thumb from side to side, suggesting he wasn't really okay. She smiled again without a clue about his gesture. He leant back into the conversation behind.

The second man replied to Edern: 'Okay, okay, I'm listening, Ed. What have you done? Give me an idea what you want me to do about it...Tell me bloody straight, mind.'

'Well, for starters, damned Jago nearly killed the kid from the bloody commune. During the Easter thing. The egg hunt.'

'So...?'

'Well, the hippies come around this mornin', smashes up our car and the barn and gnomes an' wotnot. Says I got to give 'em money to shut up. You can imagine, Wenna gets in a right state. So I clattered a couple of 'em.'

'And? Why not just call the police like a normal person would, Ed?'

'Jacob, I can't. I'm not in the position to. They says I been havin' relations with the boy...'

'ED!' hissed Jacob. 'Don't you start with these stories! Have you? I don't believe it...I won't believe it, not an upstanding citizen like Edern Hawkey of Trebrowagh. Have you been having relations with a commune boy?'

'Yes, sir, yes, I have...' Edern looked to the bottom of his empty pint glass.

'No, Edern! You have NOT been having relations with a boy child, have you?' Sergeant Merlyn winked across the table at Edern.

Edern searched the policeman's face for answers, then the penny dropped. 'No, Jacob, that is, er, yes, that is correct: I have not been having relations with no boy.'

'Sooo...' Jacob continued, 'I don't understand why we're having this conversation?'

'Well, I kidnapped him! This morning. From the commune...'

Jacob smashed his tankard down on the oak table, attracting the attention of forty or so scone-scoffing tourists. The boy held his breath in the booth behind.

'F-u-c-k s-a-k-e...' he spat through gritted teeth. 'And where is this kid now, Edern? What have you done with him, man?'

Jacob scowled and pulled at his hair. He took the longest drink from his jug, finishing every drop. 'I left 'im up King Arthur's Hall. I s'pect he's dead b'now.'

'And what in God's name do you suggest we do about it?!' He cracked his knuckles.

Trying to look anywhere except in his acquaintance's eyes, Edern muttered back, 'I don't know, Jacob. I messed up. I just thought you could clear it up. I figured cause...you owe me.'

Breathing slowly and deliberately, Sergeant Merlyn leant across the table. 'I cannot for the life of me even try to understand what kind of shit-housery you've got yourself into here, Edern Hawkey. Sure, sure I owe you a big favour, but this? This must be the holy-fucking-grail of favours...' Jacob buried his face in his hands and for a few long seconds he growled. A deathly chill shot down the boy's spine. He shivered as Jacob delivered his verdict.

'Here's what is gonna happen, Edern. Firstly, some house rules. I am repelled by your actions. Truly disgusted! So, after we are through with this business, we are equal, and we can move on with our lives. I don't owe you anything, and you never think of asking me for nothing. Ever again. We will not speak no more, nor be seen to be acquaintances. If we pass by each other with our wives or families, we will acknowledge one another in a civil manner so as never to raise suspicions, understand? Now, listen careful...'

The boy looked for the vicar, but he couldn't see her anymore. A crowd of diners from another coach had joined the back of the queue. He was sweating. Should he get up and find her? He'd be safe next to her, wouldn't he? But these men were like wild animals, and they'd just snatch him if they wanted him and probably throw him into another car and drive him to his certain death. No, he'd keep his head down, turn away from the room and keep listening. He wished the vicar would hurry though.

Jacob continued: 'As it happens, we have one of the hippies at the nick in Bodmin right now. Fella by the name of Scoob or some nonsense...'

Dad, the boy thought to himself. *Why do they have Scoob?* He started sobbing, worried about what they were going to do to Scoob. He feared the worst but was careful to stay as quiet as a mouse.

'So, I has this waster up on drugs charges. We found about a kilo of grass on him up the preaching pit...' Jacob winked at Edern as he spoke. 'Matter of fact, we also found a load of soiled children's garments up there...Oh fuck me! That was you, Ed?'

Edern replied, 'Er, no, not me...'

'Right answer, Mr Hawkey. So, we got this fella at the nick. He's on drug charges, and now we suspects him of having relations with a boy from the commune and disposing of his dirty clothes. If this kid don't come back, I guess I got no alternative than to charge the scumbag with kidnap an' murder. Trouble there, Edern? I don't got no evidence to send him down. Second thing is this: some nosy parker seen your sodding bright orange tractor by the pit on Saturday afternoon. You really are a prize fucking clown!'

'So, here's how it works. Tomorrow mornin', you present yourself at Bodmin nick, nice an' early. I takes you in, and we pretend to talk to you for twenty-four hours or so. That way people believes everything we do, and they think we take them seriously in return. We release you with no charges. Then we charge Swampy or whatever his name is. But...' He winked at his acquaintance, then sighed. '...Sadly, before we need to start putting together evidence for the prosecution, our friend has a nasty little fall in his cell. Now, if you agree to this, Ed, you are a free man. If any of this ever gets out, however, you're a dead one! I'll personally see to it that you, Wenna and Jago all disappear. Simple. End of. Understand me?'

With that the sergeant collected his car keys, and offering no further pleasantries, simply said, 'I'll see you in the morning.'

As he turned, he almost bumped into Maria, who was returning from placing her order. He apologised and noticed the boy sitting in the booth. *Hmm*, he thought, *just a perfectly ordinary, clean and nicely presented young lad out with his mum for lunch. How lovely. Lot of cuts and bruises, mind...* He smiled down at them from his great height and left Jamaica Inn.

❖

Maria stroked the boy's face, as she noticed he'd been crying. She figured that he must still be in a lot of pain. This had been an awful day so far, and by the look of him this morning, it'd been a very hard life. She wished he could talk. She prayed she could help. It was, she believed, her raison d'être to care for all the world's suffering children. Well, it used to be anyway.

'I promise you everything will be okay. I'll have a look for some more paracetamol in my bag, that'll help. Our burgers are ordered; lady said they'd be about ten minutes. We'll enjoy those and be on our way. How's that sound, eh, Mr Toad?'

❖

Edern watched the bar girl tighten her apron and push her hair out of her eyes before she left the counter and walked towards him. She huffed as she sloppily put a jug of nut-brown ale and a tumbler of amber liquor down on the table.

'Put it on me tab!' he slurred.

'Can I get you anything else, sir?' She sneered.

'Hmm, depends on what you're offering, young lady...'

'You dirty old man, you're drunk! I think that's your lot.'

'I'll drink as much as I want. I'll have another rum. I'll have two! I'm Edern Hawkey. I does what I wants.'

'We'll see what the boss has to say about that.' The girl rolled her eyes and returned to the bar.

Edern winced and gasped as he knocked back the neat alcohol from the smaller glass. He eyed the barmaid up and down as she walked away and smirked to himself. *Looks like you got away with that then, Edern. Wenna will be pleased. Jago's gonna get the belt 'cross his back though...*

◈

Despite the distraction of knowing Edern Hawkey was drinking himself blind right behind him, the boy, now ravenous, devoured his cheeseburger in a matter of minutes. The vicar took her time. She hadn't had anything like this since leaving London; she would savour it.

'Mmm, this is delicious. I see you enjoyed yours. Be sure to eat that salad...Now make sure you've had enough. Would you like a pudding?' He puffed out his cheeks and shook his head. 'Good. I'm pleased to see you've eaten well. The drive to Sussex will be a long one, my guess is at least six hours. Be sure to use the loo before we leave. It's over there at the back, behind the next booth.' His eyes widened as he turned in the direction of the booth behind him. He shook his head again and stuck his thumb down. 'Go on. Just try. It's a long drive' He grabbed the wooden pew with both hands. He wasn't going anywhere.

Maria stood up and looked over the top of the pew into the next booth. 'What an appalling state,' she tutted and looked back at the boy. 'There's a drunken old man asleep with his head on the table behind you.' The boy was frozen to his seat. 'Well, if you don't need to go, I suggest that we pay the bill and hit the road.'

At the counter, the server checked how the food had been, but she couldn't stop looking at the boy's beaten-up face. Directing her attention away, Maria pointed out the drunk man in the booth. 'I'm a bit concerned for the welfare of that gentleman over there. He seems to have fallen asleep.'

'He's a dirty old pervert,' the barmaid sneered again as she handed Maria her receipt.

'Oh, is that the case? I see. Well, thank you, lunch was lovely. See you next time.'

Maria took the boy by the hand, and they left the pub together. They crossed the car park to her little burgundy Peugeot 305, and she opened the boot and put her coat and bag inside. She then retrieved a soft woollen blanket and handed it to him, and for the first time in as long as he could remember, he felt truly safe.

As they pulled out of the car park, he couldn't help but notice Edern's tatty terracotta Chevette with no rear window. It really had been him sitting behind them, that brutal, disgusting, evil, drunken man.

Over the duration of the drive, the reality of everything that had happened to him at the hands of that wretched family began to set in. He'd been scarred for life; he'd been abused, beaten, kidnapped and forced to leave his family aged just eleven years old.

He would never forget, he would never forgive.

Act III: Three Dishes and Petits Fours Served Cold

Chapter 17

Starters

May 2024

It is said that revenge is a dish best served cold, the insinuation being that it is protracted and calculated in its planning. I've been perfecting my three-course banquet for thirty-three years. It may disturb you to discover that, by my own admission, I have made perfect with some previous and occasional practise (the ponytailed, Hawaiian shirt wearing wanker was, I think, my best work to date. More on that another time). Anyway, right now, I'm ready to prep up for a *MasterChef* finale in justice. To start with, as any good chef will tell you, the most important thing to do is to sharpen one's knives. I've found a dram of whisky usually suffices. Next, I'll ensure I have all the appropriate equipment and ingredients necessary to create my ultimate feast fatale.

Back at the cottage, I boil up some water in the little cheap kettle and select a bag of Yorkshire Gold from the caddy of beverage options. I pour the water into a blue and white striped Cornish-ware mug and let the tea brew.

Upstairs, I get out of my psychotherapist costume of loose chino's, linen shirt and leather bracelet, and then my underwear. I reach inside the shower cubicle and carefully turn it on, trying not to get the floor or my arm soaked. Unzipping my brown-leather John Lewis holdall, I take out a Morrison's plastic carrier that contains my outfit. I lay the bag on the fresh linen of the made bed and jump into the steaming shower. I decide to take an extra long and lavishly hot shower just in case any of this goes wrong. Who knows, my next wash could be an ice cold scrubbing down, next to a large and promiscuous gentleman in prison, or worse still, this could be my last.

Doubt taps me on the shoulder, perhaps I've created my own bad luck taking this shower and ordering my last supper. I brush it aside, nope, I'm not superstitious, I have a plan, and I'll follow it through. I convince myself I'll succeed. But it's true, the brain does play tricks on you at times of high stress or when the adrenalin is pumping through the veins. I find myself relishing every sip of tea as if it's the nectar of the gods. It's really not. I didn't leave it to brew long enough and it's essentially just hot water with milk in it. Isn't tea a let down more often, than not?

I tip the contents of the carrier out onto the bed. Black jeans, black socks and a black t-shirt. I feel like a superhero putting them on. For the finishing touch, this superhero needs a mask! As strange as it may sound, I have brought a vacuum-packed bag of dark peaty mud with me. Hear me out, I slice it open with my penknife and am pleased to find it's still sticky and wet. I plunge my freshly showered hand into the bag and rub my hands together before staining my face with the dirt. I look in the mirror and after a brief moment I see him, the 'ugly little black toad' smiles back at me. *Kronegyn hager du.*

'You ready?' I ask him. A tear clears a path down his muddied cheek, he nods back, he is very ready. As the teardrop disperses, a big, innocent and beautiful smile shines back at me.

Encouraged by seeing him happy, I mess up the rest of my body and arms with the mud. *Housekeeping won't be impressed.* Then I pack a small bag for the job. I must admit at this point to having second thoughts. I really don't fancy doing this. However, I've convinced myself that the only way I'll be free of this sentence is through justice. And as Edern has successfully evaded his comeuppance for over three decades, I feel it only fair that I should be in control of his destiny now.

Okay, so it's just gone eight thirty p.m. and I'm fed and watered. The idea, obviously, is to get all this done completely unnoticed. As for an alibi, I'll leave my car where it is, and the TV will be flickering through the curtains. Plus, I've been seen at the pub on a very busy night. Although, thinking about it, I've probably already been a bit slack with Pop Biddle, and maybe Donna could raise an alarm if she suspects anything. I doubt they'll care, but still, I wish I'd been a little smarter. *Oh well, fuck it!*

My plan is to walk to the Hawkeys' across the fields. It's a long way around, but I'd be very surprised if I bumped into anyone out there. I've worked out it'll take me about forty-five minutes. By the time I arrive, it'll be under the night sky. The sun finally disappears below the trees to the west of the cottage at nine p.m., signing off with an extraordinary illumination show of pinks, scarlet and tangerine. Hundreds of little marshmallow clouds gradually disperse into the midnight-blue atmosphere and, as the moon rises, night begins to fall. I carefully and quietly pull the door closed behind me and leave the cottage at nine fifteen exactly.

◈

Down at the Hawkeys' farm, Jago is washing up the dishes and pots from dinner. He has the radio turned up quite high to try to make sense of the programme he's listening to, which is discussing politics and a general election thing. For dinner, they all had ham, egg and chips. Jago loved the food but hates that his mum insisted on doing scrambled eggs. *No one else has scrambled eggs with ham and chips, and they always stick to the blooming pan.* It takes him bloody ages to scrape off all the stinking dried yellow egg! He can never understand why she doesn't have the non-stick pans. He has been washing up his entire life. He can't stand it. Still, he does it, and always with as much passive-aggressive crashing and clanking as possible. Wenna has taken herself to her bedroom, she can't make it much past half nine these days. She gets washed and into her stretchy nightie, takes her tablets, puts some cream on to soothe the shingles and, after a gargantuan effort, heaves herself onto her bed and under the covers. She has the radio tuned to Radio Cornwall as usual and relaxes by reading her *TV Quick* magazine.

◈

A dim light shines through the back window of the barn. As I'd hoped, Edern is in there; I assume he's doing some kind of late-night tinkering. So far, it appears that this is going smoothly. I was always mindful that their bastard hound could get involved, but as yet he hasn't detected me. I creep around the perimeter of the farm to save having to walk on the gravel. The cloudless, moonlit sky makes for a bright enough guide. The temperature has dropped quickly though. I carefully peer through a small window at the far end of the barn, furthest from Edern. Nobody's cleaned this for decades, I have to clear cobwebs away with the side of my hand to get a half decent view.

I see you. There's the rotten old tosser, lurking at the back of the building. He has his spectacles resting on his nose and is hunched over the workbench inspecting what looks like a teapot. As my eyes adjust, I can see that he is indeed supergluing the handle of the pot back together and is deep in concentration doing so. I despise him. For everything he did to me. And now here he is, still living life as a free man, doing what he wants. In front of me is this seemingly able-bodied aged man in a checked green woollen shirt and brown trousers fixing a teapot. But in my mind, all I can picture is that red-faced brute thirty years ago, his pants at his ankles and his bony, veiny hands around my neck.

I check in my bag. I have a heavy rubber mallet, some bolt cutters, a couple of car polishing rags and the bottle of chloroform I bought on the internet – surprisingly easily.

I draw in a deep breath. No turning back now. It's been a long time coming. Revenge will be oh-so-sweet. Actually, that's not quite true. It will be a messy and guilt-provoking plague on the rest of my life, but in this scenario revenge is just. I push the barn door open with intent, causing Edern to jump out of his skin.

'What?! What in heaven's name!' he barks. Then he begins to realise what is happening.

Here in front of him is the therapist who's been hassling him and his family for the last few weeks. Here in front of him is that same man, dressed up as the child he used and abused, kidnapped and left for dead. Here in front of him is the Grim Reaper. Here in front of Edern Hawkey are his last remaining minutes of mortality, and as the colour drains from his face, he quickly resigns himself to that end.

'Hello again, Edern.' I calmly call along the length of the barn, completely deadpan. 'I guess you know why I'm here, don't you, Edern? He tries to focus on my face. 'Allow me to remind you briefly of your last words to me, that time you left me for dead. Remember? I quote, *"I hope one day you will forgive Edern Hawkey. His only sin was to love you."*

'So, er...' I laugh aloud. 'Here's the thing. Weirdly, I was never able to forgive you for abusing me, or "loving me" as you so poetically put it. NO! I will never forgive you. In fact, I'm here tonight to avenge your crimes against me, to balance the books as it were...'

He swallows defeatedly, his eyes shiftily scan the room for an exit strategy. 'I thought you was dead? I'm so sorry.' He fumbles with the teapot. 'I thought there were something fishy about you when you came here with your questions and wotnot...' His hands start visibly shaking and he's forced to put the teapot down.

I slowly walk towards the bench where he is standing frozen to the spot, I sense his fear. I'm going to smack him so bloody hard.

He's sweating, he stutters. 'Can, can, can I sort out some money for you? You want money? Is that right? I can help. I have savings an' that. Promise not to hurt Wenna or Jago, oh please...How come you speaks?' He stumbles backwards as I close in.

His question stops my advance. 'Selective mutism,' I reply. 'Here's a story for you. Even before you got to me, you contemptible pig, I had decided that the world around me was a cruel and frightening place.' I pause and rub my chin. 'Do you know what atychiphobia is, Edern? Tell me what it is. If you get it right, I'll promise not to harm the other two. Go on...what could it be?' I put my finger to my lips in a sarcastic puzzled manner. I know the pathetic pervert won't know the answer. To be fair, I wouldn't have known it before my own therapist diagnosed it.

'Atychiphobia is an intense fear of failure. For me it manifests as extreme anxiety and self-sabotage. I was so afraid of the violence within our commune and scared that I would let my family down or never achieve the dreams they had for me, that in the end I just shut down. I figured if I said nothing, no one could accuse me of wrongdoing. I believed this to the point that something clicked OFF. The neural pathways in my brain were blocked. After that, no matter how hard I tried to use my voice, the receptors had ceased or refused to work. I could not speak. This suited me for a long time.'

The truth is, I loved being locked inside my own version of the world. I could disappear into the forest or to the streams and rivers, and the wildlife trusted me. They knew I was like them. I was *without a voice*, so I could not make decisions on their behalf. I was their equal. I was safe. Innocuous and happy in my boundaryless natural environment. I truly felt part of nature.

'Until they made me "toe the line", until the day they sent me to school...And that foolish, simple, inbred son of yours decided he could vent out his own lifetime of frustrations through bullying me! It started with the name-calling, Edern, nothing too horrid, usual crap like "toad", "ugly little black toad", "mangy cur", "dirty bastard", and on it went.'

'Then the physical cruelty. Your son, your pride and joy, took real pleasure in pinching me, kicking me, stabbing me with his compass. He'd throw stones and rocks at me. And despite being four years my senior, despite knowing I couldn't cry for help, that fat little bitch tortured me. I thought he'd kill me the day of the egg hunt. I was in fear of my life as he battered me with that stick and kicked my ribs repeatedly until I could feel my heart was being bruised. You know, I'd decided to give him the egg. Stupidly, at the time I thought he'd maybe share it with me. But he couldn't give a shit. Well, fuck him!'

Edern tucks his hands into his trouser pockets and stares at the floor.

'Look at me, old man, have the respect to look at someone when they're speaking to you!' He begrudgingly looks up, but there is no remorse, he shows no shame in his lifeless old eyes. 'And then, and then, Edern…The torture didn't stop with Jago, did it? Do you think it stopped with Jago? No, of course it damned well didn't. You, a strong, fully grown, adult male, took it upon yourself to abuse me. To rape an eleven-year-old mute kid! How do you feel about that today Ed?' I shake my head, my eyes searching his emotionless face for any sign of remorse. There is nothing. 'You still feel sexy about little boys? You revolting dirty old man. I have never, ever understood or been mentally able to come to terms with your violation. How does anyone ever learn to accept that shit?'

I feel so sick. I have to stay in control here. The memories of the pain inflicted by this sadist could easily rubber-band me psychologically back to that place I'd spent a lifetime avoiding..

Physically, he is not that animal anymore. He's not a frail man, but his best days are well behind him. His breathing becomes more obvious as he begins to totter from side to side. I sense he's going into shock.

I seize the opportunity to close in on him. I approach the workbench very slowly and deliberately, I feel myself growing in stature, I am in complete control and the old bastard knows it. Carefully, I put my bag down next to him and take his wrinkled smoker's face in my hands. He does not struggle as I squeeze his cheeks together and pull him close to my own face.

'Did you really think you'd get away with it? I feign surprise. 'Here, get this, you'll never guess what? Thirty three years ago, I was sitting right behind you in the Jamaica Inn while you discussed everything with your little bent copper boyfriend Merlyn. Do you remember that? You were practically on your knees, begging that deceitful policeman to get you off the hook. You know what? You're both a couple of little weasels.' I'm so close to him I can feel the heat of his foul breath in my mouth as I speak. 'You allowed him to cover up your dirty work, didn't you? You let him arrange a "little accident" for my father! You bastard. You fucking bastard! You left me for dead and allowed my dad's name to be desecrated throughout our communities everywhere. But that was not enough for Edern Hawkey, was it?'

I can't help myself as the rage surges through my boiling veins. I smack the side of his face so hard that it knocks him off balance. I catch him, grabbing his head again.

'NO, THAT WASN'T ENOUGH!' I spit at him, across the eyes. 'You let him die so you could live freely...' I hiss through my teeth.

He is struggling to stay upright, he is suddenly very weak, and as tears well up in the corners of his eyes, all the life in his face drains away.

I move around the bench to be the same side as him. He tries to shuffle away.

'Don't move one more inch. Don't you dare.' I pull his shirt sleeve to keep him where he is.

'So, this is how it's going to go, Ed.' I pass him a postcard I bought at the post office down in Summercroft and put a black biro in his hand. 'You write what I tell you to write.' He nods. 'I want you to simply write this: *I'm sorry, Wenna. I cannot live with myself no more...Sorry about the cake.*'

He does as I say under duress, and I place the card deliberately so that it's visible on the end of the bench nearest the door.

Next, I pull a chequered teacloth out of the bag and then the bottle of chloroform.

'Trousers down,' I order. He refuses, he thinks I'm joking. This angers me, so I thrust his forehead down onto the hard workbench with all my might. He groans as he slips out of consciousness. I am glad he hasn't bled everywhere, I don't need any mess to clear up.

I carefully remove the lid from the chloroform bottle and am immediately struck by how sweet it smells, almost like candyfloss. I pull my t-shirt up over my mouth and nose to avoid inhaling too much of it. Acting quickly whilst Edern tries to gather himself together, I douse the rag with the acrid liquid, before reaching around the old man's head and smothering his mouth and nose.

'In a minute or two, Edern, you will pass out, and when I let you wake up, you may find yourself in a rather uncompromising position...'

I hold the toxic cloth across his face until he's unconscious, then, with my spare hand I remove his brown synthetic trousers and, well, I'll spare you the finer details. I wretch, I'd expected revenge to taste sweet, it doesn't. It sickens me, and only serves to take me back to the horror, pain and ignominy of my life as their 'Ugly little black toad'.

In truth, it takes me remarkably close to the edge of reason, and for a split second I consider taking my own life with him, such is the shame I still carry. My brain spiralling in and out of sense, I snap out of it and push him to the floor. God, I need to wash my hands right now. I feel utterly revolting.

With the cloth away from his mouth, he comes round quickly. His eyes are wild with pain and confusion. He tries to garble a few last words, but nothing comes out. A rather ironic justice, I feel.

Leaning down to this pathetic, doubled-up and trouser-less excuse for a man, I whisper in his ear, 'Remember how you took me into the little church down at Temple on the edge of the moor and told me to make my peace with God? Well, Edern, I'm afraid I will not be offering you that luxury. All I need you to know is this: you are only the *starter* of my little killing feast.' I rub my hands together and wink at him. 'Mmm, for my main course I will take out your complicit and frankly revolting wife, Wenna. Then for dessert...ooh, yummy.' I can hardly contain myself, I pat my tummy. 'For dessert I'll polish off that large spotted dick of a man, Jago.'

I close my eyes and deliberately smell the air. His only answer is to smirk back at me. Arsehole.

'Goodbye, Edern Hawkey. I hope it was worth it.' With that I tear the rubber mallet out of him and smash him across the temple with it. And out he goes.

Cold.

Dead.

A blunt instrument killing. Perfection, no blood splatter. No trace.

◈

The moonlight shines through one of the windows on the house side of the barn and silence falls across the farm. I look down at the lifeless body on the floor and feel nothing. I am completely numb to my execution of him. I sit down on the floor next to the corpse and hear the child within me speak. *Thank you*, he says, and my stomach grows warm.

After two or three silent minutes, I clear my things away. I put the bottle and cloth in a carrier bag and am careful to tie it tightly. I take a clean cloth and wipe the mallet clean. Now I need to get the dead man out of the barn and into his car. I pull up his trousers and search his pockets for the car keys. Damned things aren't on his person. I need to get out of here as quickly as possible without anyone noticing. I scan across the workbench and other surfaces. No sign of them. I look out of the barn at the house. The kitchen lights are on, and I can see Jago's silhouette at the sink. I need to get to the hall by the front door. They have an ornate key-hanging thing on the wall there. It looks like a Swiss cuckoo clock but is just a piece of tourist tat. I bet the keys are hanging on that. But I mustn't wake that bastard dog up.

I manage to sneak across the drive to the Vauxhall Vectra. It's unlocked, but the keys aren't in it. Bollocks. Okay, the first thing to do is get the body in the car, then I'll have to make a bit of a smash and grab for the keys and speed away. Hopefully, anyone who hears me will think it's Edern off out someplace.

I lift the tailgate and leave it open. Back inside the barn, I get my head under the dead man's arm and lift him over my shoulder. He is as heavy as I'd imagined, and awkward. I drag him slowly across the noisy gravel drive, roll him into the boot and gently close it before tiptoeing to the front door. No one has noticed me yet. Jago is still in the kitchen, but I have no idea where Wenna is.

I softly push the door handle down. It squeaks slightly, but no one would hear it. It clicks, and I open the door, just an inch. Ugh, that smell: gravy, dog and Shake 'n' Vac. Light shines down the hall from under a door, but there doesn't appear to be anybody moving about. I can see the car keys about three feet away on the hook. I make a snatch for them, knocking a second set onto the hard floor with a clank. The dog starts barking. Bollocks!

'You alright out there, Pappy?' comes the voice from the kitchen.

Thinking quickly, I feign a dreadful Cornish accent: 'Yarp, jus' popping out a mo.'

I run to the car, start it first time and drive away. Jago waves through the window and calls down the hall to his mother, 'Dad's off out again Ma...'

'Jesus Christ!' I shout to myself. 'I've done it! I've killed him...Wooooooooooohooooooooo!' I cry out the window into the darkness as I leave the drive and make my way through the narrow country lanes up to the kaolin mine.

Turning the lights off when I arrive at the access road to the mine, I find the gates are shut. Luckily, they're very flimsy wire swing gates, and they won't stop anyone with this kind of intent. I reach for the bag and, leaving the car running, I take the bolt cutters and make quick work of the chain which binds the gates together. I cautiously drive up the track, guided by the moonlight on the chalky white unmade road. I'm on the opposite side of the pit from where I was earlier. Blimey, what a day! I pull the car to a halt near the top and walk to the edge of the mine. The bank is incredibly steep, and in the dark I can't even begin to see the bottom of the pit.

This will do.

Carefully, inch by inch I manoeuvre Edern's car to the very edge of the cliff so it's practically hanging over the precipice, I pull the handbrake on, leaving the engine running, drag his stiffening body out of the boot and shoehorn him into the driver's seat. The front end of the car rocks slightly but settles once Edern's in a seated position. I secure the seatbelt, lean over the dead man and select drive. The car jolts forward. I release the handbrake, quickly step back...and over it goes, into the abyss. The scene is slow and noisy; at first I guess the car is still upright as I hear the underside scraping the ground, then as it loses control there are a few rapid-fire crunches as the plastic parts of the bodywork shatter, splinter, crack and snap. After that come the heavy thuds as it begins to roll and tumble. Each roll creates an almost thunder-like boom out here in the serene starry Cornish night. Then the cackling of some foxes, followed by one final muted thud and absolute silence.

He's gone. I wonder how, or where they'll find him. Still strapped in? Half way up the escarpment, severed into many bloody parts scattered across the site? Who knows? I hope it's the last option.

I don't rush back to the cottage. Instead, I revel in the sounds and activities of the nocturnal world as I trudge across the fields and back past the farm I saw earlier this afternoon. I don't believe any single human noticed my movements, on the other hand, the owls have almost certainly witnessed my activities, but they'll never tell anyone. I make myself laugh with the thought they couldn't give a hoot about Edern Hawkey's death.

Chapter 18

Soused Malt Loaf
May 2024

Early next morning I struggle to open my eyes, it feels like they're glued together. Oh! Right, yep, I see. The pillow is caked in mud, it takes a minute or two to become compos mentis and recall last night's events. I should have washed my face. I check my phone to see the time. It is almost eight a.m. Someone will find that car soon, and any sporadic pieces of Edern lying around the pit. I'd better get moving. Today is going to be a busy one: Three in one day. Never done that many before.

I turn on the shower and head downstairs to put the coffee on. I bought some croissants a couple of days ago and they've become a bit hard, so I put the oven on to soften them up.

After my shower, at eight twelve a.m., I receive a notification from Parcelforce to advise me that the parcel I sent a few days ago has been delivered. Excellent, I feel a nervous buzz in my stomach.

❖

Down at the Hawkeys' farm, Wenna was in the middle of saying goodbye to Jago, who's off to work at the nursery, when a red van trundles down the drive. At first, she thinks it may be Edern, who's been out all night, again. In fact, it's the post lady. She pulls to a halt by the gate and winds the window down.

'Mornin', Mrs 'Awkey,' she beams and waves from the car window. 'Got a package for you today, needs a signature. Must be important.'

'Mornin' Trish, I isn't 'spectin' nuffin'.' Wenna's eyes light up. 'Cor, 'tis excitin',' she coos.

The woman goes to the back of the van and produces a perfectly cuboid parcel secured with red-and-white 'Fragile' tape.

'Says to take care, fragile, innit.' She raises her thick, square eyebrows as she passes the parcel to Wenna.

Wenna tries to sign the Trish's handheld delivery-tracking device but only succeeds in creating an illegible squiggle.

'Thank you, young lady. Have a lovely day.'

Wenna looks at the label and is overwhelmed to discover it's addressed to her. She can't resist giving the parcel a delicate shake. It seems reassuringly weighty. Beside herself with expectation, she takes the gift into the kitchen and puts it in the middle of the dining table. She'll make a nice cup of tea, then open it. What could it be? It doesn't have a return address on it. What a surprise this is.

Brutus rests his head on the table and gives the package a good sniff. He baulks a little and plods back to his blanket filled basket in the corner of the room. Wenna puts her tea down on the table and pulls up a chair.

'Right then, what 'as we 'ere then?!'

She carefully unwraps the brown packaging paper to find a cardboard box. Seeing the box is taped up, she reaches across to the side table for a penknife. She scores the Sellotape and opens the flaps. She is absolutely flabbergasted to find inside an exquisitely painted, ornate Japanese lacquered box. She can't recall having ever seen anything so beautiful. It is roughly half the size of a shoebox.

She puts it in front of her on the table and sits back with her tea and sighs in admiration. 'Well, Wenna, must be your birthday or summat,' she says aloud. 'Let's see what's inside...' She lifts the lid and gazes in.

Inside the box, wrapped in a high quality clear cellophane and tied with a dark-green silk bow, is one of the finest examples of a well-baked, dark, sticky and fruity malt loaf she's ever laid her beady little eyes on.

'Oh my goodness! Someone knows me well. I will absolutely be having a sumptuous slice of this for my elevenses! With butter on.'

I treat my warm croissants to a generous smothering of delicious local butter that the pub provided. It is more than delicious, it's indescribably creamy. You know how people bang on about Guinness being better in Dublin? Well, there is something incredibly special about Cornish butter. It's just different, in a good way. It tastes of cream and salt, and there's a godly golden shine to it…Ah, just take my word for it.

I have a second mug of black coffee from the moka pot, which makes my lips feel oddly fizzy. I think the adrenalin is already pumping. I take the time to strip the bed of the muddied linen and dutifully load it all into the washing machine. I search in the little cupboard under the stairs and am grateful to find an iron and ironing board.

After dressing in a freshly pressed white cotton shirt and some loose cream trousers, I brush my teeth, rinse away the yellow coffee and put together a Cluedo-like collection of items I'll require later. This includes, in no particular order, a length of rope, a shovel, a family bucket of quicklime, a set of handcuffs and a replica pistol – a Walther PPK as it goes, yep, just like Bond.

I arrive at the Hawkeys' house at ten fifty five a.m., bang on time for coffee and cake. I know Edern isn't there, and unless I completely misjudged this, I'm pretty certain Jago'll be at work at the posh garden centre.

It feels natural to make my return cheery, to act apologetic. Last time I was officially here, I'd lost my patience with them, but now I imagine you understand why. I pull up next to where I took Edern's car only a few hours earlier. Stomach churning, I beep the horn to signal my arrival. The old bag will think it's her husband/ brother/ lover/ whatever, getting home. I get out of the car at the same time as she opens the door.

'Cooey, Doctor,' she calls, waving from her waist. She appears to be in a particularly good mood and quite welcoming. 'I never 'spected to see you 'ere again. Everything okay, Doctor?' she asks.

'Yes,' I say, returning her wave. 'Good morning, Mrs Hawkey.'

'Wenna...'

'Yes, of course, good morning, Wenna.' I purposefully bend down to touch my toes; I want her to notice me stretching. 'I thought I'd just swing by to say, sorry about the other morning, and to say goodbye really. I'm going home tomorrow. Nobody else about?'

'Nope. Jago gone 'a work, an' bloody Edern left yesterday evenin' and never been back.' As she says this, I notice I left the bloody barn door open last night. *Very sloppy*, I think to myself.

'Oh, is that normal?'

'I dunno what be normal with him these last few years. You ask me, he's gone round the twist, lost his marbles. 'Ere, strangest thing happened s'mornin', Doctor! I hears a car coming down the drive earlier an' I thinks it's Ed popping home, lost his keys or wotnot. Turns out it's the post girl.'

'The post girl?'

'Yarp, 'er – Trish the post, odd lookin', with the fish lips and the yellow hair, eyebrows like sausages.'

'Oh, and this is strange...how?'

'I'm jus' gettin' 'a that bit, if you'll stop your buttin' in. Now then, she says, "I 'ave a parcel for you Mrs 'Awkey." Well, Doctor, I looks at her like she's an alien or someone from Devon or something. No one has delivered a package for as long as I remember to the 'Awkeys. But wait, gets even better...Can you guess what it was, Doctor?'

'Er, hmm, a cake?' I put my fingers to my mouth and pretend to nibble an imaginary morsel.

'Well, you'll never guess, the package was...What? Wait, how'd you know?'

'I didn't. I could just see how excited you are, and I know you love your cake.' I smile. 'Was it a Dundee cake by any chance?'

She lifts her face, satisfied that I wasn't correct. 'Nope. Malt loaf! A dark, moist and curranty malt loaf. An' now we can share a slice together. With a nice bid-a'-budder on it.'

I dip to touch my toes again. 'Can't, I'm afraid, Wenna, just started a diet. Very disappointing. You know how I love a good malt loaf.'

She stares at me as if I've lost my mind followed by one of her customary shrugs. 'Please yourself. I'll 'ave your piece too.' She chuckles and shows me into the house. The keys

I knocked off last night are hanging back in their regular place. It is a very strange feeling to be welcomed into the house of the man I murdered only hours earlier, but at the same time I feel brilliantly victorious.

'Wanna frothy coffee, or a milky tea, dear?' she asks as she shuffles down the smelly, dismal hall.

'Frothy coffee, Wenna, nice and hot, please.'

'Comin' up. Now go sit in the lounge an' we'll 'ave a natter. For old times' sake.'

I can hear the radio in the background, bleating on about a competition of some kind. No sign of the dog, which I am pleased about. Over the sound of the radio, I can hear Wenna humming 'Who Knew' by Pink – very surreal. I guess they repeat these songs over and over on local radio.

When she returns to the lounge, she is grinning from ear to ear. She presents the ornate box out in front of her to show me.

'Here it is, Doctor. Did you ever see such a thing?' She puts it up to her nose and inhales. 'Mmm, that is perfect. Have a whiff, Doctor. Smells like almonds.'

That'll be the cyanide then, I congratulate myself as I pretend to sniff the cake.

'Delicious,' I offer. 'You simply must have a slice, Wenna. I wonder why they sent it? Someone obviously thought you deserved it.'

'Could have been Angela down at me 'airdresser's. I gave her some words of advice about her relations with her old man when I was there last month.'

I shrug my shoulders in the *Hawkey* fashion and watch in anticipation as she cuts herself a hearty tranche of the deadly loaf. She lays the cake on her plate and slathers a thick coating of butter on the top.

She wobbles her jowls in awe. 'Mmm, now that,' she points repeatedly to the prepared malt loaf, 'that could send a weaker woman than I to an early grave. Naughty but nice.' She chortles. So do I. At her, not with her.

'Go on,' I encourage her, raising my eyebrows, 'taste it. I bet it's as good as it looks!'

She picks the slab up between her chubby little thumb and forefinger and puts it to her salivating mouth. She licks her pale, thin lips in preparation and clamps her teeth around the cake.

Her eyes close for the longest time before she looks across at me with a gaze of pure happiness.

'Well…?' I enquire.

She licks her lips as she draws her conclusions. 'I might say it's a tiny bit bitter, Doctor, but mmm, so fruity and moist. Best I've had since we went to Camborne ten year back. *That* is a lovely loaf, to be sure.'

I sip my awful coffee and watch her wolf down her last supper. Rather like my cheeseburger thing, I felt it only fitting that she should have a portion of her favourite fare before dying. Let me be clear here, I don't despise her in the same way I do Edern and Jago. However, over the last thirty years, I've never been able to forgive her for her complicity in allowing my abuse to go unreported.

I follow her hand as she licks her finger and dabs at the remaining crumbs on the plate.

'You used to feed me there, Wenna,' I say calmly, nodding in the direction of the window.

'What do you mean? I gives you cakes in 'ere last week...'

'I mean, when I was younger, I used to come to that window, and you'd always give me something to eat. Sometimes a piece of cake, sometimes a Ryvita, or even a bag of pork scratchings if I was lucky.'

She tips her head to one side like a puzzled dog, and I watch as she begins computing who I am. She is very confused.

'I never fed no one through no fenister. What are you talkin' about? You can't be my little toad...can you? You? You're my little grubby warty toad? Give over, you isn't.' She wobbles her cheeks. 'Never is! I heard you was missin'. They says you were kidnapped or wotnot. Edern said you was most likely dead by now.'

I smile demonically, nod encouragingly and wink. 'Well, here I am. It is me, or rather, it was me. I was your ugly little black toad. And now I'm back in Trebrowagh with the sole purpose of exacting my warty revenge on you and your family.' Cracking my fingers, I speak with deliberate and slightly sarcastic menace. I want her to understand that there will be no avoiding this fate.

She frowns at me in disbelief. 'Stop talkin' skollyon! You ain't the toad boy. He couldn't speak no words. What's wrong with you, comin' here scarin' old ladies?'

'I'll scare old ladies! Did you know what Edern was doing to me back then? Did you know he raped me?'

'Oh nonsense!' She shakes her jowls from side to side.

'True story. I tell you, he invited me into the barn to do some craft, woodwork or something. He locked me in. He abused me. He raped me! That dirty old pervert hurt me. He physically and mentally destroyed me!'

Wenna nervously adjusts her tights and puts her cup down on the side table. She is agitated. Her face has become very pink, and she can't stop shaking her head, unable to process the situation at all.

'I don't believe you. You tells me the police up Truro sent you.' *Oh Wenna, poor, simple Wenna...*

'I don't believe you are...is...was...the Toad! I don't believe you had s'gustin' relations with Edern! S'gustin', dirty talk. I don't believe none of it! GET OUT!'

'There you go again.' I put my head in my hand and feel my pulse racing. 'Protecting your brother as you've done your whole life. *That* is unbelievable!'

Her face reddens. I imagine she has always felt a degree of discomfort or shame when exposed as the incestuous wife of Edern Hawkey.

'When I was young, I loved you, Wenna. I mean, I trusted you. I always came to you for help, to be safe. I would come when we had no food at home. I'd come to you to escape from Jago after he'd hit or beaten me up. He was a very cruel boy.'

She growls at me, 'Jago never done nuffin'!'

'God's sake Wenna...he hurt me almost every day. Until the point I refused to go to school, fearful of the pain and embarrassment of the beatings. Your malignant, good-for-nothing oaf of a son tortured me as much as, if not more than your husband did.'

She is seething; I can hear her panting. She hasn't a clue what to do.

'Anyway, as I say, I only want justice. Call it revenge if you like. For thirty-odd years I've suffered. I think it only fair that I take three lives as my settlement. The three lives that stole mine. A life for each fucked up decade I've managed to survive. Sound fair to you?'

'I didn't do nuffin'! I want no part of these murders. Nor does Jago or Edern.'

'Edern's dead.' I crack my knuckles again.

She exhales heavily. 'STOP, Doctor! You're frightenin' me. I didn't do nuffin'.'

'Precisely! You did bugger all. You let those arseholes get away with whatever they wanted! You covered up for them, you complicit old bag.'

'DEAD?! Why is he dead? Where? Oh, Wenna Hawkey, I declare I feel all queer...' She slumps back into the La-Z-Boy and begins sobbing. 'I had such a nice mornin' too...'

'I don't need to go into the details,' I tell her, 'but I killed him in the barn last night. Then I drove his body over to the china clay pit beyond St Kres and dumped him. He's gone Wenna, he can't coerce you anymore.'

'Oh Lord, say it ain't true. I loves him so much. Now there is only Jago and Pascoe an' me. Oh, please, Lord, make it stop. Please.' She struggles to catch her breath.

I check my watch: eleven thirty five a.m. Another few minutes and the cyanide will begin to make its presence known. I feel obliged to give her a smidge of dignity and, kneeling at her side, I present her with a box of tissues from the half-sideboard.

'I hope you understand why I'm doing this.' I speak quietly to soothe her in her last few moments of consciousness.

'I feel so hot, not too good, Doctor. My palms is sticky. Oh Lord, Edern, my love...'Tis the shock. I'm gonna phone Jed the policeman.' She tries to get up out of the La-Z-Boy but hasn't the energy, and she slips back down. 'You 'as broken my heart, Doctor. Now Jago will be an orphan boy. I hates you!' she snivels.

'Don't you worry about Jago, Wenna. I'll make sure I take care of him.' I smile.

'I feel a bit sicky, Doctor,' Wenna whines as she holds her stomach tightly. 'I has such a sudden temperature.' She starts convulsing. Her spasms are more violent than I'd expected. She almost tips her huge armchair over as she jerks in torment.

I notice the foamy saliva building up at the corners of her mouth. 'It's the cyanide. I poisoned your malt loaf. I couldn't bring myself to physically harm you, Wenna, so I thought I'd send you off with a tummy full of yummy cake. There's a chance you might recover, but I'll need to get you to bed and call a doctor out for you.'

She is visibly weakening as her heart begins to slowly fail and her central nervous system starts to shut down.

'Let's get you to bed.' I put her arm around my shoulders and help lift her out of the chair, she's a bloody heavy old girl. Wenna sobs uncontrollably as we take the few steps down the dark hall to her bedroom, and I help her lie down on the bed.

Within minutes she starts retching. I run to the kitchen to get her a bucket and put it at the side of the bed. She makes a horrendously forced sound as she begins throwing up. The smell makes me wince, but I hold her hair back from her face as she projectiles into the blue mop bucket. Moments later she's starting to fade in and out of consciousness. I tell her to try to remain calm. She can only mumble incomprehensible sentences now. I make out the names Jago, Ed and Nell. She clenches and releases her fingers as the pain rushes through her boiling arteries. Then, as quickly as it started, her body stops writhing, and after one final groan from her stomach, silence fills her chintzy room.

I close her eyes, pull up her blankets and feel for her pulse. She is gone. The house falls silent, bar the soft padding of the dog in the hallway and the ticking of the alarm clock on her bedside table.

'Goodnight, dear Wenna.'

I deliberately leave her door open. It is highly likely, and my fantasy, that if she goes undiscovered for more than three or four days, the dog will starve and have no choice but to eat the old crow.

Chapter 19

Ding Dong Bell

Ding dong bell,
Pussy's in the well.
Who put her in?
Little Johnny Flynn.
Who pulled her out?
Little Tommy Stout.
What a naughty boy was that,
Tried to drown a pussycat,
Who ne'er did any harm,
But killed all the mice in the farmer's barn.
– Lang. 1580.

I decide to leave the malt loaf and the Japanese box for the investigators. I take the packaging cardboard and paper as I don't want it traced to the post office, although it's more than likely that Parcelforce would have a timeline on the thing. Ah, bloody shoddy again. I convince myself they've no reason to consider such a hypothesis and tell myself I'll get better at this. Practice makes perfect.

It's getting on for twelve thirty p.m. and according to the *First Bus* website I need to intercept the number ninety three from St Columb at three twelve. Jago will be on that one. He'll be heading home with a head full of the day's futile stories about sandwiches or moss or gravel...Dumb bastard. For now, I'll make my presence known back at the Blue Rose, where I'll definitely try something new off the menu.

I park in the same space I used yesterday, make sure nothing relevant is visible in my hire car, and go through the heavy oak door and to my favourite table. Pop Biddle acknowledges me with a nod and a half arsed grunt, which I return with equal gusto. The weather outside looks nicer than it is. It's changing; nowhere near as hot as it was yesterday. The sun is still shining, but the westerly wind is starting to pick up, making the air cooler and a bit clammy. It's now cloudier too, not grey, but there's certainly more action in the stratosphere this lunchtime.

I put my car keys down on the table and check my phone is in my pocket. It is. I turn the airplane mode off, I am traceable again. I order a pint of Guinness.

'Would you pull it straight through, please?'

Donna isn't at work this afternoon, instead, the girl from housekeeping is tending the bar. She looks at me as if I've walked in dressed as a member of the SS at an upper class fancy dress party.

'Got a proper job 'ere.' She winks at the old men sat at the counter. 'Straight through? It's Guinness. That ain't right.'

'Yes, please, just like it that way.' I spare her the lecture.

'How's Anchor Cottage, sir?'

'It's absolutely perfect, thank you, very homely. I had a cosy night last night, watched *Skyfall* and went to bed. It's so quiet around here.'

'Mostly is. Last night were a bit rowdy, probably cause of the sun. You know 'ow people get in this country when the sun comes out...'

'Madness,' I reply. She shrugs.

I take the menu back to the window seat and check my phone for anything remotely interesting. Nothing. Six Facebook birthdays to acknowledge, that sort of crap. To be honest I don't really use social media a great deal, I feel that it makes me idle and exposes how disingenuous I am. Of far more interest is the omen, an enormous seagull outside the window. It just crashed out of the sky into a collection of bottles, glasses and ashtrays that someone has tidied together. After a lot of frenetic flapping of wings, everything smashes onto the ground, and this frightens the bird, which *kee-haa*'s and takes off again in terror. This may not be a popular opinion, but I like seagulls. I find them quite beautiful, they're enormous, brave and amusing. If they were rarer I bet we'd be fascinated by them.

I really want the cheeseburger, but in the end, I figure I'll go with the 'Catch of the day'. I silently mouth across the room to the waitress, 'Catch of the day?'

'North Atlantic cod.'

'Oh, not local then?'

'Couldn't say...'

'No problems. I'll come to the bar.' I cross the empty pub. 'Hi, I'll have the fish finger sandwich with tartar sauce, please.'

'That's cod too.'

'Yes, yes, I read that. Could I get that with a side of chunky chips, please.'

'Sure, fifteen mins. Anything else?'

'Jug of water, please.'

'No problem.' She disappears into the kitchen.

Seeing me standing there, Pop taps his crook on the edge of the copper bar. 'Lot of sirens this mornin' over by the A30. Back o' Carter's farm. Probably a pile-up or something...'

There's something about Pop; I can't quite put my finger on it, but I always feel that he knows things aren't quite right. He plays the devil's advocate well. He knows I know something about the sirens. Yet, he's complicit in letting me get away with it despite his suspicion. Quite the mischievous character.

The girl returns from the kitchen, putting her hair up with the biro she just used to take my order. 'I 'eard they found a car down the bottom of the pit this morning. Dave "The Boat" says it's a suicide job. Car all mangled up and that. Surprised it didn't catch fire.'

Pop raises his eyebrow in my direction. 'That so, Jenny? Wonder who that be then? Someone local, I 'spect.' I feign a passing interest, and he turns back to his lunchtime beer and says no more.

Jenny, the house girl, isn't finished though. I can tell she is one for a bit of gossip and a natter.

'I reckon it could be Davy Yellen. He got done for all thems pills he were sellin' down Newquay. They was gonna sentence him at Cambourne next week. Or might be that old lesbian teacher, she looks proper depressed all the time. 'Ere, what car was it, Pop?'

He looks up for a second, looks at Jenny, then me, then around the room. 'Vauxhall. Silver one.'

'Oh, oh goodness, you know who 'as a silver car, don't you? Oh shit, oh, Pop, I know who 'as a silver car...You-know-who, he has a silver car.'

'Don't talk such skollyon, Jen, most 'alf the cars in Cornwall are bloody silver. Could be anyone. Ain't healthy to keep goin' on.' Thankfully, Pop takes the heat off.

Jenny brings my jug of water over with a small tumbler and my cutlery. 'Pervert lives by 'ere got a silver car. 'Ope it's him. He ain't no good to no one,' she offers.

I quietly agree with her. 'Yeah, I hope so too. All they deserve, those types.' I wink.

The fish finger sandwich is top class! To start with, the bread is fresh, white and soft on the inside with a gum-shreddingly crunchy crust. Cut thick. The fish fingers are handmade goujons cut from lovely long fillets of a dense, flaky white fish. They are deftly seasoned, and the batter is oh so exquisitely light, maybe some kind of tempura. The sauce has the correct balance of bite and piquancy with a glorious herby finish. And the chips – fuck me! If you're ever within twenty miles of the Blue Rose, then promise me you'll go there, if solely for the chips. You can thank me later. Oddly, I have never seen or even heard the chef. I've noted a couple of young kp's grabbing a crafty cigarette, or a wisp of watermelon vape by the trade door every now and then, but never the chef. Anyway, whoever you are, please accept my compliments.

I take my empty plate back to the bar and offer my thanks to the kitchen. Jenny asks me if I'll be eating at the pub this evening. I can see Old Man Biddle's ears prick up.

'Got a date tonight. Should have suggested here, shouldn't I? She's booked somewhere in Port Isaac, Outlaw's Kitchen or some such, menu looks great. So no, I won't make it this evening. Sorry about that. But I'll be in to check out in the morning. Do you do breakfast?'

'Nah, we don't. Should do, probably enough people would come for it.'

'Shame. Okay, thanks very much. I'll try to pop back for a pint before my date. See ya, Pop. Thanks, Jenny. Need to pop out to grab a deodorant.'

I wink, turn on my heel and stride out into the sun. *That's a neat alibi*, I congratulate myself, and head to the cottage to freshen up. It's two twenty p.m. near enough. I'll leave at three p.m. on the dot. I can't wait to see that ridiculous chubby little fuckwit again!

◆

Jago, blissfully unaware of his parents' untimely passing, begins cleaning up his area of the kitchen where he's been preparing sandwiches all day. A couple of smart ladies from St Agnes were most flattering about his food and left him a five-pound tip. *That will be going straight into the savings jar at home.* He is incredibly pleased about it. His manager, a precocious teenaged boy named Quentin, praised Jago for his 'High standards and perseverance in the face of adversity'. Jago is feeling enormously proud.

Hanging up his apron on the back of the fire door, he turns out the fluorescent lights and leaves the kitchen through the farm shop.

'See you next week, Quentin. Bye, girls. Keep up the good work.' He smiles and waves to all his colleagues, who do their best to ignore him as he makes his way out to the bus stop.

Jago is pleased to see it's Bernie driving the bus today. Bernie is always cheerful and greets his passengers by their name if he knows them.

'Afternoon, Jago. Busy day at the office?' he asks as Jago boards the number ninety-three to Truro.

Jago twiddles his fingers and thumbs together. 'Really good, Bernie. Some posh ladies gave me a fiver too.'

'Ooh, well, you can give that to me for me early Christmas bonus,' jests the driver.

Jago looks embarrassed and isn't quite sure if Bernie means it or not. 'You're alright,' he says and makes his way to his usual seat. Three rows back and on the left. He sits there so he can see out across the fields and in the shop windows when they drive through Trebrowagh.

Behind him, a schoolkid who's somehow got out of his lessons early blows a plume of watermelon vape at the back of Jago's head and laughs as he exclaims, 'Sorry, not sorry, fat man.'

Kids can be so cruel, Jago thinks to himself, but chooses not to be wound up by the boy. Bernie scowls at the lad through the rear view mirror.

❖

I know where he'll be getting off. The stop is about a hundred and fifty metres from the entrance to the Hawkeys' drive. I pull into the layby just as the bus comes over the brow of the hill. It passes me and then slows and stops to let Jago alight. He gets off, waves and starts to trundle away from me towards his drive. I let the bus disappear before getting out of the car.

'Jago! Jago!' I shout, waving my arms like a lunatic.

He turns around and begins walking towards me. 'What you doin' here?' He's immediately on my case. To be fair, he's always been a bit suspicious of me.

'Quick, Jago, hurry! We need to get to the hospital in Newquay!'

His face drops. 'What?! Why? Is it Mother?'

'Yes, Jago, it's Wenna, she's had a fall. Edern's down there already. He asked me to wait for you and bring you in when you got home. Come on, man, get in!'

He ups his pace. I get in the car and, leaning across, I open the passenger door for him. He has worked up a sweat and huffs and puffs as he shoehorns himself in. I start the car and we pull away quickly.

'She gonna be okay, Doctor?'

'Who? Oh yeah, Mum. Yes, I think she'll be resting now.'

'How long till we get there, Doctor?' He frowns.

'Not long, Jago.'

I press the central-locking button and head out onto what was the old A30. The skies are shifting as clouds roll and tumble in from the west, the ears of corn in adjacent fields bending in the increasing wind.

'Wait, you missed the turning,' exclaims my tubby little passenger as we speed past the A39 Newquay turn off. 'You're driving pretty fast, Doctor,' he yelps and snatches the door handle.

'Yeah, sorry, Jago, I seem to have missed that junction. Never mind. We're not going that way anyway. Fancy a road trip, old buddy?'

'What you talkin' 'bout? Why ain't we going to Mother? Are you mad?'

I look over at him and frown through my eyebrows with wide, wild eyes like Jack Nicholson in *The Shining*. 'Could be, Jago...' I flash him the whites of my teeth. I am going to enjoy this one.

Realising he's been tricked into getting into the car, Jago starts panicking. 'Can we stop, sir? I just want to go see my mother, be sure she's okay. Please, sir.'

'Mum's going to be absolutely fine as long as you help me out, Jago. I need you to assist me with something.'

'What is it? I just want to go 'ome.'

'Jago, I'm afraid you can't go home. Not yet. Not until you've helped me with a few things.'

'I'll jump out the car!'

'Well, you won't. I've locked it. Besides, your big fat head would explode if it hit the road at this speed. Then you'd never see Mummy again!'

'I'm frightened. Why are we going so fast?'

He's right, I am hammering it! Adrenalin must have snuck up on me. I slow back to the speed limit. I don't want to attract any attention.

'Ding dong bell, Pussy's in the well...' I start to sing the nursery rhyme. 'Why'd you put Pussy in the well, Jago?'

'I don't understand what you mean. I ain't never put no cat nowhere.'

'I'd argue you did!'

'I never!'

'Did.'

'Did not!'

'You did, Jago. I was there. I witnessed it first hand.'

'Why do you speak so odd? I don't know what you're talking about. What cat did I assposedly put in the well?'

'Me!' I shout, raising my eyebrows. Then, taking both hands off the steering wheel, I thump my chest three or four times. 'Fucking me, Jago. FUCKING ME! I was the fucking pussy!' I scream, my eyes bulging out of my face. I've never screamed at anyone or anything so aggressively in my life.

He bursts into tears. This forty eight year old, pasty, plump baby can hardly catch his breath. 'I really don't like this sir. Car makes me feel sick. Please stop.'

Calmy, I continue, 'It's about cruelty to animals. Helpless, innocent animals. Animals who cannot speak for themselves...'

'What is?'

'The nursery rhyme, Jago! It's about cruelty to animals. Little Johnny Flynn, or shall we call him Jago Hawkey, put Pussy, who for context we'll call *Me*, in the poxy well. Jago was a big bully! He tried to kill Pussy, he wanted to drown Pussy. Jago picked on the little pussy because the little pussy was too small to fight back. This little pussy couldn't say a word to defend himself...'

Sweat soaking through his clothes, Jago sits bewildered, sobbing into his hands. He isn't getting any of this through his thick skull. I let out a primal scream from the very pit of my soul. He pushes himself as far back into his seat as he can.

'Well, little Johnny Flynn, that pussy is now a lion, and boy oh boy is he hungry...' I roar into his face, and we narrowly miss clipping a van coming in the other direction. I need to calm down if I'm to get this done without any fuckups.

We continue east along the A30, passing through Bodmin, and sticking to the old road and then increasingly narrow country lanes, we make our way across Bodmin Moor to the village of Temple. The weather out on the horizon is not dissimilar to the day Edern kidnapped me and dragged me out here to die. The darkest blue-black clouds roll and tumble across the plains. When the sun can break through, oblique rays illuminate rock faces, changing the stone from drab grey to bright silver. Jago is trembling and has succumbed to submissiveness. The primal screams have numbed and shocked him.

I pull up next to the rectory, Maria's old house. It's just as I remembered it. I wish so much she was still in there. She kept the most perfect home whilst I lived there with her. The hamlet was so peaceful, and life was pastoral and agreeable growing up here. I've come to terms with her loss, but returning has opened the wound, and it stings and is bittersweet. The modest church is not as pristine as I remembered it. The privet hedges need reshaping, and part of the stone wall next to the gate has crumbled away, allowing nettles to grow from the verge through to the graveyard. I expect the door will be open, I don't believe it's ever been locked in 600 years. The church was a true haven for all who passed by.

I tell Jago to stay where he is while I go to the boot and get out my bag of goodies. I check around for signs of life. Nobody is here. Looking down the lane, I see the red phone box is still there; it looks from afar as if it is now a defibrillator station. *Who for?* I ask myself. There is no one here anymore. I take the handcuffs and pistol out of the bag, walk around the side of the car and tap on Jago's window with the butt of the gun.

'Come on, Tubs, out you come.'

He's frozen in his seat. He pushes the lock button. 'I ain't comin' out. You're a dangerous man. I ain't comin' out.'

I put the PPK in my back pocket and pull out the car keys, which I wave at him. I press the unlock button, pull his door open, drag him out and push him to the ground. I take the handcuffs from the bag.

'Now you're making me angry,' I say as I roll him over and lock his hands together behind his back with the cuffs. He wheezes and starts coughing.

I get on top of him, my knees holding him down. He tries to wriggle free, but he is completely disabled without the use of his hands. I grab his jaw with both hands and jerk his head back, forcing his face to the sky.

Leaning in, I whisper, 'You really don't have a clue why this is happening, do you? Smell me, Jago – do I still "smell of dogs"?'

'I swear on my own life that I don't know what I done to you…I'm sorry I got cross when you was bein' nosy about the news cuttings in the pantry and wotnot…'

'Jago, you don't need to be sorry for that. I'm asking you to think back a long, long time ago and ask yourself what you did wrong…Did you hurt anyone? Anything?'

Little shit tries to bite at my hands, but I just grip his throat tighter. I could throttle him here and now. I'm tempted, but I plan to put him through the same hell that his father subjected me to. 'You don't have to tell me what you've done, but I'd recommend you ask for forgiveness when we kneel at the altar. Thirty three years ago, your father brought me here. He asked me to pray for my life. At that point, aged just eleven, I was wholly innocent. I had nothing to pray for. At that point in my life I'd never done anything wrong, to anybody. And do you know what? The gods spared my life that day. Let's hope they look down kindly on you.'

'Why'd Edern bring you here?'

'Oh, you know, just to murder me…Thing was though, Jago, your dad was a coward, just like you. A bully, a paedophile and a coward.' I slip my hand into my trouser pocket and bring out a small yet heavy, shiny golden egg. I hold it in front of Jago's face. 'Do you recognise this, Jago?' To be fair, it's not the original one, I think this one is brass.

He whines. I can feel his breathing quickening. 'No!'

'No? No what? No, you don't recognise it? Or no, you don't want this to be happening?' He continues to whimper. I get up and roll him onto his back. 'Open wide,' I tell him as I prise his mouth open and force feed him the golden egg. I hold his mouth shut and squeeze his wet, snorting nostrils together, forcing him to swallow it. 'There you go you greedy, selfish little piglet. Now we pray. Oink, oink.' I kick him in the ribs as he done to me so many times when I was young. 'Get up, Jago! Get the fuck up.'

He yelps and reluctantly rises, and I push him towards the chapel door. I try the handle, and with a heart warming and familiar wince of iron, the latch unlocks.

It's cool inside, and eerily dark. My memories of the place are of a building filled with nature and light and love. Maria and I would spend our spare hours making it the most inviting place on Earth; she would laugh that we'd created a piece of heaven down here on the edge of hell. Whoever looked after the chapel now was not blessed with the same love of life that Maria had had. Today, I find it austere and puritanical. I loathe it, yet there is a kind of poetry about it being Jago's turn to pray, that I'd bring him to such a solemn place. The signs don't look good.

I lead him to the altar and impel him to get on the floor. There are no prayer cushions on the pews anymore. The stone floor is cold, grey and unforgiving. 'So, here we are, Jago Hawkey. I'll now repeat your dad's words to me thirty-three years ago: *Now is the time to make your apologies to the Lord. If you ever think'd you done a bad thing, or told a lie, then you says sorry now and the gods give you a safe passage to the next place.'* I deliver this in my dreadful Cornish accent. 'I should add, Jago, that at that point in time, I was convinced I was going to die. I believe Edern was too. Thankfully, I did make my prayers, and perhaps miraculously, I survived. Now it's your turn to bow your head and beg forgiveness...'

He looks to me for assurance. I nod, and he lowers his head.

'Dear Lord, I asks that I stays alive, and so do my mother and father, and Brutus. We never done nuffin' wrong to nobody,' he sobs.

I roll my eyes at this compulsive liar and begin to address the altar myself. I never completely believed in Maria's faith, but I do understand the cathartic release of owning my wrongdoing. If I can be at peace with my own sense of justice, then I can easily split myself mentally from my revenge and file it away with all my other ugly thoughts and deepest secrets. The truth is – or rather, my truth is – I feel no remorse for murdering Wenna and Edern. In this moment I'm completely ambivalent about it. As far as I'm concerned, they're gone, a risk to nobody anymore, and I'm freer than I ever remember being. Therefore, I reason, finishing off this bumbling idiot is just the icing on that giant slab of malt loaf. No harm in shitting him up a bit then...

'Dear Lord,' I begin. 'I know you will forgive me for what I plan to do to this man beside me. I believe you'll understand I must take vengeance on him for the suffering he caused me as a boy.' Sure, I'm camping it up for the show...'It pains me, dear Lord, that you have asked me to sacrifice this portly little lamb for my peace. Why, oh Divine One, do you want his still-beating heart?'

Jago gasps and tries to get to his feet. I pull him straight back down, smashing his knees on the floor. I am having fun with this one. Careful to hold Jago's gaze, I continue. 'Forgive me for slaying that demon Edern Hawkey...'

Jago cries out, struggling to get away. I have a firm hold of his handcuffed wrists, but he is thrashing about like a wounded shark. 'Don't lie!' he screams. 'You ain't killed Edern. You ain't! I don't believe it.' He is now crimson in the face and begins to try to throw me around, like a dog that won't release a rope. He's a very strong man, but I have him incapacitated. From side to side, he pulls.

'Forgive me, Father,' I finish as I slap him repeatedly around his repellent, stout head. This brings him out of his stupor and he begins to calm down. I lead him to the door, and we walk out into the impending storm, towards the car. I need him to comply, he's a real handful, and now he knows Edern's dead, he's like a thing possessed.

'I need you to do what I say, Jago. If you won't listen to me and do as I ask, then I have no choice but to murder your mother.'

'Leave her alone. Please, mister. Why do you want to hurt us Hawkeys?'

He is so dim. 'The golden egg, Jago, the egg didn't remind you of anything? It doesn't remind you of the time that you robbed me of that golden egg? The same time you savagely attacked me. ME. I'm the UGLY LITTLE BLACK TOAD!' I slap both of my hands on my chest. 'Kronegyn hager du!'

He rubs his stomach, which must be complaining about the brass egg I'd just force fed him with. 'I don't believe you! He's, he's dead. He can't talk. You ain't the Toad.'

Save me, Maria! He must be the thickest person in the entire country.

I take my canvas shoulder bag and the shovel from the boot of the car. I thrust the spade into his chest.

'You're carrying this.'

I snatch his handcuffed hands and grip them around the handle, and with a big old hammy wink and an insane smile, I proclaim, 'C'mon, Johnny, we're going to dig a well.'

Chapter 20

Dessert

May 2024

I know Bodmin Moor as well as anyone, after all, I'd spent my childhood there.

After we'd left the Jamaica Inn, back in 1991 on the day Edern Hawkey had intended to murder me, the Reverend Sherrington had, at my request, taken me all the way to East Sussex. You'll recall that after deciding not to kill me, Edern had tossed me an Ordnance Survey map of a town called Bourne. He'd written a woman's name on the map and circled an address. I'd shown this to Maria, and she'd decided she'd take me there. As a child, I wouldn't speak. Communication was made through visual clues, actions and sometimes drawings. Maybe the nod of a head, a thumbs-up or down, smiles and tears.

Anyhow, to cut a long and not particularly interesting story short, we'd arrived at the location maybe eight hours later, exhausted and starving. Maria parked her Peugeot on the High Street next to an enormous Catholic church. I remember this because she mumbled some choice curse words about the Catholics having so much money. I thought this most ungodly. That memory always makes me happy. She took me to the church door and showed me inside. It was vast, with the highest ceilings and most ornate glass. Not like the tiny chapel in Temple.

Next door to the church was our destination, a pub called the First In Last Out. I recall thinking the name was scary. I guess every minute of those few days was harrowing for the eleven-year-old me. The pub was cosy, there was a fireplace in the middle of the bar which glowered and hissed. Men chattered and argued and laughed and scoffed. Women whispered and cackled. The sound was, I remember, quite intense and abrasive. But I liked the smell; the bitterness of beer, the sweetness of cheap perfume and the toasted smell of cigarettes. It was wonderful.

Maria didn't appear to like it. She spoke to a petite bar lady and a barbarian of a beardy landlord. 'I'm looking for someone. I wonder if you could help me, please.'

The barman, noticing Maria's clerical collar, was immediately compelled to assist. 'And who might that be, Vicar?'

'I...' She put her arm around me and pulled me into her waist. 'We - are looking for a lady by the name of Mc-Cormick. I believe her Christian name is Margaret.'

'Margaret?' He rubbed the top of his lip and the bottom of his nose simultaneously, in thought. ' Margaret Mc-Cormick...hmm?' He looked at the little lady beside him for answers, but she stuck out her lower lip and shook her head. Then the penny dropped, and his face lit up. 'Ah! Haha! You mean Maggie Rocket!' He roared with laughter before bellowing her name across the crowded room whilst pointing at an inebriated lady bent double in the corner of the pub. The merry men of the establishment were apparently unable to keep their hands away from her body, and it was Maria's opinion that this 'Maggie Rocket' was in no fit shape to meet the boy. Not now, not ever!

'That harridan is Margaret McCormick? Well, we must be mistaken, sir. I apologise for wasting your time and bid you all a good evening. Goodbye.'

Without a second thought, the vicar turned me around and marched me out through the wooden front door.

'We're getting fish and chips and heading straight back to Cornwall. Tonight.'

And that was that. She drove me back to Temple and moved me into the rectory. For good. It was Maria and my amazing therapist who encouraged and patiently taught me to speak again. Maria also informed me, when I was old enough, that the drunken lady in the pub was my aunt. But these are stories for another time. Point being, I grew up on this land and know it very well indeed. So, for now, I'll take you back to the edge of Bodmin Moor and my hike with Jago Hawkey...

The drizzle soaks through my shirt and trousers as we march across the moor. I know there's never anyone around these parts after schooltime on a weekday, particularly if it's going to storm. It's just me, Jago and the larks. Jago is struggling to keep hold of the shovel. He has no free hands to move the drenched hair from his hot and sticky face. I sense this is irritating him, as he keeps trying to flick it out of his eyes with sharp jolts of his head.

'Come on, Chunk,' I call back to him. He must have dropped back twenty metres. I don't want him doing a runner, so I stop and wait.

'Where we goin'?' he moans.

'A magical place,' I reply.

'Why?'

'To dig a well, Jago. I told you this an hour ago at the church.'

'I don't wanna dig nuffin'!'

'Well, you're gonna dig sumfin'...' I mimic him and his Cornish drawl.

'Where is it?'

'Out there...' I point to the horizon, where the mauve sky bleeds into the heather and granite.

We continue trudging across the squidgy ground, and as we walk, I run through my usual reality checks.

Should I do this? I mean, I'm pretty deep in here already. Will I get away with it? From previous experience, I know this can plague me for months. In this scenario I believe it all stacks up. Edern's body with accompanying suicide note will be found within hours. The police will, initially at least, suspect him of poisoning Wenna. The cake and box are still in the house. The only problem as far as I can see is Jago. He'll be a missing person's case. Well, from my experience no one really puts too much energy into those, unless the loved ones of the missing person kick up a fuss. Anyone who cared about him is dead anyway, so I envisage a lacklustre search at best. He's almost fifty, they'll conclude he just walked into the sea after discovering the deaths of his parents. Good, I doubt it'll catch up with me.

How do I feel about killing him though? I mean, shit, I feel sorry for him, I really do. The guy never really had a chance, did he? Picked on and mollycoddled by his mum and largely ignored by his father – though who knows what other evil deeds Edern inflicted on the little sod. From childhood he's been the primary subject of ridicule at school and around Trebrowagh. And even today at the garden centre, Jago has been a lifelong laughing stock. No positive experiences of love and relationships outside of his family. An awful existence really.

Maybe I should give him the opportunity to apologise for his part in my pain. After all, more often than not we ignore, or don't hear, those silent cries for help. But, you know what? Balls to them, ultimately, each member of that messed up family played their part in laying the foundations of this rather unhinged shadow side that's grown deep inside me. And if that slithery, tar-ish hate is ascending, then exoneration has probably gone into hiding. Jago had, by his own admission, chosen to treat me like shit. He'd led me to this lifetime of insecurity and personality disorders. This is his stuff, his fault. Arguably, while I'm at it I could and should blame him for my catalogue of failed relationships.

Nah, fuck it. I'll kill him.

I am also mindful of the time. I want to get this done, make it to Jamaica Inn before closing time and return to Anchor Cottage for a clean-up and to pack my bags. My little vacation is rapidly coming to an end.

I snatch the shovel from him and push him towards the mound in front of us. 'King Arthur's Hall!' I announce triumphantly, hands on hips. My exclamation appears to irritate a pair of ravens who've been devouring a small muntjac deer. This amuses the onlooking crows, who hop in beak first to seize the sinewy leftovers.

The lichen-encrusted blue-black stones stand ominously at the top of the ridge, like foot soldiers guarding their castle. I have looked upon this place many times over the years. I used to sit near the summit of Rough Tor and look over to the site, watching the birds of prey circle above the monoliths. But I've never once been back here since the gods spooked Edern and inadvertently saved my life. I look now to the heavens. I wish for my own dramatic explosion or biblical downpouring, you know, for dramatic effect. I like that kind of thing. Not today though, just heavy, rolling black clouds with their promise of rain hanging precariously close to our heads.

'Here we are, Jago. Breathe in the ghosts of the Round Table,' I say. The petrified sloth stares blankly back. I run to the lowest point in the enclosure. 'Here!' I propel the shovel blade first into the peaty soil. 'This is where we'll make our well. Come down here now and I'll remove the handcuffs.'

Jago stumbles down the slope towards me, he presents his hands, and the key clicks in the lock. I take the cuffs from him as he shakes his hands out and exercises his fingers.

'Right then, oddball, I suggest you start digging...' I present him with the spade. His first move is to swing it at my head. Of course it is! Fortunately, this had been pre-empted, and I catch the handle mid-flight. 'You naughty little runt!' I tut and push him away, pulling the fake gun from my pocket. Pointing it inches from his face, I pull back the safety catch with a satisfying clack and wave him into action. He gets the idea, and all credit to him, he digs an excessively big hole. True, I need to encourage him from time to time with a flashing of the pistol, or the threat of shooting his mother. But now, here it is. Our perfectly man-sized well.

I pat him over firmly on the shoulder. 'Good work, Jago. I knew I could rely on you to get the job done.' It's pretty deep.

He stands up to his waist in the hole. 'What we gonna do with it now?' he asks.

'Jago, Jago my man, did Wenna send you to Sunday school? Let me quote something from the Book of Proverbs *"Whoever digs a pit will fall into it, and a stone will come back on him who starts it rolling."* Understand? He shakes his bland head at me. 'You don't. Clearly. I'm going to bury you in it, dear friend!' I stroll casually towards him, and once again draw the pistol for encouragement. 'Put out your hands, please.'

He flares his nostrils, huffing nervously in short bursts through them, but does as he's told. I carefully put the handcuffs on him again, ensuring they're locked. His palms are sweating.

'What you want me to do, sir? Promise you ain't gonna shoot Wenna...'

'I promise I will not shoot Wenna. Now, Jago, I want you to get down on your knees, please.'

'I don't like it, Doctor. I don't want to...' he whimpers.

I pull a handkerchief from my trousers. 'Okay, Jago, here's how this works. I'm going to ask you to apologise for bullying me. I want you to say sorry for every time you pinched me, kicked me, for every name you called me. For trying to kill me, and for every rock you threw at me. Then I'll consider whether I'm going to kill you.'

The birds of prey cry in the sky, and within seconds there are four of them circling us below the cloud line.

'I never done nuffin' to you! I don't know who you are,' he cries back at me.

'Enough is enough! You know who I am. You know very well. You know what? I'd go as far as to say that you recognised me the moment I turned up at your house four weeks ago. You're not as stupid as you make out. You're a bully, Jago Hawkey, and in my experience, bullies appear to be dumb, but the truth is, you're extremely divisive and cunning. So, Jago, remembering that you don't want to be in this situation, for one last time, I'm going to ask you to apologise. For everything you did to me when I was young.'

I can see him thinking, plotting how to get out of this. He looks up at me, his expression turning gradually from one of defeat and terror into a broad smile, then a grimace and finally, the nastiest, cruellest smirk I have ever seen.

'FUCK OFF, TOAD!'

I can't take any more. I walk to the hole, jump in and punch him to the ground. I force the handkerchief into his mouth.

'Now *you* don't speak. You can't plead with me to stop. This is what you deserve.'

I smack him around the head with the butt of the pistol and he falls forwards onto his face. I climb out of the well and pick up the first large granite rock I see. Recalling every single pebble and rock he ever projected at me, I throw it at him with all my might. He lets out a deep and defeated grunt as it crushes his shoulder, knocking him back down.

I pick up another; this one is bigger. I pull it back behind my head and launch it at his. It connects with a sickening crack as the side of his skull smashes. He tries raising his cuffed hands to the wound but can't reach. He begins squirming and scratching around at the base of the well. The third rock hits him across the bridge of his nose, tearing open his left eye, and with a sigh he falls forward onto a rock, his teeth crack loudly as his head hits the stone. 'Sleep well Jago Hawkey.'

Stoned

to

death.

I sit at the edge of the well and dangle my legs over the ledge, looking at the bloodied, crumpled mess of a man below me. I throw up, there's no stopping it. It's as if my body is ejecting poison from within me. Feeling strangely purged, I sit there for twenty minutes. In floods of tears, I cry and cry. I cry out loud, I sob peacefully into my hands. I can't tell you if they are tears of sadness, remorse, joy or relief. Maybe all the above. But I take solace in knowing that this pussy has finally put little Johnny Flynn in the well.

All the Hawkeys are dead. I'd like to say I'm relieved. I'm not. The only thing I feel at that moment is remorse. It's all a fucking waste. ALL OF IT. I wish none of it had ever happened. I wish I'd never ventured onto their godawful farm all those years ago. I wish they'd been better people. But they took everything from me. They plundered my future for their own warped pleasures. Now they are gone, physically, but I fear their memory will not be as easy to remove.

After a while I clamber back down to the shallow grave. Diligently, I remove the handcuffs and lay him flat. I pour the lye mixture over his face and the wound on his shoulder. I don't need anything digging him up for dinner. I kick myself for not having thought out this disposal properly. However, once I've covered him and filled the torn earth with some moss and reeds, I feel confident that Jago Hawkey will now lie with Arthurian royalty for time immemorial. A court jester for our time. *The worms will get fat on you. Goodbye.*

The light is drawing in by the time I get back to St Catherine's church. The plethora of birds in the ancient yew tree are relentlessly calling everyone home to roost. Inspecting the broad trunk of the tree to find the scar of love my girlfriend and I carved into the bark a lifetime ago, I'm cheered to find it still there: *JG 4 GT*. That must be thirty years old. I wonder where she is now? I know she went to France after university, but that was the last anyone heard. It's doubtful she's the Facebook type, so I'll probably never know. Bet she's still the most beautiful girl in the world.

I put the canvas bag back in the hire car. Checking no one is around, I put the shovel next to the ones the gravedigger used to use, in the lean-to at the back of the chapel. Feeling the urge to speak with Maria, I take myself back into the little chapel. Sitting right at the back, near the door, I lean my head back against the stone wall and gaze at the rafters. I tell her what I've done, how I know she'd be furious and yet pleased for me. It is peacefully silent, until the busy scurrying's of two church mice interrupt my meditation. They peer up at me from under the pew in front, before scuttling back to their hole. After explaining everything to the spirit of my surrogate mother, it is time to proceed to the final act of revenge.

Outside the door, a rather chunky ginger tomcat sits looking at me, seeking permission to enter, perchance to eat. I quote Revelation 1:18: *'I am the Living One; I was dead, and now look, I am alive for ever and ever! And I hold the keys of death and Hades.'*

The cat circles my ankles and purrs. I duly oblige and let him in through the door to feast.

Chapter 21

Jamaica Inn
May 2024

When I was young, I'd have this recurring dream. In fact, there was something nightmarish about it. The dream was very childlike in its design, cartoonish if you like. I guess that the four year old brain does not have the complexity to create intricate landscapes. In this case a man, my father, was running across a rudimentary scene: green hills, round trees, et cetera. He was being pursued and shot at from above by giant, red, cursor-like arrows. I never saw one hit him. He always escaped, but the panic for me as the dreamer was palpable. He was my hero. No man should have taken him from me, yet *that* man had orchestrated my father's death, in his custody. That man would pay dearly for his crime.

I drive past the Jamaica Inn at just after nine forty five to check how busy it is. From my seat it is noticeable that the car park is empty but for one or two vehicles. Dusk is giving way to night, and I can see a few glimmering lights are on inside, but it is certainly not overly busy. I pull over in a layby five miles down the road to check the rope and to secret the pistol under my shirt. I wait a further thirty minutes to let the sunset become night and head back. The inn is so far out on the moor that there is extraordinarily little, if any, light pollution.

There is only one truck left by the time I return, a sort of pick-up truck, maybe a Hi-Lux, it's irrelevant. I park on the verge a hundred metres from the front of the pub, then pack the rope into my bag and cover my face as best as I can with the peak of a baseball cap pulled down low. I sneak around the periphery of the car park and surreptitiously place my bag just inside the open door to a seemingly disused garage. There isn't much noise coming from the pub, and it would be surprising if there are any patrons in there. The wind whips around the courtyard, sending the metal pub sign into a frenzy. The snap hooks and rope weights on the flagpole chime and clank as the gale and driving rain stream in from the moor. This is turning into a grim night indeed.

The heavy oak front door is protected from the downpour by a stone portico. At the entrance I remove my hat – a gentleman doesn't wear his hat indoors. I push the door and enter the vast bar-cum-dining room. It's not as big as I remember, but I was rather small back then and everything seemed enormous. There's one couple in a booth by the rear windows, pushing their dinner around half-emptied plates with forks. Otherwise, it is empty, but for the gigantic, hunched figure of the landlord standing at the helm, polishing a tiny glass with a crisp white tea towel.

'CLOSED!' he booms across the bar.

Undeterred, I smile and slowly make my way to the bar, where I put my car keys and soaked hat down on the cold brass counter. I size up this giant, leathery old man. His hands, although cruelly carved by arthritis and discoloured from the proliferation of liver spots, are huge, his forearms look like Popeye the Sailor man's, and his haunted pale grey eyes cut through the warm yellow light of the pub with a ghoulish glint.

'A pint of Tribute, please,' I say.

'I said, we're closed.' he replies, folding his sturdy arms.

'And I, quite politely, asked for a pint of beer. I'll repeat my request for you.' I smile and give him a thumbs-up. 'A pint of Tribute, please, landlord.' I raise my eyebrows sarcastically.

He puts the clean, empty glass down in front of me and stares through my soul. 'I don't suppose you heard me right, boy. We are closed. Now, I'd like you to leave. Please,' he says with a calm and menacing tone.

'Can't do that, Jacob. I'd just like a pint with you, please.'

He frowns and runs his tongue around the outside of his teeth and gums. 'Who are you? What's your name? What do you want at Jamaica Inn?'

'My name...' I pause and look around the empty building for dramatic effect, 'is Stuart Dowie...'

His eyes narrow and I can almost hear him thinking. 'I don't know you, Stu-art Dow-ie,' he sneers, overpronouncing the name.

'People know me as Scoob!' I flash my teeth and shrug.

He points at me in my seat, intimating that I should not move an inch. He then calmly lifts the bar hatch and hooks it open. He walks past me, menacing and deliberately close to my back. I don't turn around, even as he puts one of his massive, trowel-like hands gently upon my shoulder. He continues quietly over to the disinterested diners, crouches down at the end of their booth and speaks convivially with them. I cannot hear a word he says.

He returns slowly, the giant passes threateningly close behind me and then is back behind the bar. Reaching for two crystal cut rocks glasses, he breaks the silence only to bid farewell and thanks to the diners as they scurry out the door.

He puts the glasses to the dark rum optic and drains down two doubles. He puts one in front of me, careful to put down a beer mat first. He then moves to the front door with his glass in hand. He looks out of the window and, satisfied the customers have driven away, he draws the curtains and bolts the door shut. He takes a long slug of his rum as he approaches me, gazes lovingly at the now almost empty glass, and then proceeds to encourage me. 'Down the hatch.'

I'm not going to show him any weakness and knock the rum back in one go.

Jacob returns behind the bar, swipes my glass and refills the pair of them. He puts the rums on the bar and leans forward on his elbows. 'So...Scoob...I'm going to tell you a story. I picked up the keys to the inn here fifteen years ago, same day I retired from the police force.' He looks lovingly around the interior of his 'castle'. 'This place had always been in my dreams, ever since my old mother told me that we 'ad ancestors what used to own the inn. I've had a very peaceful relationship with my pub and my customers over that time. So...you might imagine my chagrin when some cocky little fella turns up as I'm closing up one night and starts goin' on about a distressing incident that may or may not have happened on my watch many years ago at Bodmin nick. Consider what that does to a proud old man. Well, I'll tell you, stranger, it makes my fucking blood boil!' He bears his yellow, crooked teeth. 'I've just had to let that lovely couple have their dinner on the house. They will never return, for fear this is a den of iniquity.'

He looks over his shoulder behind him, and then to the ceiling. 'I'll continue. I will now be late to bed, and Mrs Merlyn, God bless her, will berate me for opening beyond my licence. Maybe she will expect I have been chatting with the village harlot. It is certain that your visit will bring out the shrew in her, and no love will be shown to me tonight.' He takes a sip of his drink. 'With all that in mind, I'm hoping that you will now offer me a very reasonable explanation for your presence, before I take it upon myself to knock you from here to high heaven! You can start with telling me why in God's own name you're here, and secondly, who the hell you think you are?' He straightens himself upright and downs his rum. Again.

For a man in his mid-seventies, he's a formidable figure. But the reality is that I'm very much the younger, faster and fitter of the two of us. He is an ogre, it's true, but his schtick doesn't really bother me. I've done my homework, I know what to expect of Jacob Merlyn.

Picking up my glass, I swirl the caramel liquid around the bottom of the tumbler. I inhale the rum, it smells divine. Mmm, I'm getting rich notes of toffee, honey and vanilla, and on tasting it I'm then hit by oak and cinnamon. It's a very classy rum.

'Nice. Pusser's Rum. May I congratulate you on your choice of tipple.' I wriggle into the stool, to get comfortable, which is almost impossible on these wretched wooden things. 'Now then, allow me the honour of telling you a story, Mr Merlyn. Once upon a time, it was the first of April 1991. No joke, I sat here in this very pub. In a booth just over at the back there.' I point to the rear of the pub; the booths have gone, but two dining tables are still there. 'Picture the scene. Two drunk, haggard and dishonest men sat behind me discussing their foul play. In secret, or so they thought, Mr Merlyn...' It's my turn to put the fear into him. I slam my empty tumbler onto the counter. '*You* may remember a busload of tourists came in. Do you remember that, Jacob?'

Pushing his bottom lip out, he shakes his head.

'Well, let me help jump start that memory. You, Jacob Merlyn, were discussing ways in which you could help your friend, or acquaintance, Edern Hawkey get away with kidnap, rape and murder. Remember that day? Anything come to mind, Mr Merlyn? Kidnap! Rape! Murder?!'

'Curse you! Who told you these lies?' he growls and curls his lip. 'How dare you bring your devilry into Jamaica Inn!' His eyes bulge as he puffs his chest out.

'How about Scoob, Jacob? Remember him? Did he have his "little accident" down at Bodmin nick? Was Stuart Dowie the scapegoat for Edern Hawkey? Let me enlighten you as to who Stuart Dowie was...He was my dad! You killed my hero! You fucking murdered my father...You want to know who I am, old man? I'll tell you who I am. I am the angel of death, and this, you bent old bastard, is an amazingly simple transaction. You robbed me of a normal, happy life and in exchange, I figure, it's quite reasonable that I'm owed yours.'

Jacob seems more suspicious than afraid. 'How do you know about these things? It ain't natural.'

'I was behind you, you arsehole. I just told you. I listened to every word of your conversation with Edern Hawkey. Then I sat and watched you get up and leave.'

'The boy with the vicar lady...' The penny drops. He growls at my apparent insolence. He takes a bottle of rum from the back of the bar, undoes the lid and pours himself a large glass of neat rum. 'But I don't understand who you think you are? You say you're Scoob's son. But I can tell you Scoob didn't 'ave no kids. Scoob lived in a hippy commune with a bunch of useless, workshy druggies. He had a girlfriend, some redheaded girl. She 'ad a son. He couldn't speak. But no, I didn't get rid of him. You ask me it's Edern Hawkey you should be talkin' to.'

'Already did that, Jacob. I killed him, last night. He's at the bottom of a china clay pit now, probably a burnt-out husk. Don't worry about Edern.' He frowns, slowly rotating his bottom jaw.

'Stuart Dowie was my dad, I can tell you that. The boy who couldn't speak...well, he's sitting at your bar.' I give him a cheap wink. 'As for you, PC Persil, you killed my dad and now I'm gonna kill you. Justice?' I weigh up the air with my hands before reaching under my shirt and withdrawing the pistol.

For a split second Jacob looks fearful, but the longer he has to inspect the gun, the more amused he becomes, it starts with a cracked smile, then a couple of huffing chuckles which cause his head to nod, finally he roars with laughter.

'Oh, you silly little man. If anyone knows a fake gun, it's me. You stupid little prick.' He throws his boulder-like head back in disbelief, and, reaching under the counter, he produces a stumpy-looking sawn-off shotgun. Cocks it open, checks there is a cartridge in each bore. Closes it with a snap and sticks the end millimetres from my forehead.

'Oh dear, oh dear.' He roars, 'Do you think you can come up to my pub in the middle of the night, threaten me with a toy gun, tell me I'm a bent copper and expect to walk away? Fuck me. You're unwell. I mean, you must have lost your fucking mind. Do you want me to call a doctor or the police first? You total fucking spastic!'

He prods me hard in the head with the barrel of the gun. It smarts. He is clearly enjoying himself. I'm not. *Oh shit! Shit, shit, shit.* I don't know what to do. I'm fucked. I look him in the eye, stony faced. It's fight or flight.

Then he really turns my world upside down.

'Sure, your mother was a proper piece of work. Coral, weren't it? That 'er name? She always 'ad it in for me. She used to call me the Devil in uniform. That's coz she knew I knew...Do you follow?' He leans in towards me, licking the rum off his lips.

'Not sure I do,' I reply. I'm looking for a way to get that gun out of my face. I'm really stuck here. God, his breath stinks.

'You were born in Somerset weren't you? All communes and bongo drums. Well, your mother got knocked up by one of them hippies. A real piece of work he was!' His grin widens, his teeth are as yellow as the old map parchment on the pub walls.

'Well, my lad, if you really are the Trebrowagh urchin, your soap-dodging mother had you way before she shacked up with Scoob. You really wanna know who your daddy is? He reads my eyes, and whispers as if he's telling a foul joke.

'Go on, think. Who owed your old mum money? Who were always desperate to shut her up? Always hangin' around Biddle's farm, getting too close to the kids?' He taps the side of his head. He's loving this.

Now, if what you're telling me is true about killing Edern Hawkey, I'm afraid to tell you...' He pauses and sips his rum and smirks. 'You just murdered your father. Haha, You just done away with Edern bloody Hawkey...Bit of a family reunion eh?' He shouts over his shoulder. 'ANNIE!' And with that he swipes the side of my head with the barrel of his gun.

I make a grab for the edge of the bar, it's too late, I can't see straight. I must have passed out, because the next thing I know I find myself being dragged by my feet across the cold hard flagstone floor to the door. The gigantic old man is engaging every muscle in his body to pull me out of his pub. He doesn't have the gun. I look back to the bar. Yes! It's still on the counter. The odds shift slightly back to me.

Then it dawns on me. Did I just hear that correctly? Edern Hawkey was my dad? I just killed my own father and didn't realise it. I feel so sick. Why would he have treated me as he did? Did he know I was his son? He must have. Was I *the other little thing*? That explains the extortion money.

My neck freezes and I can feel the blood running hot through my hands. Okay, I tell myself, now is not the time to process the news about Edern. I have to survive. I need to get rid of Jacob. He knows too much now and will certainly have me arrested. Or worse.

◆

Have you ever thought that you were being looked after? Celestially, I mean, beyond existential boundaries. The idea that there is a design for your life. You know, the whole guardian angel thing? I know most of us, myself included, feel like we're being shadowed by a relentless black cloud half the time. But every so often, as happened when Edern changed his mind about killing me after the skies opened, something happens, something that can only be described as divine intervention. And when that happens, you have to accept that yes, there is a plan for you, and this isn't it...

❖

At the back of the bar is a door, the sign on which reads *Private – No Public Access*. Well, it so happens that right at that moment, that very door opens with such violent force that the shotgun falls to the floor and the cocked trigger fires as it hits the ground, and the cartridge sends pellets flying everywhere in the building, except into me.

Jacob cries out in pain, lets go of me and drops to the floor clutching his knee. I wriggle free and quickly roll away from him. In the open doorway behind the counter stands a tiny, grey, ghoulish figure. A small woman of about eighty, dressed only in an ivory-coloured old-fashioned nightdress, screams across the room like a cockney fishwife.

'OH, MY GAWD! What in 'eaven's name is goin' on 'ere?! Jacob Merlyn! You've been shot! You better have good reason for gettin' me out of bed – else I'll be filing for divorce at first light, you mark my words man.'

Jacob is writhing around in the doorway yelping in agony. Now is my chance. I dive across the room, duck below the counter and retrieve the gun. I pull back the trigger and raise my head above the parapet. I point the barrels straight at the old hag.

'WHO the FUCK are YOU?' she barks.

She has a face like a baby drinking vinegar and scrawny little talon-like fingers. She's like the evil Mary Berry. She puts her hands on her hips and starts tapping her foot as she waits impatiently for my answer. I have never in all my life seen such an angry little human. I look back at the door. Jacob is in a right mess, he isn't going anywhere. I turn to face the old crow and pull the trigger. The power of the shotgun tears a hole straight through her chest, blowing her off the floor, back through the door and up the first three or four steps. Wow! I didn't expect that, she pretty much just exploded before my eyes.

Jacob desperately tries to get up but can't get any grip as he slips around in his own blood on the wet stone floor. I'm well aware he will rip me limb from limb if he can lay his hands on me. He roars and he wails, yet, thankfully, he cannot move. I step over him and make my way to the garage, where my bag and the rope are. I leave the bar door open so I can keep half an eye on the bastard. Hastily, I tie a noose. I need a good place to hang it. Aha. Poetic. I spy an old, half covered Rover 3500 SDI panda car, it must be his. After tying one end of the rope around the front axle of the car, I sling the noose over a rafter in the barn ceiling of the garage and go to collect Jacob. I sidestep him as he makes a swipe for my leg.

Behind the bar, fresh pieces of Mrs Merlyn are scattered everywhere. It's quite shocking how powerful that gun is. Whilst I rummage for more ammunition, I pour two more Pusser's rums and put them on the countertop. I check under the bar, from where Jacob produced the shotgun. Bingo! Not only is there a box of virgin ammunition but also a basic video CCTV recorder. I take two new cartridges and load the weapon. Then I eject the VHS tape from the unit and put it with the drinks. I take a long sip from my glass. Damn, it tastes good, and it's a tonic for the nerves. *Good rum.* I head back to the doorway to take Jacob his glass. He falls into silence as I approach, almost grateful for the drink. Sadly, and agonisingly for him, I pour it over his shredded knee. He screams in horror. I pick up the video tape and the gun and usher Jacob out of the door towards the outbuilding. He howls in pain as he slithers across the wet car park, the gravel agitating his wounds. He hasn't any real alternative as he has the loaded shotgun inches from the back of his skull.

In the garage and in complete shock from having seen his wife blown away, his bawling gives way to silence. He doesn't speak, and, curiously, accepts the noose as I tighten it around his broad throat.

'Stand up,' I instruct, gesturing for him to move.

He lifts himself up, grimacing as he avoids putting any weight on the shattered knee. Then, with a straight face, in an apparent act of salvation, he turns to me and in the calmest of voices he proceeds to help me get away with it.

'Be sure to clean your fingerprints off that shooter when you're done. You'll find some rubber gloves on the workbench at the back there. Put a pair on, then try and get my dirty fingerprints on the barrel and the trigger and leave it by Mrs Merlyn. Police will be certain I got pissed and done me old lady in. They know we have a "lively" relationship. They'll expect I hanged myself in shame. I'm sorry about Edern. It pains me what that man done to you. In all my years in the law, I never had the misfortune to meet a more repellent man than Edern Hawkey and believe me when I tell you I've met my fair share arseholes over those years. I hope you find your peace, young man. I'm sorry about all of it.'

He bows his head and never once looks at me again. I can't help but find his resignation most bizarre. I can only surmise that a proud man like Jacob Merlyn recognises and accepts when his time has come.

I reach into the panda car and release the handbrake. A solid push with my boot, and it slowly rolls backwards just enough to pull the noose tight. Jacob's joints crack and creak as he's raised into the air by his neck. His huge body struggles for an eon before letting go.

As he advised, I prudently clean the weapon using a rag I picked up off the bonnet of the car and plant as many fingerprints from the hanged man on the weapon as I can. I reach for my bag, put the VHS tape inside and return the gun to the bar. I finish my rum, clean the tumbler of any prints, bid goodbye to the various parts of the vile Mrs Merlyn and, as silently as I arrived, I leave the Jamaica Inn.

Driving back to St Kres across the unforgiving moor, I find myself struggling to contain a sense of grief at discovering Edern was my biological father. Oh fuck! Jago was my own flesh and blood. Jesus! What a mess. I knew I should have understood the naivety in Jago. This is too much. There are so many questions. I should have realised. It was all there to see. It explains why Coral felt that Edern owed her. And bloody hell, I feel absolutely dreadful about Mrs Merlyn. God, do they have family? She's the first person I've killed whom I hadn't planned on hurting. I've botched this right up. Damn! Thankfully, she's given me a watertight alibi in Jacob. For a moment back there, I thought I was going to be the dead man. Merlyn could have blown my brains out if he wanted to. I'm pleased he's gone though. There must be a special place in hell for bent coppers, and if there is, Sergeant Jacob Merlyn will surely dine at the top table.

But the Edern business...That disgusting man, even in death he continues to haunt me. They are all dead though. And through revenge, I am free. I have been heard.

I drive vigilantly back to the cottage, avoiding attracting any interest, and am careful to park a hundred yards away from the pub car park. I cover up the bag, lock the car and go silently into the cosy little house. I'm exhausted. Completely spent. My heart aches. I fall asleep in front of the television watching an *Inbetweeners* repeat, the one where they go to Jay's dad's caravan in Camber Sands.

Chapter 22

Farewell Cornwall, my friend
May 2024

After an idiot check of the room, I'm confident I've left no trace of myself, nor any incriminating evidence related to either the Hawkeys or the Merlyns.

Apart from the obvious, I've enjoyed my stay here. If the opportunity ever presented itself, I'd return, if for nothing else than the chips at the Blue Rose. I've hung out the washed linen and tidied the kitchen. Having taken a refreshing shower and dressed in neatly pressed navy cotton shorts and a cream polo shirt, I push my sunglasses onto my forehead and leave the building. With my bags packed and the clock agreeing it's ten thirty a.m., I stroll over to the pub to check out.

The sun is beating down again this morning. A sharp contrast to last night. Always the same down here, so very changeable. It's the topography of Bodmin Moor which upsets the meteorological apple cart. But I am pleased to have a clear drive home. With it being a Thursday morning, I should have a decent run. I'll hit Bristol just after lunch and the M4 should be straightforward until the South Circular.

In the car park an unkindness of ravens has convened to observe my departure. They know everything, they always have and always will. A word of advice: if you want the universe's support, look after the ravens. The pub is dark inside, the sun yet to reach the little leaded windows. Nobody is in the bar, but I can hear female voices nattering in the kitchen...

'Dad says Edern poisoned Wenna an' topped 'imself. Police found a suicide note an' wotnot.'

'I heard the son done it.'

'Fuck knows. He's a weirdo an' that. But they dead now, just like the two up over Bodmin way...Dark...'

I give a customary cough to attract attention. Donna comes out hugging a hot mug of tea.

'Oh, morning, sir. You checkin' out? Sorry about us; we just had some murky news this morning. That car they found down the pit was that Edern 'Awkey. Suicide, they say. And he murdered 'is wife. I always knew they was wronguns. No one seen their boy, mind, so...' She shrugs in the fashion I've become accustomed to around here. 'Sorry, forgot my manners. How was your stay, sir? S'nice little cottage, no?'

'It was most rewarding. In fact, I think I'll return next year, if that's okay with you?'

'Course it is. We like good people like yourself in these parts. Now then, that's gonna be, let's see...two hundred and fifty pounds for the room, thirty-five pounds for cleanin', and then you 'as, hmm...' She tots up the bar receipts on a small Casio calculator. 'You 'as one hundred and seventy-seven pounds ninety-five for food and drink...so...that is...'

'Make it four hundred and fifty pounds and have a drink on me. And make sure you get one for Pop, will you?' I slide the cash across the bar. Donna counts it and nods. I hand her the key on its clunky wooden keyring, and we say our goodbyes.

'Oh, can I grab a couple of bags of the biltong, please.'

'Sure. Six quid, please, sir.'

'Thanks, Donna,' I call as I leave the building. I open the biltong and scatter it across the car park as a little hush money for my raven friends. They caw and croak their appreciation. You never know, one of them could be King Arthur, he was reincarnated as one. Apparently. One of them hops onto the bonnet as I start the engine. It looks into my eyes, then takes off over the roof of the pub.

There is something about Cornwall, something that gets into your heart and never truly leaves. It makes driving away difficult. I always feel like it doesn't want me to take my secrets with me. Well this time I've left her a little something extra.

Just outside of Bodmin, a roadside sign for 'fresh cut flowers' catches my attention, and I pull into the layby. A middle aged lady and a young boy are laughing away with each other as they arrange heads of campion amongst pretty pink dog roses. They seem surprised to hear my car coming to a halt, and they dart behind their pretty red and white wooden flower cart and stand to attention. They both have huge grins across their faces, which in turn makes me feel warm inside.

'Good morning, sir.' The lady glows, presenting her flowers as if they were fine jewels at an ancient souk.

'Morning,' I reply, inhaling the intoxicating perfume emanating from their colourful little stall. 'You have some beautiful flowers here. Absolutely stunning.' I look at the boy and ask him how much. He doesn't say anything.

'I'd like a large bunch of the roses, and yes, add a few sprigs of the campion. They were Mum's favourite.'

The boy proceeds to lay the stems on a large sheet of brown paper, whilst the lady cuts some green ribbon.

'Lovely. So how much will they be, please?' I ask the boy again.

'Tommy don't speak, sir. He just makes beautiful things.' The lady forces a cracked smile past her apologetic eyes.

I take my wallet out of my trouser pocket; I have forty pounds left in there. I put it down on the cart in front of the boy.

'Your flower arrangement is the prettiest I've ever seen. I hope this covers it...I hear you loud and clear, my friend.' I wink knowingly at him.

He bows his head and scrunches up his nose like one of Fagin's' minions. I take the bunch and continue my journey. Looking in the rear view mirror, I watch the two dancing in circles together as they disappear from my sight. *Who will buy my beautiful roses...*I can't help but hum it.

Not even five miles further on, I take the familiar turning off the A30, rumble over the cattle grid and onto Bodmin Moor. The moorland cows and ponies begrudgingly move off the road and I trundle down the narrow lane to Temple. I half expect St Catherine's to be crawling with police, but the hamlet is as peaceful as it ever was. I park by the phone box and take the flowers from the back seat. There's a car on the drive at the rectory. I'd love to know who lives there now. I wonder who has my old room. I close my eyes and can hear the doves cooing. Keeping them shut, I can make out other familiar sounds; the distant rumble of a tractor, the hum of the A30, a woodpecker...and, softly on the wind, I hear her voice. Her beautiful voice.

'Come in, darling, your dinner is ready. Come now, or it'll get cold...'

She 'steps on my grave.' I shudder as the ice cold spirit passes through me, and the hairs on my arms stand up in the breeze. She was the kindest, funniest and best person in the world. I know she is watching out for me. I wish I could go in and sit at the kitchen table. What would we have? Well, it's almost eleven, so that means croissants and coffee. Actually, it was always hot chocolate for me, until I was nearly fourteen, when she put out two coffee cups one morning and I spoke to her for the first time: 'Thank you, Mum.'

An unfamiliar ashen face appears in the lounge window and breaks my daydream. Careful not to make any eye contact, I wave and turn down the hill to the church. It is necessary to clear some old flowers away from the gravestone and fill the rose bowl with fresh water. I put Tommy's arrangement of flowers into the vase, kiss my hand and touch the headstone. She would have loved them. She adored campion, especially the way it smelt so much stronger in the evening to attract moths.

'I'm sorry Mum. I miss you, Mum. You'll hopefully be pleased that I'm finally as free as you are now. I promise I'll be back soon. Love you.'

❖

It's almost five by the time I get back to the city. I need to return the car to Danny at the arches rental place in Sydenham before he closes for the day. He appears from his little hut, grinning from ear to ear, with a can of Sprite in one hand and the other in the pocket of his navy-blue quilted gilet. He swaggers as if he was in the band Oasis.

'Been to see ya daughter up Warwick again, mate?' he asks. His Estuary twang pricks my ears, it's so whiny in comparison to the hearty and warm West Country accent I've become accustomed to again.

'Yes, Danny. Lovely time, thank you. Car ran great. Smells a bit funny though...bit like a Snickers bar...'

'Oh, that! Yeah, one of the kids dropped a jar of peanut butter in the back. Can't get rid of it.'

'Oh, I'm really sorry Danny, I had a bit of an accident. There's a smudge of blue paint on the front bumper.'

'Oh don't worry 'bout that mate, it'll buff out. What ya do?'

'Killed a Smurf.' Danny squints at me in disbelief.

I take my bags and transfer them to my classic old alpine-white BMW, which is at the back of the car park.

'Cwoar, lovely motor that,' says Danny, rubbing his thighs.

'See you next time,' I call through the window as I head home, accompanied by a heady soundtrack of John Coltrane and that straight-six engine.

Next morning, I swing the Beemer into the parking space reserved for 'Dr Greene' in the car park at the rear of my clinic. I grab the miserable Pret tuna mayo sandwich I'd swiped on the way and feel a sense of warmth as I approach the familiar green gloss door. Unable not to give the brass plaque a little sheen with my cuff, I smile at being safe again.

Entering the familiar clinic, my receptionist, and life support machine, Helene peers over her scotch bonnet red, super-trendy, handmade cat's-eye specs.

'Nice holiday, sir?' She arches an eyebrow and pouts.

I shiver, I can't shift the image of my half brother's face as he fell forward in that pit. 'Most satisfactory,' I reply, placing an 'I love Penzance' biro on her desk.

'Good, well, your first client is due in at ten, sir. I've put his file on your desk. He's the kid with the night traumas and the messing...Glad you're back, Jack.'

Afterword

We are, I think guilty as a global collective of not listening to the silence of our natural world. We think we can bury our crimes, but the Earth, like our memory does not forget those wrongs.

Now the dust has settled, and order has been restored, I ask you to close your eyes and picture thousands of acres of tropical rainforest being bulldozed in front of you, watch as the towers of tangerine and umber smoke billow into the sky. I want you to hear the endless orchestra of chainsaws, I apologise if the cries and screams of millions of displaced and tortured animals cannot be heard, they seldom can be. They are easy to ignore. But look closer, they could so easily be our own children and families. As the Orangutang in Borneo cannot protest at her home being razed to the ground to make way for palm oil plantations, neither would the antagonists of this story listen to the Toad's silent narrative. Without his voice, he was useless, disposable. Used and discarded for their own gains. Tragically they failed to notice, he was the same as them.

Look West to California. Picture the desperate faces of interviewees sobbing into the cameras in the aftermath of the January 2025 Los Angeles wildfires. These are faces we recognise – our own. Faces, collectively as guilty and complicit in the burning down of their own homes, as much as any vengeance nature could unleash.

Sir Isaac Newton simplified his Third law of motion: 'For every action there is a reaction'. And so it is with the environment. That it doesn't have voice or agency does not mean it should not be listened to. Ignore her mute signals at your peril. She will bite back.

Just as the ugly little black toad did.

The Jack in the Greene
Part Two

Left with more questions than you started with? Well friends, my contract with you is to provide those answers and more. Over the course of two further instalments, we will follow Doctor Jack Greene and his biological mother Coral McCormick as they escape the idyllic and verdant Dordogne for a new life in East Sussex. Why does Jack find himself gagged, bound and fingerless in an abandoned caravan on a cliff overlooking Loch Fyne in Argyll & Bute? Does every road lead back to Bodmin? What of Maria? Here, for a taste of the ensuing trials and tribulations of your new favourite sociopathic psychologist, is the first chapter of The Jack in the Greene; a study of three religions, of finding his voice, and of learning the art of murder...(Due 2026).

Beltane

Wednesday 1st May 2013

Though it was still dark, the sun would begin to rise soon. One could hear the distant soft rhythmic thumping of bodhrans and other skin drums floating across the Bourne valley. Listening carefully you could piece together the muted rummaging's, coughs and murmurs and conclude that a handful of residents of the narrow streets of the sleepy fishing village below the hill were beginning to wake. Doors quietly creaked opened and clicked closed, the occasional jingle of flat sounding bells tiptoed along narrow and twisting snickets.

A giant as tall as the bedroom windows of the timber framed cottages was aided through the High Street, and up to the castle in silence by four men. Their faces painted with soot, one of them wore an archaic headdress; a complete stag's skull with antlers and hide still intact. This was worn as representation of the 'Horned God'; consort of the Triple Goddess – He is the God of nature, wilderness, sexuality and hunting, one of the two primary deities of Neopaganism.

A party goer from the night before staggered and tacked his way home. He drunkenly attempted to kick a discarded drink can across the road. The rattle attracted the attention of a seagull, who immediately began to laugh. Within minutes every gull in the vicinity had joined in with the mirthful chatter, the shrill squawking would not dampen until lunchtime.

Over the channel to the east, the edges of large cumulus clouds were becoming visible, outlined with fuchsia and peach as the sun began its slovenly rise. As the minutes ticked by, more and more shadowy figures convened at the Maiden's Parlour to 'Dance in the Dawn' and celebrate the arrival of summer. A large circle of worshippers interlinked hands around the edge of the green, and they began to gently sway as they sang:

'Feathered winds come dance with me
Lift me from the ground.
Join my waltz, my spirit, freed
As we're upward bound.
Tongues of flame come jump with me
Ye purifying fires,
Join my joy, my playful glee
As we move yet higher.
Tears from seas, come sing with me

Roll from out the caves,
Join my verse, my body cleansed
In your healing waves.
Mother Earth come laugh with me
Set aside your toils
Join my chant of forests green
Secure me in rich soil.
Earth and Air, Fire and Sea
I call you all, come dance with me!
Grant me now a sacred space
While working magik in this place.

※

The chain of hands was broken by the Horned God, and the Giant then ushered into the circle. He was followed by 'Jack O' the Green – A huge, verdant cavorting woodland sprite, decorated in flowers, ribbons and greenery. He darted around the inner circle colliding with the revellers like a whirling dervish, smearing their faces with green paint from his fingertips as he went. Finally, Hannah the Witch was granted entry, and the Morris troops would clatter batons and smash bells until daylight.

Beyond the Maidens' Parlour at the cliff edge, two men also dressed in suits of green and brown ribbon were having a heated but hushed discussion. They cursed and pushed at each other, whether they had been drinking it would be difficult to have said, but certainly, they acted with the carefree bullishness of the inebriated. Then one of the men, using all his strength was successful in pushing the other over the edge. The pagan celebrants were too noisy and entranced in their own merry making to hear the man's cries as he fell 100ft onto the rocks below, nor did they notice the antagonist rejoin the party. Beltane was upon them, and for one of their gathering, a sacrifice had already been made.

Acknowledgements

In no particular order I have a few people to thank for getting this book out of my head and into your lives.

There is no way, absolutely no way I would be writing an acknowledgements page without the help of the industry professionals I've been blessed with on the way. So a huge round of applause ladies and gentlemen, for Helen Thomas (Editor), Charlie Wilson (Proofing) and Toby Stevens (Cover design). I think I should mention the collective Alliance of Independent authors, whose wealth of knowledge surrounding everything self publishing and beyond is indispensable. One single thread on their forum is worth the subscription in a flash.

Ah, dear Annette, my own therapist over the last decade and a half (don't worry, she contains my anxiety, I'm not likely to stick a rubber mallet up your bum). She kept me going through biblical amounts of self doubt and also provided me with an insight into the world and working mind of the practising psychotherapist and psychologist.

My family, Dad, Mum, Daughter and Maria have perhaps been the strongest supporters of my whimsy, and for their sufferance and help, I thank them from the bottom of my heart.

And finally a special thanks to Nigel Carr, whom I do not know, but whose Google review of St. Columb Post Office made me laugh so much I had to write it into the story. He gave them a 2.5 rating. If you happen to know Nigel, tell him I owe him a pint.

Thank you everyone, love Tom.

Printed in Dunstable, United Kingdom